Praise for *The Moonshine Shack Murder*
and the Southern Homebrew Mystery Series

"*The Moonshine Shack Murder* is a charming cozy mystery that will warm you from the inside out and keep you guessing till the end!"
—Kate Lansing, author of *Mulled to Death*

"A creative storyteller, the author quickly builds a delightful and engaging community . . . Kelly skillfully devises an intriguing mystery. The Southern Homebrew series starts with a 100-proof story."   —Fresh Fiction

"The mystery is captivating, the characters are a delight . . . and the author's trademark humor brightens up even the most stressful scenes."   —Open Book Society

"This series is off to a fantastic start . . . I can't wait to return to Chattanooga and The Moonshine Shack for a sample or two and whatever trouble Hattie gets herself wrapped up in."   —Escape With Dollycas Into A Good Book

"I loved everything about this book—the characters, the moonshine, the animals, the quick wit and snarky dialogue."   —Storeybook Reviews

"Fast-paced, clever, and filled with humor."
—Socrates' Book Reviews

"Family pride, friendship, romance, and a little hooch make *The Moonshine Shack Murder* a fun start to a new series."   —Cozy Up with Kathy

Berkley Titles by Diane Kelly

THE MOONSHINE SHACK MURDER
THE PROOF IS IN THE POISON
FIDDLING WITH FATE

Fiddling with Fate

A Southern Homebrew Mystery

DIANE KELLY

BERKLEY PRIME CRIME
New York

BERKLEY PRIME CRIME
Published by Berkley
An imprint of Penguin Random House LLC
penguinrandomhouse.com

ISBN: 9780593333266

First Edition: April 2023

Printed in the United States of America
1 3 5 7 9 10 8 6 4 2

Book design by George Towne

Fiddling with Fate

Chapter One

By late August in Chattanooga, Tennessee, folks have had their fill of the summer's relentless sunshine, heat, and humidity. Fortunately, though, they hadn't had their fill of bluegrass music or moonshine. That's why I was up early this Saturday morning, scurrying about my tiny mountainside cabin, getting myself ready for the opening of the Hamilton County Bluegrass Festival. I'd donned my usual firefly-green T-shirt that bore my moonshine brand's logo, a pair of old-fashioned denim overalls, and sneakers with gel inserts and arch supports. I'd be on my feet all day at the festival. Best to be prepared. For the final touch, I pulled my brown curls up into a carefree ponytail, swiped a few coats of mascara on my lashes to accentuate my dark-brown eyes, and applied a light coat of lip gloss. *There. All done.* No sense putting much more effort into my appearance. With the outdoor temps still lingering near ninety, makeup would melt off my face.

Besides, I wasn't the glamorous type to begin with and, at just over five feet tall, I was better off going for girl-next-door rather than gorgeous.

My gray cat, Smoky, eyed me from atop the kitchen counter, where he lounged. Unsanitary, I supposed. But I'd scolded the cat and removed him from the counter a thousand times before and learned it was a futile endeavor. The instant his paws hit the floor, he'd jump right back up onto the countertop. I bent over and put my face in his while scratching behind his ears. "Be a good boy while I'm gone, okey dokey, Smoky?"

The swish of his tail said, *Nope. Not even gonna think about behaving.* He'd probably spend the day sharpening his claws on my couch, shedding on my bed coverings, or kicking the litter out of his box.

I gave him a kiss on the head and headed out to my fluorescent-green glow-in-the-dark van. In the daylight, it just looked crazy bright but, come nighttime, you couldn't miss the van as I made my way around town, advertising my wares as I went about my business. My first order of business today was to pick up my granddaddy from the Singing River Retirement Home. If not for Benjamin Hayes having lovingly taught me how to make moonshine, I wouldn't even have my Moonshine Shack shop. I owed everything to him. Well, maybe I owed some to his father, who'd first taught him the secrets of moonshining, and to my Irish ancestors who'd preceded him, bringing their whiskey-making know-how over with them from the mother country when they'd immigrated long ago and settled in the mountains here.

I motored down the winding road that led from my cabin into the beautiful city of Chattanooga. Granddaddy waited on a bench in front of the one-story stone retirement home, clearly eager to start the day. He might be almost ninety years old, but he was like a little boy when it came to our moonshine. He loved talking up the 'shine with customers, drawing them in with his folksy charm. Today, he'd enjoy the fresh air and music. Bluegrass was his favorite, especially the classics like "Rocky Top," "Mountain Dew," "The Wabash Cannonball," and the fast-paced instrumental "Foggy Mountain Breakdown."

When Granddaddy spotted me approaching, he pushed himself up to a wobbly stand and stuck out a gnarled thumb as if attempting to hitch a ride. *Forever the jokester.*

I unrolled the window, raised a hand in greeting, and called, "Hey, Granddaddy! Ready to hear some good music?"

"Sure am, Hattie!" he called back. "Ready to sell lots of 'shine, too."

Like him, I hoped for big sales today. Since I'd launched my brand and opened my Moonshine Shack, things had been a roller-coaster ride. Not long ago, the former owner of the Irish pub located across the street from my shop was found dead on my store's stoop, and my moonshine had also later been implicated—wrongly— in a poisoning death. But things had bounced back and were on an upswing now. Only time would tell how far up the swing would go. The festival was a perfect opportunity to introduce my 'shine to more folks. There was sure to be a big crowd of both locals and bluegrass fans from around the region. With any luck, they'd spread the word about my 'shine when they went back home to their cities and towns.

I hopped down from my van and helped my granddaddy into the passenger seat. Though he fussed at me the entire time and insisted he didn't need my help, he'd have never gotten into the seat without a little boost from me. As we drove off, he waved goodbye to a trio of women working a puzzle on the veranda. "See you later, ladies!"

They waved back, one in particular treating him to a bright smile filled with perfect teeth. She'd clearly polished her dentures. They were as white as her curly hair, which she'd swept up into a wild knot atop her head. With her curls and carefree smile, she resembled my long-gone granny.

I glanced over at Granddaddy. "Something going on between you and Louise?"

"Her name's Louetta," he snapped, "and nothing's going on. How could you even ask me that? She sits by me sometimes on movie night and we share a popcorn, but that's all."

Fighting a grin, I asked, "Do you plan in advance to sit together at the movies?"

"No," he said. "She asks me if I'm going to watch the show and, if I say yes, she saves me a seat. But there's no plan."

Sure sounds like a date to me. "I think you've got yourself a girlfriend, Granddaddy."

"No, I don't!" He sent a heated look my way and scowled. "I'd never cheat on your granny."

The poor, naïve fool. He might not realize he was dating Louetta, but I was pretty sure she thought she was dating him. Besides, you couldn't cheat on someone who'd been gone for over decade. His heart would always belong to Granny, but I'd bet even she wouldn't mind seeing him enjoy some female companionship. I dropped the subject, though. No sense getting him all riled up. He was difficult enough on his best behavior, and I'd never forgive myself if he suffered a stroke or heart attack on my account.

We drove on to Market Street, turned down the back alley, and parked in the Moonshine Shack's rear parking lot next to the single-horse trailer I'd repurposed as a portable moonshine bar. I'd spotted the old trailer behind the barn where my boyfriend, a mounted police officer, boarded his horse. The paint had faded, the metal had begun to rust, and the tires had been worn bald. Like the old gray mare, the trailer wasn't what it used to be and had been put out to pasture. When I'd approached the owner of the boarding facility about buying the trailer, he'd barked a laugh. "Hon, you don't want to put a horse in that old thing. The floor's likely to cave in."

I told him I wouldn't be using it to transport a horse, but rather planned to repurpose it as a mobile moonshine bar. He'd barked another laugh. "You millennials. You're always turning things on their heads. You've got imagination, I'll give you that."

Speaking of giving . . . "How about I give you fifty dollars and you give me the trailer?"

"Sold!"

As fast as he'd accepted my offer, I had to wonder if instead I should've asked him to pay me fifty bucks to haul the thing away. My friend Kiki Nakamura and I had laid some plywood over the floor of the trailer to cover the holes. We'd also painted the outside a beautiful midnight blue with the word MOONSHINE in glow-in-the-dark fluorescent green across each side. Kiki, a graphic artist, added a white crescent moon and a scattering of brilliant stars. When we finished, I had an adorable portable beverage bar that I could use to serve my moonshine at outdoor events. The cost of the trailer and paint was less than the price for renting a commercial food trailer a single time. I didn't need all the bells and whistles of a fully outfitted food truck anyway. There was no need for running water, gas, or electricity. Moonshine could be stored at room temperature, and ice could be kept cold in plastic coolers.

Today would mark the trailer's debut. I couldn't wait to see how things would go at the festival! After attaching the trailer to the hitch on my van, I headed through the back door of my shop and into the storeroom. Granddaddy used his cane to hobble inside to help me. In light of his age and balance issues, his help consisted primarily of telling me to be careful and making sure I packed enough jugs of his pure Granddaddy's Ole-Timey Corn Liquor, which I sold in earthenware jugs sealed with a cork. I also packed up multiple cases of my fruit-flavored moonshine, which was sold in mason jars. I loaded a portable table, folding chairs, sun canopy, chalkboard sign, cups, and napkins into the trailer, as well as large beverage coolers that contained iced tea, lemonade, and a sour fruit punch. I packed cleaning supplies, too, in the event of spills. To fight the heat, I'd ordered two small battery-operated fans online. The fans went into the van, as well.

Materials in tow, we drove to the riverfront area and made our way to Ross's Landing, a riverside park with a natural amphitheater, pier, and marina. I flashed my vendor badge at the attendant and was allowed to drive my van through the checkpoint and onto the festival grounds. A covered rectangular platform had been erected at the end of the grassy area to serve as the main stage. While bluegrass music typically did not include instruments that required electricity, microphones and speakers would nonetheless be needed to amplify the sound. To that end, men strung electrical cords, set up speakers, and hung lights. Food trucks and trailers rolled slowly along, easing into their assigned places. Merchandise vendors milled about on the other side of the lawn, setting up their booths along the perimeter of the grass.

Granddaddy glanced about. "Where's our space?"

"We're booth number thirteen." When I'd received the booth assignment from the event organizer, I'd been tempted to ask for a different space. After all, the number thirteen was supposed to be unlucky. But I'd refrained. After all, we make our own luck, don't we? At least, I liked to think so, for the most part anyway. Unexpected things could happen, of course, but it was childish to fret about something as silly as a booth number. Besides, the spot was close to the stage, where we'd be highly visible. I'd been fortunate to land such a prime spot.

We continued past booths ten, eleven, and twelve. I pointed when I saw four orange cones marked with the number 13 designating the perimeter of our space. "There we are."

I pulled into our space and we climbed out of the van. The first thing we did was set about erecting the pop-up canopy in front of the trailer so my customers could enjoy some cool shade while waiting for us to prepare their drinks. Laying the parts out on the grass, I screwed the support poles together and attached them to the canvas canopy in the appropriate places. But as I tried to erect the tent, the supports collapsed in on each other. *This is a two-person job.*

Granddaddy shifted his cane to his left hand and reached out with his right. "I'll hold the poles while you tie 'em down."

While my grandfather held each corner pole in place, I used a mallet to hammer the plastic support stakes into the grass. When we finished, I took a few steps backward to admire our handiwork. I held my breath as a light breeze kicked up and the wind filled the canopy, attempting to whip it about, but the covering held its ground. I released the breath—*phew!*—and raised the mallet in victory. "We did it!"

"Did what?" came a familiar woman's voice from behind me.

I turned to see Kiki approaching with a large rectangular cooler on a dolly. Kiki was one of the most reliable, supportive, and thoughtful people on the planet, though her punk-rock garb sometimes threw people off. Today, she sported a bright-red romper with torn fishnet hose and battered combat boots. She'd topped things off with a bright-yellow bowler hat adorned with a pink silk rose in full bloom on the brim. She looked like an escapee from clown reform school. One side of her head was shaved close to her scalp, while the dark tresses hanging from the other side cascaded over her shoulder. She'd adopted the punk look after studying abroad in London during college.

I explained the source of my pride. "Granddaddy and I set up the shade tent all by ourselves."

She eyed the canopy and shrugged. "Big whoop. I just lugged fifteen tons of ice from my car." She quirked her head to indicate the cooler.

"And I can't thank you enough." Though I seriously doubted her math, I stepped forward and enveloped her in a warm hug.

Now that the canopy had been installed, we situated my grandfather on a folding lounge chair in the shade. Leaving Granddaddy to hold down the fort, Kiki and I went to her Mini Cooper in the public parking lot and retrieved the additional two coolers of ice she'd picked up for me that morning. Her car was painted to resemble the Union Jack flag. For such a small car, the Mini held a surprising amount of cargo.

We stacked the heavy coolers on the dolly and rolled them back to my moonshine trailer. The trailer was seven and a half feet high, six feet wide, and ten feet long, just big enough to hold the six-foot table and stack the coolers beside it for easy access. After covering the table with a vinyl tablecloth for quick cleanup, I stacked the cups upside down on the tabletop, where we could grab them to prepare the drinks. Kiki set the napkin dispenser beside it. I uncorked a jug of the unflavored moonshine and placed two jars of each flavored moonshine on the table in easy reach, replacing their aluminum lids with pour spouts. Things were warming up inside the trailer, and my skin felt clammy. I strategically positioned the two fans on the floor, angled upward and turned to maximum power to provide us a small measure of relief from the heat.

Today, we'd be serving three moonshine drinks that Granddaddy and I had concocted together. The first was called Blueberry Bluegrass Tea, and consisted of iced tea with a shot of blueberry moonshine, garnished with fresh blueberries and an orange wedge. The next we'd deemed Rosemary Lemonade. It, too, was simple. Lemonade with a dash of my grandfather's unflavored moonshine, garnished with both a curlicue of lemon peel and a sprig of fresh rosemary. The Sucker Punch consisted of two-thirds fruit punch and one-third ruby red grapefruit juice, with a dash of cherry moonshine, a dash of peach moonshine, and a dash of apple pie moonshine, garnished with a strawberry. An extra shot of 'shine could be added to any drink for only a dollar more.

Being a professional artist, Kiki naturally assumed the role as sign-maker, using colored chalk to list our drinks on the chalkboard before setting the sandwich board sign up in front of the trailer. As much as I would have loved to sell bottles of my moonshine here, my permit allowed me to sell only ready-to-drink beverages. That said, I had a stack of coupons at the ready, providing a ten percent discount to anyone who ventured into the nearby tourist district and visited my shop on Market Street. Nora, the blonde, midthirties sales clerk I'd hired a few months earlier, was running the shop today, with help from a student from the University of Tennessee at Chattanooga, my alma mater.

Kiki glanced around. "Nobody can miss you right here by the stage. How'd you land this primo location? You know someone on the planning committee? Bribe them with free moonshine?"

"Nope," I said. "It was sheer dumb luck."

Next to us was a booth selling big Bavarian pretzels. The smell of the warm dough enticed my taste buds. *I know what I'm having for lunch.* Farther down was a line of food trucks and trailers with offerings ranging from barbecue to hot dogs to healthier plant-based fare, the aromas of their foods drifting along on the breeze and making my stomach growl. The merchandise vendors lined the opposite side of the lawn. Directly across from my moonshine booth was a vendor selling T-shirts, while the adjacent booth offered sunglasses, sun hats, and sunscreen. Another sold artisan soaps and lotions.

We'd just finished setting up when the gates opened and music lovers began to stream onto the lawn. Some had brought lawn chairs with them. Others carried blankets or beach towels to sit on. Others simply flopped down directly on the grass. Boats began to pull up at the pier on the river, too, the occupants taking up positions on their decks, planning to enjoy the concert from the comfort and privacy of their vessels.

At noon, the first band took the stage. The group included five performers with various stringed instruments, including a banjo, an upright bass, a violin, a guitar, and a mandolin. Though it was much too hot for the full western suits worn by traditional bluegrass bands, all were dressed in jeans, white dress shirts, and classic black string ties. By then, my grandfather had eaten both a pretzel and a corncob-on-a-stick, drunk a full cup of our Blueberry Bluegrass Tea with an extra shot of 'shine, and fallen fast asleep in the lawn chair, his cane resting across his belly as he dozed, snoring softly. Onstage, the musicians tuned their instruments. The portly fiddle player tucked the instrument under his chin, put his bow to the strings, and played a few quick notes. The guitarist ran through a scale. The banjo player treated us to the first few notes of the classic "Dueling Banjos." The bass stood taller than the man who plucked its strings. As his fingers moved, the instrument offered what sounded like a deep and dire warning—*doom-doom-doom*.

After playing a few bars on his mandolin, the lead singer stepped to the microphone to check that the equipment was working properly. "Testing, testing. One, two, three."

An earsplitting squelch came from a nearby speaker. *EEEEEERK!* My hands flew to cover my ears. Kiki crossed one eye inward and stuck her index fingers in her ears. Meanwhile, my grandfather shot up out of the lounge chair, launching his cane into the air. "Mercy!"

While I helped to resettle my startled grandfather on

his chair and rounded up his cane, the sound technicians and equipment crew made a few adjustments onstage and the singer stepped back to the mic. Fortunately, we were prepared this time and protected our eardrums as best we could. The second sound check went off without a hitch. The singer apologized for nearly causing a mass aneurism earlier. "Sorry 'bout that squeal, folks. It'll be all good sounds the rest of the day. I promise."

A female emcee in cowgirl boots and a ruffled denim dress sashayed up to the mic to get the party started. "Howdy, folks! Welcome to the Hamilton County Bluegrass Festival. Let's give a big welcome to our first performers, the Quintucky Pickers!"

With the headliners scheduled to perform much later in the day, the audience was still relatively meager and offered only scattered applause, but the lack of fans didn't dampen the musicians' spirits. They launched into their music with absolute abandon, as if they were born to play bluegrass.

Customers began to wander over to the moonshine booth, and Kiki and I greeted each one with a smile. Granddaddy ventured into the trailer to help us out. Kiki processed payments using a fanny pack full of cash and a handheld card scanner attached to her phone for credit and debit card payments. As she called out the orders, Granddaddy scooped ice into cups and handed them to me. I filled the cups with the appropriate mixer and shots of 'shine before handing them to the waiting customer, along with a discount coupon that could be redeemed at my shop. "Enjoy your moonshine!" I called after them as they left the booth.

Between sets was our busiest time. When the line dwindled, Kiki stepped out in front of our booth and danced an improvised jig using Granddaddy's cane as a prop. No one could ever accuse my friend of being shy, that's for sure. Once she'd drawn people's attention, she'd use the cane to point to the booth, cup her other hand around her mouth, and call, "Step right up and get your 'shine on, folks!"

As a line formed once again and Kiki handed the cane back to my grandfather, I gave my friend a smile. "You missed your calling, Kiki. You should've been a carnival barker."

"It's never too late," she said. "Maybe I'll take it up in my spare time."

As the day wore on, band after band took the stage. The crowd and the noise level grew until Kiki was now having to cup her hand around her ear to hear the orders as the customers called them out. At one point, the line at our booth was at least two dozen people long. It seemed the more people that there were at our booth, the more people wanted to know what was drawing such a crowd. We sold more moonshine drinks than I dared dream of! In the early days, there'd been times when not a single customer would enter my shop for hours, and I'd wondered whether starting my own moonshine business had been a mistake. But today told me otherwise. Launching my 'shine brand and shop was one of the smartest decisions I'd ever made. We were making money hand over fist. Patrons had even tucked quite a few dollars into the tip jar Kiki had put out. She'd be going home with a nice bundle of cash at the end of the night.

When we had another lull, Kiki stepped out in front of the trailer again. With no sign to spin, she improvised, tossing her flower-trimmed hat high up into the air, where it could be seen from far and wide. She caught the hat on its return—most of the time anyway. She added spins and jumps and cartwheels for fun. A few times her hat fell to the ground nearby and, once, it landed atop the canopy. She grabbed Granddaddy's cane and jabbed at the underside of the fabric until her hat toppled over the edge of the cover and she could round it up again. Her amusing antics caught the crowd's attention, and soon we had a new line of customers at the booth.

Around four, my eyes spotted a beautiful chestnut mare strolling along the back of the crowd. On her back was Chattanooga Police Officer Marlon Landers. Marlon was tall with an athletic build, eyes the amber color of mahogany, and short buckskin curls fashioned in a stylish contemporary pompadour. He was also my boyfriend. *How lucky am I?*

We'd met a few months earlier, when he and his horse, Charlotte, had *clop-clop-clopped* up the back alley to my shop. I'd been instantly smitten—what woman wouldn't be?—but I'd since learned there was much more to him than a strong physique and a chiseled jawline. He was a good guy, patient and even-tempered, a true public servant and seeker of justice. He was smart, too, well respected by his superiors at the police department. He had a good sense of humor, as well. He'd even earned my granddaddy's approval. It hadn't been an easy feat. Back in the days of Prohibition, Marlon's great-grandfather, the Hamilton County sheriff, had arrested my granddaddy's daddy for selling illegal hooch. At first, Granddaddy had held a grudge against Marlon. But eventually, even my stubborn grandfather had to acknowledge that, despite our families' intertwined and contentious history, Marlon was a stand-up guy.

Marlon and Charlotte pulled to a stop at the back of the crowd, where he could look out over the audience. With his mirrored aviator sunglasses on, it was difficult to tell where he was looking. But when I raised a hand in greeting and he raised his in return, I knew he'd been looking my way. My insides warmed and my head went as light as if I'd just downed a shot of my 'shine. Marlon and moonshine had the same effect on me. Both made me giddy.

Marlon and Charlotte turned and headed our way, coming up behind the booths. When they reached my trailer, Marlon dismounted, sliding off the horse with ease and grace. I quickly filled a cup with half lemonade and half iced tea, making him an Arnold Palmer. I left out the moonshine, of course. He couldn't drink alcohol on duty.

I handed him the cup through the open window of the trailer. He gave me a smile in appreciation as he took it. "Looks like things are going well. You've had a line at your trailer since I arrived."

"It's gone better than I could've ever imagined!" My assistant, Nora, had texted me from the shop to let me know that several of the coupons I'd handed out today had already been redeemed there.

Granddaddy used his cane to lever himself to a stand and walked over to pet Charlotte. He ran a hand over her neck. "How you doin', pretty girl?" Once he'd greeted the horse, he gave Marlon a nod in acknowledgment.

Marlon said, "You're looking good, Ben."

"That's the problem with getting old," Granddaddy said. "People tell you that you're looking good rather than good-looking."

Kiki pshawed and waved a dismissive hand. "C'mon now, G-Daddy. You're the hunkiest hunk in your entire retirement home."

"I don't know about that," Granddaddy said, "but at least I can still dress myself, boots and all."

I leaned over, ducked my head, and whispered, "He's got a new girlfriend named Louetta."

"I heard that!" Granddaddy stomped his foot. "And I do not have a girlfriend!"

"Of course you don't," Kiki said. "That's crazy talk." Once he'd turned his attention back to the cups, she cut me a look and wagged her brows.

The emcee took the stage once more to introduce the next band. "Lots of you folks have been looking forward to hearing our next band play. They're a band of brothers, from right here in Chattanooga. We've got big brother Brody Sheridan on strings; middle brother Josh Sheridan on vocals; and baby brother Garth Sheridan on the jug, stovepipe, washboard, spoons, jaw harp, and harmonica. Put your hands together and give a big welcome to everyone's favorite up-and-coming bluegrass band, the Bootlegging Brothers!"

As the trio climbed up to the stage, the crowd erupted in a roar, especially the women. It was easy to see why. The Sheridan brothers were an attractive bunch, with dark glossy hair, nicely trimmed chinstrap-style beards, blue eyes, and sun-kissed summer tans that had warmed their skin to a nice brown. They weren't tall men, but they were solidly built with broad-shouldered, formidable frames. They sported tweed newsboy-style caps, dark-blue vests over lightweight plaid shirts, and blue jeans with boots. Their look was a casual yet creative mix of traditional bluegrass attire and hipster chic.

With big smiles, Josh and Brody made their way to the stage. Brody brandished his fiddle in one hand and his banjo in the other to elicit more cheers. As Garth ascended the stairs with his washboard tucked under one arm, his stovepipe in one hand, and his jug in the other, the toe of his boot got caught under an extension cord that had pulled loose. The musician lost his footing and stumbled onto the stage. The crowd sucked air in a collective gasp. His jug fell from his hand and hit the stage with first a *crash* then a *tinkle* as it exploded into shards.

Josh grabbed Garth's upper arm to prevent his brother from falling, too. Once Garth had been righted, he stared down at the shattered jug for a moment before looking up at the crowd with an *uh-oh* expression. Brody cut a sharp look at his brother before grabbing the mic. "Looks like we'll be playing without our jug tonight."

I cupped my hands around my mouth and hollered, "Don't worry, Garth! I've got you covered!"

Chapter Two

Grabbing a jug of my Granddaddy's Ole-Timey Corn Liquor, I exited the trailer, yanked out the cork, and poured the high-proof moonshine out onto the grass.

My grandfather put his hands to his head. "What in the world are you doing, Hattie? You're wasting my 'shine!"

"No, I'm not!" I said. "I'm saving the show!"

When the 'shine slowed to a drip, I scurried over to the stage and held up the empty jug to offer it to Garth Sheridan. He reached down to take it, giving me a big grin in return. The crowd burst into cheers as I rushed back to my booth.

Garth carried the jug over to a microphone. He put his nose to the jug, sniffed, and grimaced. "Hoo-ee! That must've been some strong hooch!" He raised the jug to his lips and blew into it. The jug responded with a resonant *hoo*. "This jug sounds even better than the one I dropped." He raised the jug in salute and looked my way. "Thanks to my shining star at the moonshine booth for the new jug. I hope you'll come back after the set with your phone number." He blew me a kiss and the entire audience turned their heads to look my way, as if following the kiss through the air.

With a thousand eyes on me, my face warmed with a blush. Even so, I realized it was best to play along. I reached up, pretended to catch the kiss Garth Sheridan had blown my way, and applied my fingers to my warm cheek, as if placing the kiss there. Garth released a loud "Whoop!" and, with that, the band launched into their first song.

Sensing eyes on me, I turned to see Marlon holding Charlotte's reins a few feet away. His face wore a frown. It might have been my imagination, but Charlotte seemed to be frowning, too. Marlon and I had just recently put a label on our relationship, and flirting with another man in front of a huge crowd of people did not comply with the fine print on that label.

With the Bootlegging Brothers' first song under way and the audience now focused on the stage, I offered Marlon an apology by way of a contrite cringe and palms raised in an *I'm sorry but what else could I do?* gesture. His face softened. He tossed back the rest of his drink, dropped the empty cup in the trash can, and blew me a kiss himself. I grabbed his kiss from the air and applied it to directly my lips. The grin he sent my way said he'd forgiven me. *Good.*

Kiki sighed. "Kate loves the Bootlegging Brothers. Shame she couldn't be here."

"Sure is."

While Kiki and I had met waiting in line for the jungle gym at recess in elementary school, Kate had become our good friend a few years later, in high school. She'd recently given birth and, though she'd originally planned to attend the festival today, her baby boy had come down with an ear infection that had brought her life to a grinding halt. While I hoped to have children one day, I had to admit it was a good thing I didn't have one now. I'd never be able to manage my moonshine business and take care of a kid. It was hard enough keeping up with my cat's demands.

I watched as the band performed. Brody moved the bow on his fiddle, sliding it back and forth over the strings with amazing speed, producing lively notes to the delight of the crowd. He sure knew how to work the instrument. If not for the fact that the boy in the classic country song identified himself as Johnny, I might have thought Brody was the fiddle player who'd bested the devil down in Georgia.

After a couple of minutes, the song ended. When the applause died down, raucous shouts came from across the field. A group of young adults were playing around on the pier, trying to push one another into the Tennessee River. They were having fun but, still, someone could get hurt.

"I'd better get over there." Marlon swung himself up into the saddle in a fluid motion. He doffed his riding helmet. "I'll check back with you later." With a nod, he and Charlotte trotted off in the direction of the river.

Traffic at the moonshine trailer slowed during the Bootlegging Brothers' performance. Seemed everyone wanted to hear the band. Brody was as adept on the banjo as he was on the fiddle, and Garth moved among his home-spun instruments with talent and skill as well. The crowd clapped and sang along to one of the group's more popular songs, "Get Off My Lawn," a tongue-in-cheek ballad to the insistent weeds that repeatedly sprang up no matter what a person does to prevent them. Granddaddy sang along, too, raising his cane each time the song reached the chorus and hollering, "Get off my lawn!" It was nice to see him having such a great time.

As Garth launched into his jug solo—*hooooo-hoo-hoo-hooooo*—my grandfather beamed. A couple stepped up to the moonshine booth, and Granddaddy pointed at Garth with his cane. "Hear that sound? That's my jug he's using up there."

I was tempted to point out to my grandfather that he'd initially chastised me for pouring out his moonshine, but it wasn't worth starting an argument. But as I watched Garth play the jug, clearly marked with the label that read GRANDADDY'S OLE-TIMEY CORN LIQUOR, an idea began to take shape in my mind. I'd been looking into new marketing options and had even bought commercial time on a local country music radio station. It would be an expensive proposition, but I couldn't rely solely on passersby and word of mouth to grow my business. I'd been planning to simply speak during my commercial, but a jingle would be much more likely to catch the listeners' attention. *Who better to sing a jingle for my Moonshine Shack than the Bootlegging Brothers?*

When the band wrapped up their set, I jotted my name and phone number on a napkin and turned to Kiki. "I'll be right back."

Her mouth dropped when she saw the napkin in my

hand. "You're *actually* going to give that musician your phone number? And you're leaving *now*?" She gestured to the line forming in front of the trailer.

"I'm not interested in dating Garth Sheridan," I said. "I have a different kind of partnership to propose to him. I'll be right back."

She glanced at the line again. "You'd better!"

Napkin in hand, I scurried over to the stage. I intercepted Garth as he and his brothers circled around to the back to pack up their instruments. Panting from my sprint, I held out the napkin.

He looked down, saw the name and phone number written there, and grinned as he took the napkin from me. "Glad you came back to see me, Hattie."

"I have a business proposition for you," I said. "For all of the Bootlegging Brothers, actually."

"You do?" Garth cocked his head. "What is it?"

Josh and Brody turned around and looked at me expectantly, too.

"I bought airtime on local radio to promote my Moonshine Shack. I'd like y'all to sing a jingle in my commercial."

I ran my gaze over them. Josh's face hadn't changed. Garth's brows rose and his eyes gleamed with interest, but Brody quickly shut him down with a firm shake of his head. "No. No way. Absolutely not."

Sheesh. I hadn't necessarily expected them to say *yes* immediately, but I hadn't expected such staunch resistance, either. "What's your objection?"

Brody crossed his arms over his chest. "Because the Bootlegging Brothers aren't sellouts."

"But you wouldn't be selling out," I insisted. "Music and moonshine go hand in hand, especially bluegrass music. You know how many bluegrass songs mention moonshine?"

Brody grunted. "How many?"

I didn't have an actual number, of course, so I simply said, "A lot of them."

Garth backed me up. "Bro, our band is named after moonshine runners. It could be a good fit. C'mon, man."

At that, Brody uncrossed his arms. His eyes narrowed as he seemed to be thinking things over. He turned to their middle brother. "What do you think, Josh?"

Though the middle brother was now in the position of tiebreaker, Josh merely shrugged one shoulder, refusing to cast the deciding vote.

Garth exhaled sharply, and his jaw flexed with frustration. "This could be our chance! We've been wanting to get on the radio but, without a label backing us, none of the stations will play our songs. A commercial could get the band some attention, maybe even land us a recording contract."

Brody cocked his head. "How would people know it was us singing the song?"

"You'd tell them," I said. "After you sing the jingle, you could say something like 'Head over to the Moonshine Shack, and tell 'em the Bootlegging Brothers sent you.'"

Brody seemed to be wavering. He hooked his thumbs into his belt loops and rocked back on his heels. "How does the jingle go?"

"I don't know," I said. "I haven't written it yet." Not to mention I had no idea where to even start writing a song, nor a lick of musical talent.

As if he'd read my mind, Garth said, "I'll work with her on it."

Brody asked, "How much will we get paid?"

I had no idea how long it would take for them to practice the song and record a good take, so I figured it would be best to offer a flat fee rather than an hourly rate. I also had no idea how much a gig like this would normally pay. I did the only thing I could. I pulled a number out of the air and hoped it would be enough. "A thousand dollars. That's over three hundred bucks for each of you. Three hundred thirty-three dollars and thirty-three cents, to be precise."

"Actually," Brody said, "that's not precise at all. You left a penny unaccounted for."

Garth rolled his eyes. "You can have the extra penny, bro."

I stuck out my hand before Brody could change his mind. "Deal?"

"Deal." He shook my hand, albeit with a hint of reluctance. But at least we had an agreement. I obtained Garth's contact information, added his phone number to my contacts, and documented the terms of our agreement in a quick message sent to his e-mail account. Lest they change their minds, I figured I should move quickly. Besides, my commercial was scheduled to be recorded on Wednesday morning at nine A.M. After confirming they'd all be available to record at that time, I turned my attention back to Garth. "Are you available for a jingle-writing session tomorrow? We could meet at my shop. I open at noon."

"It's a date." Garth gave me a coy grin. "Looking forward to working with you, Hattie."

I was looking forward to working with him, too, but not because he was attractive. I wanted to get the word out about my wares, grow my business. The fact that Garth's face would be nice to look at while we bandied jingles about was simply a bonus.

I hurried back to the moonshine booth and relieved my grandfather of his bartending duties. Once we'd served everyone in line and could catch our breath, I told Kiki about the deal I'd made.

"Way to seize an opportunity," she said. "You've really got a nose for business."

"I only wish I knew something about songwriting."

"How hard can it be to write a jingle?"

I supposed I'd find out when I met with Garth tomorrow to work on it. Realizing Marlon would be none too happy if I met with the guy alone, I said, "Want to join in?"

"On your songwriting sesh?" she said. "Sure. I'm always up for exploring a new creative outlet."

My dad came by at five o'clock to pick up my grandfather. Although my father drank his fair share of my moonshine, he'd never been interested in making the stuff himself. Seems skills and interests sometimes skip a generation. I thanked my dad and gave my grandfather a kiss goodbye on his grizzled cheek. It had been a long day for Granddaddy, but he'd been a trooper.

By the time the festival wrapped up that night, Kiki and I had sore feet and sticky shoes from the lemonade drips, but we also had a small fortune to take home with us. I split the day's profits fifty-fifty with her, and she kept everything in the tip jar. After she counted her take, she let loose a whistle. "Who knew moonshining would be so lucrative?"

"Be sure to set some aside for the revenuer," I teased. "Otherwise, they'll come for your art supplies and your cats."

"Nobody better dare try to seize Kahlo or van Gogh. Not unless they want a fight to the death."

I felt the same way about Smoky. Meanwhile, if I were taken away by the authorities, I'd be lucky to get a tail swish out of him.

After Kiki and I packed up my van and trailer and hugged goodbye, I headed back to my cabin, dragging the trailer with me. It was late and, after the busy day we'd had, I was exhausted. I'd unpack the trailer tomorrow.

Chapter Three

The following day, I'd just finished hauling the table, chairs, coolers, and leftover moonshine from the trailer into the storeroom at the Moonshine Shack, when I heard a rap on the front door of my shop. I ventured from the back room onto the sales floor to see Garth Sheridan at the glass with a banjo case in one hand and a tall, hard-sided rolling case beside him. My guess was that the rolling case held his long stovepipe, washboard, and other improvised instruments. He wore boots, jeans, a souvenir T-shirt from an Emmylou Harris concert, and a big smile on his face. His dark-green pickup truck was parked at the curb behind him. A bright-yellow safety vest with reflective silver strips hung over the top of the seat. It reminded me of the vests worn by school crossing guards.

I walked to the door and unlocked it. "Good morning!" We'd agreed to meet up at noon, but it was only a quarter till. "You're early. Morning person?"

"Not at all." He slid me a sly smile. "Guess I was just eager to get started."

I felt my face warm with a blush. Was he implying he'd been looking forward to seeing me? Perhaps I was just flattering myself. A lot of women would kill to spend time with Garth Sheridan, but I had no interest in him other than as a means of promoting my moonshine. My heart belonged to Marlon. Garth was probably just excited to be writing a song and working on some music, even if it would be only a short commercial jingle. As he'd told his brother the day before, this commercial might not only sell my 'shine. It could be a break for the band, too.

As long as I was already at the shop and had unlocked the door, I figured I may as well open up for the day. I turned the cardboard sign in the window around so that it now read OPEN. I held out a hand to indicate the stools at the sample table. "Why don't we work there?"

Garth strode over and perched atop a stool. After he took a seat, I circled around behind the bar, grabbed a jar of my apple pie moonshine, and held it up. "Want a shot to get your creative juices flowing?"

He grinned. "I thought you'd never ask."

I poured a shot in one of my sample glasses and slid it in front of him. He picked up the shot glass, tossed back the liquor, and swallowed, closing his eyes and giving his head a hard shake. When he opened his eyes, he said, "That stuff burns. But in a good way."

A smile skittered across my lips. I slid the jar back onto the shelf behind the sample table, took a seat on a stool facing Garth, and readied a pen and notepad. "I know nothing about songwriting. Where do we start?"

"We can start with a tune and set words to it," he said, "or we can start with words and give it a tune."

"You got a tune in mind?"

"I do. It came to me on the drive over." He proceeded to unsnap the locks on his banjo case—*snap-snap*—opened it up, and removed the instrument.

"I didn't realize you played banjo, too."

"I'm not near as good as Brody on strings," he said, "but I can riff." He positioned the instrument and played a few bars to warm up, speaking over the sound. "Brody uses the three-finger picking method Earl Scruggs invented, but I prefer the traditional clawhammer style."

Who knew there was more than one way to play a banjo? Not me, that's for sure.

Garth plucked out a lively tune. It was upbeat and catchy, but much longer than the fifteen-second time slot I'd purchased.

"I like it," I said, "but we've only got fifteen seconds of airtime."

His jaw dropped. "*Fifteen seconds?*"

The quick segment would cost a small fortune and was all I could afford at this point, but I would be embarrassed to admit that fact. Instead, I said, "That's all I agreed to for now, until I see the results. No sense buying a lot of commercial time if I don't get a good ROI."

His brows inverted in a perplexed V. "What the heck is ROI?"

"Return on investment."

"Ah. So, it's a fancy term for 'payoff.'"

"Exactly."

Garth plucked a few notes on the banjo. "We could shorten the tune, just keep the chorus."

"Works for me. I liked the sound."

"Now for the lyrics." Garth cocked his head, gazing intently at me. "What's your story?"

"What do you mean?"

"Bluegrass music always tells a story. Your jingle should tell yours." He gestured around the shop. "How did the Moonshine Shack come to be?"

I told him the basics. About my Irish ancestors, who brought their whiskey recipe over with them from Ireland. About my great-grandfather, who was arrested during Prohibition. About my granddaddy, who'd taught me how to make 'shine. I pointed to the newspaper clipping I'd hung on the wall. The article detailed the arrest of Eustatius Hayes and featured a grainy black-and-white photograph of my great-granddad wearing both a scowl and handcuffs, while Marlon's great-grandpa stood beside him, grinning ear to ear after finally capturing the region's most elusive moonshiner.

Garth's eyes narrowed and his head bobbed as he appeared to be thinking. He reached out, grabbed my pen, and turned the pad toward himself. He rapidly scribbled off a few lines. When he finished, he turned the pad my way so I could read what he'd written. As I leaned in to read, my nose caught a whiff of his body wash. Sandalwood, if I wasn't mistaken, with just a hint of musk. *Nice.* Still, I wouldn't trade it for Marlon's signature scent of fresh hay and saddle leather. On the page, Garth had written:

> *I met a moonshiner named Hattie,*
> *Who learned to 'shine from her granddaddy.*
> *Her liquor's the best, it outshines all the rest!*
> *Get it at her Moonshine Shack!*
> *She's a shining star! Get a jug! Get a jar!*

Underneath the lyrics, he'd written lines to be spoken in a voice-over: *Visit the Moonshine Shack on Market*

Street in Chattanooga and taste the hooch that put Hattie's great-granddaddy in the hoosegow! Tell 'er the Bootlegging Brothers sent ya!

When I looked up, he said, "I thought Brody and I could softly repeat that last line several times while Josh does the voice-over. What do you think?"

It was perfect. Simple. Clever. Catchy. "I think you're a musical genius, Garth."

The door opened and in walked Kiki with our good friend Kate Pardue. Kate was tall, blond, and fair, and to my surprise she was without the baby she'd recently given birth to. Looked like her husband was on daddy duty today. She had a gaga look on her face, her eyes wide and bright, her jaw slack.

Before I could even introduce her to Garth, she began to fangirl, putting her hands to her mouth to stifle her squeal, then using those hands to fan herself as if she feared she'd burst into flame on the spot. She spoke as if the musician were merely an apparition. "I can't believe it! Garth Sheridan is right here in your store!"

"Yes," I said. "I am fully aware of his presence." Maybe *too* aware, given that I was in a committed relationship but nonetheless had thoroughly enjoyed that sniff of his soap.

Garth chuckled good-naturedly and stuck out his hand. "Who might you be?"

"I might be Kate," my friend said on a breath.

Garth fought a grin.

Kiki was less magnanimous. "She might also be starstruck."

Garth said, "Don't get all worked up over me. I'm just like everyone else. Put on my jeans one leg at a time."

Kiki wagged her brows. "Do you take your jeans off one leg at a time, too?"

"Kiki!" I snapped. "Behave!"

Luckily, Garth laughed, unfazed by her suggestive banter.

I looked from Kate to Kiki. "I'm glad y'all are here. We've already worked something up. Let us know what you think." I held out a hand, inviting Garth to sing the jingle.

Before he started singing, he said, "Remember, I'm primarily a musician, not a vocalist. But I'll do the best I can."

The guy was much too humble. Even if he wasn't the Bootlegging Brothers' lead singer, he sang backup in all of their songs and had a darn fine voice. Of course, to fit the song into the short time frame, he had to spew words as fast as an auctioneer. After singing the jingle at warp speed, he read the voice-over while in the background I softly chanted, "She's a shining star! Get a jug! Get a jar!"

Kate bounced on her feet and clapped her hands. "It's perfect!"

"Wow," Kiki said. "You nailed it."

Garth said, "I just got to work some on the music now. Brody will play a little banjo riff, but I'd like to add some of my own sound. Course, with only fifteen seconds to fill, I'm thinking I should forget my other instruments and stick to the jug. What do y'all think?"

Kate just nodded, a ridiculous grin on her face. Kiki said, "Seems appropriate."

"I agree," I said. "I only wish more people could see you playing the jug of Granddaddy's Ole-Timey Corn Liquor. It would get even more attention for our brand."

Kiki said, "Why don't I snap some photos of the band

in front of the Moonshine Shack? You could have them made into promotional posters or postcards or whatever."

It was a great idea. I turned to Garth. "You think your brothers would agree?"

He issued a soft snort. "Josh never seems to have an opinion. Brody will agree if there's something in it for him or the band. I think I could convince him that being featured in promotional materials for your moonshine brand would be good for us. It's not often a band like ours gets an endorsement deal. Advertisers usually want the big names."

Kate pulled herself together enough to say, "The Bootlegging Brothers are a big name around Chattanooga."

Garth shrugged. "Big fish, small pond. I'd like to be a big fish in a big pond someday."

I could relate. "That's how I feel about my moonshine. I'd love to see my small-batch operation go nationwide. Maybe even international."

"Yup," Garth said. "If you're gonna dream, you might as well dream big, right?"

My friends pulled up stools and we spent a few minutes singing the jingle while Garth blew on the jug at various times. We finally decided on a single blow after each of the first two lines—*hoo*—and a double blow after the line that mentioned the Moonshine Shack—*hoo-hoo*.

When we'd done all we could for the time being, Garth packed up his instruments. "I'll get with my brothers later today, and we'll work on the music and the timing. Once we've got it down, I'll record a video and send it to you, get your approval before we head to the radio station to record it."

As he turned to leave, Kate reached out to touch his arm. "Can I get your autograph before you go?"

"Sure." Garth picked up the pen and notepad, ripped off the page with the jingle written on it, and scribbled on the next clean page. *To Kate—Keep shining bright! Fondly, Garth Sheridan.*

When he ripped off the page and handed it to her, she cradled it to her chest. "Thank you so much!"

"My pleasure."

As soon as the door swung shut behind Garth, I turned to Kate. "You seem nearly as crazy about Garth as you do about Dalton." She loved her son more than life itself.

My comment seemed to bring her to her senses. She folded the paper with the autograph on it and slid it into her purse. "My baby boy will always be my number one."

I hadn't seen her son since last week. As quickly as babies grew and changed, I'd probably missed a developmental milestone or two. "How's he doing?"

"He's as cute and sweet as ever! He can hold his head up for a few seconds at a time now." She proceeded to scroll through approximately three million photos of her son on her phone, all taken since the last time I'd seen him.

Kiki and I oohed and aahed over Dalton's pics. I said, "He's growing like a weed."

"He is," Kate acknowledged with a touch of melancholy. "He's starting to babble. It's all nonsense so far, but I'm working with him on 'mama.'"

My work on the jingle done for the time being, I turned my attention to tending my store. I'd recently attended the Chattanooga Choo-Choo Model Train Convention and bought my grandfather a fun toy train. We'd decided to install a track around the ceiling so that the train could circumnavigate the shop. The train gave off a soft *choo-choo* noise and imitation smoke. It was a cute and kitschy addition to the shop's décor. I switched the train on. It was halfway through its first loop of the day seconds later when the door opened and three middle-aged women entered.

Kate glanced in their direction. "We should go. We don't want to be in your way. Brunch soon?"

"For sure."

With that, my friends said goodbye and left me to handle my customers.

I greeted the women. "Welcome to the Moonshine Shack. Would you like to sample any of the flavors?"

One of the women put a hand to her chest and eyed her friends. "Would we?" she teased. "Why, yes. I think we would!"

After the women tried several samples, each one bought a jar of my fruity 'shine to take home with them. One chose the apple pie flavor. Another chose blackberry. The third chose the candy apple flavor, which combined the apple pie flavor with cinnamon. That flavor had been Marlon's idea, and it had been a good one. The candy apple 'shine was quite popular.

"Thank you!" I called to the women as they headed to the door. "Come back soon!"

That evening, Garth sent me a video clip of the Bootlegging Brothers singing the jingle he'd composed. Brody picked his banjo, Garth blew on his jug, and Josh sang the words. The lively, catchy song was sure to bring me some new business. I responded with a thumbs-up emoji and a face-with-hearts-for-eyes emoji to let him know I loved their performance. Asking them to sing a jingle in my commercial had been a darn good idea.

* * *

When I arrived at the radio station on Wednesday morning, I expected things would go smoothly. Brody was in a cantankerous mood, however, and soon disavowed me of that notion. After Kiki and I followed the station's audio tech and the band members into the recording booth, Brody sat his banjo case down, crossed his arms over his chest again, and turned to his brothers. "I'm having second thoughts. Once this commercial hits the air, the Bootlegging Brothers will be forever tied to her moonshine. What if people don't like her 'shine? It's already got some bad press."

He was referring to a recent incident in which a man was poisoned. While my moonshine was implicated at first, it was later cleared.

Before I could even open my mouth, Kiki came to my defense. "People are smart enough to separate the two."

"Besides," I added, "people love my 'shine. I get lots of repeat business."

I hadn't planned on paying the band until the recording session was over, but with Brody poised to blow things up I figured it couldn't hurt to show him what he'd be giving up if he walked away from our deal. I reached into my purse and pulled out the envelopes of cash I'd withdrawn from the bank the day before. I'd marked the one with the extra penny with Brody's name. I handed that envelope to him and gave each of his brothers an unmarked envelope. Brody ran a finger under the flap of his envelope to loosen the adhesive, and glanced inside. The bank teller had given me primarily hundred-dollar bills. I'd been tempted to ask her for the full amount in smaller bills, but I'd thought the hundred-dollar bills would take up less space in my small purse. I felt glad now that I hadn't gone for twenties. The hundred-dollar bills seemed more impressive.

Brody pushed the flap back into place, folded the envelope in two, and shoved it into his back pocket. "Let's get moving. I've got important things to do later."

As if recording my commercial *wasn't* important? Kiki turned to me, pretending to be removing her camera from its case. Under her breath she muttered, "Brody's a bluegrasshole."

The band spent a minute or so warming up before doing a couple of practice runs through the song. Kiki snapped photographs of them as they worked. When they felt ready, the audio technician circled around to sit behind his electronic sound board. He signaled the band with a countdown on his fingers, then pointed at them to go. They performed the jingle perfectly, and Josh recited the voice-over at the end with just the right amount of enthusiasm. Enough to sound upbeat and excited, but not so much that it came off as cheesy. When the tech played the song back to us, we all exchanged glances and nods of approval. The engineer said, "It's rare to get things right on the first take. Good job, everyone."

With the recording session now a wrap, I was eager to know when the jingle would hit the airwaves. "When will the commercial start running?"

"I've got some open spots this afternoon," the guy said. "I'll get it slotted right away."

"Wonderful!" I'd anticipated it would take several days before the commercial would air, but technology enabled things to move at warp speed these days. I could hardly wait to hear my jingle play on the airwaves! The commercial was a sign of progress for my business, and I felt proud that I'd pulled it together.

The Bootlegging Brothers, Kiki, and I left the station, but not before I left a case of moonshine for the radio station's staff to share. Couldn't hurt to build some goodwill and show them how delicious my 'shine was.

We caravanned to the Moonshine Shack, the band following my van in their vehicles. Garth was directly behind me in his dark-green pickup truck. Josh, too, drove a pickup, though his was black. He followed Garth, while Brody took up the rear in a bright-blue sporty Jeep Wrangler. Once we arrived at my shop, we gathered again on the shop's front porch.

As Kiki whipped out her camera again, Brody exhaled sharply. "Seems to me we're giving you more than we bargained for. You paid us to sing a jingle, not appear in print ads."

Garth cut his brother a sour look. "C'mon, bro. We already talked about this. The exposure will be good for the band. Maybe we'd even be able to quit our day jobs soon. That's the goal, isn't it?"

Kiki said, "I take it you don't like your day jobs?"

Garth shrugged. "They're okay jobs, but they're just a way to pay the bills. Brody's a barber, I'm in maintenance for public works, and Josh drives a paver for the highway department. Wouldn't break any of our hearts to leave our jobs behind and do our music full-time."

I'd felt the same way about my previous job. Though it was a good position and I'd liked my coworkers, moonshining had always been my dream. I knew I'd never be truly content unless I pursued it. Garth's job with public works explained the yellow safety vest in his truck.

Garth turned back to his brother. "Don't ruin this for us, Brody."

Brody crossed his arms over his chest once again.

Sheesh. He crossed his arms more often than a genie granting wishes. "I'm not ruining things for us, Garth. I'm looking out for my little brothers. It's what a good big brother should do."

"I appreciate that," Garth said, "but Josh and I aren't kids anymore. We don't need you making decisions for us or fighting our battles. We can take care of ourselves."

Rather than waste time with further argument, I decided to put a quick end to the matter. It was clear the guy was vying for more money and, in all fairness, he had a point. I hadn't paid them to appear in a print ad. "How's another hundred dollars each sound?"

Garth said, "Sounds great to me."

Once again, Josh merely shrugged. Seemed the guy opened his mouth only to sing.

"One-fifty each," Brody countered. He pointed to a display of Granddaddy's Ole-Timey Corn Liquor. "Plus a jug of 'shine."

I hesitated a moment to make him sweat a little, even though I knew I'd accept. I cocked my head and narrowed my eyes as if thinking it over. Finally, I said, "You drive a hard bargain, Brody. But you got yourself a deal."

After Brody had nearly balked at the station and insisted on an additional payment for the photos, I didn't entirely trust the guy. My earlier e-mail to Garth documented the terms of our jingle arrangement, but there was nothing stipulating the terms of this photo shoot. I searched for a photo release online while Kiki posed the Bootlegging Brothers on the front porch of my shop and snapped a series of photos featuring the band along with jugs and jars of my moonshine. On a website that featured legal forms, I found a short, standard contract that granted me the copyright to all of the photos taken today, as well as the right to exploit them for commercial purposes at my discretion. I typed the payment amount and date into the blanks on the form and printed out three copies of the contract, one for each of the Bootlegging Brothers to sign.

When Kiki finished taking photos in front of the shop, we went inside and took a few photographs indoors, too. As she downloaded the photos to my computer for viewing, I handed each of the band members a copy of the contract and a pen.

Brody held his pen aloft and extended his arm in a gesture intended to hold his brothers at bay. "Don't mean to sound untrusting, Hattie, but we've been burned before. Played three sets at a backyard birthday barbecue and the guy paid us with a worthless check that bounced. He never did make good on it. We'll sign once we get our cash and liquor."

Knowing this bit of history, I felt less insulted by his reluctance to sign right away. "I'll get your money right now." I strode to the stock room, unlocked the safe, and removed $450 in cash. After locking the safe again, I carried the money to the counter. I placed the bills on the countertop, grabbed a jug of moonshine from the display, and set it atop the cash. "Sign the contracts and we'll trade."

Brody frowned, but he scribbled his name on the contract, left it on the counter, then lifted the jug of 'shine to grab their cash. Garth and Josh signed their contracts and handed them directly to me. As Brody divvied up the money and slid his share into his wallet, I rounded up two more jugs of moonshine for his brothers from the store display.

The men set about packing up their instruments. When he'd finished, Garth caught my eye. "If you don't already have plans for the weekend, come out to the River Pearl Winery. We're playing there Saturday night. Got a four-weekend run. Our brother-in-law got us the gig. He's digging a pond at the vineyard."

Brody whirled on Garth. "Tate Hutchinson is not your brother-in-law!"

Kiki's brows rose in interest. I, too, was curious why Brody had reacted with such fury.

Garth said, "Well, what would you call Tate, then?"

Brody snarled, "If I had to call him anything, I'd just call him by his name. He's not our kin."

Garth turned to me and explained. "Tate is married to Brody's ex-wife, Camille."

"Ah, I see." That explained why Brody's carotid arteries were throbbing like the bassline at a nightclub. But Brody was technically correct. Tate Hutchinson wasn't their brother-in-law. He wasn't related by marriage or blood.

Turning back to Brody, Garth said, "Whatever you want to call Tate, we owe him for landing us the winery gig."

Brody huffed again. "Oh, I know what I want to call him."

Garth slid a discreet look my way, his eyes alight with amusement. Seemed he enjoyed pushing his big brother's buttons.

Our business concluded, I held out my hand. "Thanks so much, guys. I hope these ads bring us all success."

"Me, too," Garth said. He took my hand and gave it a shake, then lifted my arm up and turned it, leading me to dance a little two-step with him. Not that I really minded. His playfulness was charming. He'd make some other woman very happy someday.

When Garth released me, Josh merely shook my hand but said nothing.

Brody shook my hand, but his grip was as flimsy as his face was sour. "I still think you got the better part of this bargain."

Garth groaned. "You're killing us, bro."

Chapter Four

As the three brothers headed out to their vehicles on the street in front of the Moonshine Shack, Kiki and I took seats on stools behind the sales counter to look at the images on the computer. Although Kiki was an amateur photographer, she'd taken a photography class in college and her artist's eye gave her an edge.

I leaned in to get a closer look. "Kiki, these photos are fantastic!" She'd posed the band members and arranged the jars and jugs of moonshine perfectly. I turned to her. "I should pay you for your time."

"Nah." She waved a dismissive hand. "Just give me a photo credit."

I leaned over and gave her a one-armed hug. "What did I do to deserve a friend like you?"

"Who says you deserve me?"

We slowly went through the images, looking each of them over carefully and comparing them. We'd choose a few to add to the Moonshine Shack's website and have one of them enlarged into a poster I could hang in the front window.

In one of the pics, Kiki had caught Brody mid-blink, and his eyes were at half-mast. "Put that one on your website," she said. "It looks like he's enjoyed a lot of your moonshine."

"As amusing as that might be, Brody might not appreciate me posting a bad photo of him." I squinted. "Garth looks good in all of these photos."

"That's because he looks good all the time," she said. "You at all tempted to go see him play at the winery?"

"I am," I said, "but not for the reason you think."

"Uh-oh." She eyed me intently. "You've got that *I just had a great business idea* look on your face again."

"What does that look like?"

She rotated her eyeballs in a googly-eyed style and let her tongue loll out of her mouth.

"I do have an idea," I replied. "I only hope the owners of the vineyard will agree it's a good one."

"Don't bore me with the details." She slid off her stool. "Just let me know if you need me to help."

"Will do. And thanks again, Kiki." She tolerated me giving her one more hug before she flounced out the door.

Once Kiki had gone, I attached a small speaker to my cell phone and streamed the radio station, eagerly waiting to hear my commercial play. I spent the rest of the morning uploading the pics of the Bootlegging Brothers to my website, ordering posters online, and working up a proposal for the winery's owners. I figured I'd have better luck pitching my idea in person. After all, it's harder to say no to someone sitting right in front of you than it is to reject them via e-mail or on the phone. I e-mailed the owner of the vineyard and requested an in-person meet-ing, promising to take no more than fifteen minutes of her time. To my delight, I received a response that afternoon inviting me to come out for a meeting the following morn-ing. To my further delight, I heard my jingle play on the radio that afternoon. It sounded cute and catchy, just as I'd hoped. Time would tell if it brought customers to my door.

At ten Thursday morning, I gave Smoky a scratch be-hind the ears and a kiss on the nose and headed to the winery. The vineyard sat a few miles west of downtown Chattanooga, on the eastern side of Raccoon Mountain Road. The road ran along the Tennessee River, providing a beautiful view as I motored along.

As I approached the winery, the view of the river was marred by strands of rusty barbed wire strung along un-finished tree limbs that had been stuck in the ground as improvised supports. In several places, the fence posts had fallen over and the barbed wire lay strewn across the weeds, dirt, and stones. Among the long, wild grasses and weeds rose a dilapidated farmhouse. Any paint that had been applied to the boards had long since peeled off, leav-ing them a weathered brownish gray. An elderly dark-skinned woman with white hair sat on the porch. She looked frail and tiny, the top of her head barely reaching the upper rung of the ladder-back rocker. She held a glass of what appeared to be iced tea in one hand and a book in the other. A furry black-and-tan mutt lay at her feet. The dog appeared equally old and frail, its snout gray, its eyes cloudy. Both appeared content, however, happy to enjoy a warm summer day on a shaded porch. The beautiful Ten-nessee River rolled by behind them. The road curved close to the river there, and the land the house sat on was much wider than it was deep, a long and thin stretch. There were only a hundred or so feet between the road and the bluff above the river behind her.

I turned my attention back to the road as I drove past and approached the turn-in for the vineyard. The entrance was marked with a wooden sign painted a deep burgundy color that resembled red wine. The words RIVER PEARL VINEYARD AND WINERY were spelled out in pearlescent-white paint. The edges of the sign were lined with irregular stones painted in the same pearlescent paint to resemble river pearls. I pulled my van up to the automatic gate that stretched across the entrance. The gate bore the iridescent-white paint, too, and gleamed like I imagined the gates to heaven would. I unrolled my window. A light breeze carried the smell of smoke into my van. A tall pile of brush burned in the distance, sending up orange flames and thick smoke. Not an unusual sight in rural areas, where landowners needed to clear their properties for planting or as a safeguard against wildfires.

A security keypad stood atop a metal pole next to the drive. I pushed the button on the keypad to contact the office. *Bzzzt.*

A few seconds later, a cheerful female voice came through the speaker. "How can I help you?"

"Hi," I said to the disembodied voice. "It's Hattie Hayes. I have an appointment to meet with Pearl Kemp."

"That's me," she said in a singsong lilt. "Come on in, Hattie."

The gate unlocked with a loud *click* and slowly swung open to allow me onto the property. As I drove into the vineyard, I ran my gaze over the expansive property. *What a bucolic view.* Tall forsythia bushes lined one side of the driveway, their foliage all green now but sure to bloom bright yellow early next spring, one of the earliest harbingers of the season. Trees were scattered about, mostly live oaks providing shade for the picnic tables situated underneath their expansive limbs. Near the front of the acreage was an old-fashioned wood barn that had been converted and now housed the winery's tasting room. The barn, too, sported a shimmery-white hue. A spacious covered deck extended out from the barn. The wood was stained in a rich, dark shade that provided a nice contrast. Durable aluminum tables and chairs, all in white, filled the deck. Rolls of thick, clear vinyl were mounted along the interior edge of the deck's cover. The vinyl panels could be rolled down in inhospitable weather to form makeshift walls, enclosing the space so it could be used in all four seasons. For now, the vinyl walls were raised so that patrons could enjoy the view of the grapevines and the river on the other side of the road. Bright flowers in wooden wine barrels and hanging baskets added color to the retail barn and deck.

A wide raised platform sat at the end of the deck. I knew from reviewing photos on the winery's website that the platform was used both as a stage for performers and as a place where people could exchange wedding vows, toast a couple's golden anniversary, or announce the winner of a company's employee-of-the-year award. Offering the deck as a private event space was a good business move, a way to eke more profits out of the place.

In the distance stood a second barn. Unlike the barn that had been converted into the charming tasting room, this barn was a large prefab metal structure, unattractive yet functional. A two-story rustic stone house sat even farther back, tucked away among a stand of trees, only a few windows and a chimney visible between the branches. I surmised the home belonged to the vineyard's owners. *What a beautiful place to live.* Living on-site would make for a short, convenient commute, too.

The acreage between the two barns was filled with row after row of grapevines. A man drove a green John Deere tractor through the vineyard, the attachment on his tractor straddling the vines as it removed the precious fruit. On the far side of the vines, a sizable area had been cleared down to the rocky soil. A man worked a school bus–yellow excavator with rubber tracks rather than tires, digging a hole and dumping the buckets of rocky soil into a cart hitched to the back of a pickup truck. I recalled Garth saying something about the husband of Brody's ex building an ornamental pond out here. I wondered if the guy driving the excavator might be Tate. Or maybe he was one of the other two crew members, who were working with shovels, smoothing out the debris that had been dumped into the cart.

I drove to the white barn and parked in the gravel lot. As I climbed out of my van, I spotted a midnight-blue pickup truck parked at the end of the lot. An empty flatbed trailer was hooked up to the trailer hitch behind it. On the driver's door was a removable magnetic sign that bore the logo for Paradise Pools, Ponds & Patios. The truck must belong to Tate or one of his crew.

I climbed out of my van, bringing my purse, computer bag, and moonshine samples with me. The door opened as I approached. A woman stood back to allow me in. She wore a gauzy white blouse with white jeans and white ankle boots in a pointy-toed cowgirl style. She looked to be in her mid to late fifties. Her once strawberry-blond hair was now streaked with white, the resulting shade one which, in wine terms, would be called a rosé. She'd pulled her hair back into an easy, carefree ponytail secured with a barrette, the style revealing the freshwater pearl earrings dangling from her lobes. Her fair skin was spotted with a combination of small freckles and larger age spots, but she hadn't tried to hide either, aging gracefully and naturally. Her smile was just as genuine. "Good morning, Hattie. I'm Pearl Kemp."

I extended my arm and we shook hands as I introduced myself. On closer inspection, I noticed her wrist bore a freshwater pearl bracelet, and a large river pearl pendant hung from a silver chain around her neck. Her accessories tied nicely into the winery's name and theme.

When she released my hand, she waved me inside. "Come on in and take a seat."

The inside of the barn was decorated in faux grapevines that encircled the posts and hung from the trusses that supported the roof. Intertwined with the grapevines were strings of faux pearls. White wooden tables and chairs were scattered about. In the center of each table was a small votive candle inside a holder formed from pearlescent mussel shells. A wide service counter stood along the far wall. Behind it were two doors. One was open, revealing a basic commercial kitchen area. The other door was made of glass and led into a walk-in wine cooler filled with bottle after bottle of wine. A wide, locking arm spanned the front of the door. As an added measure, a metal security panel composed of crisscrossing lines forming diamond shapes was embedded between the panes of glass on the cooler door. With each bottle of wine priced at anywhere from twenty to fifty dollars, there had to be thousands of dollars' worth of wine in the cooler. They were smart to protect their investment. *Maybe I should install security bars on the windows of my shop.*

Pearl held out an arm to indicate a chair, and I sat down, placing my bags on the wood floor beside me.

Once she'd taken a seat across from me, I gestured around the place. "Is the winery named after you?"

"In a sense." She went on to tell me that she was named after her grandmother Pearl, whose name reflected a favorite pastime of her grandmother's parents in the early 1900s. "Back then, people would go pearling in the rivers all over Tennessee. It was something they did for fun, part hobby and part treasure hunt. Back then, the pearls were produced naturally by the mussels that lived in the river shoals. But then dams were built, which did away with the shoals, which did away with the mussels, which did away with pearling. Most freshwater pearls produced now are cultured."

Seemed so much of what was deemed "progress" wreaked havoc on the environment. *What a shame.*

"So," Pearl said, folding her hands on the table and leaning toward me, all business now. "What's this exciting proposition you have for me?"

I'd promised to be respectful of her time, so I got right to the point. "A Wine and 'Shine night. I got the idea after the Bootlegging Brothers recorded a jingle for me. Garth told me the band will be playing here this weekend."

"I've heard your jingle on the radio." She proceeded to sing the refrain, adding jazz hands for fun effect. "She's a shining star! Get a jug! Get a jar!"

In a gesture of feigned arrogance, I raised a hand to fluff and toss my hair. "I'm the shining star they were singing about."

"Good to see you haven't let it go to your head."

We shared a laugh. I was glad to know the song was as catchy as I'd thought, a cheery earworm. I reached into my computer bag, retrieved a copy of the written proposal I'd prepared, and handed it to her. I went over the bullet points, offering her options. "We could make it a friendly competition, your bottles and my jugs and jars going head-to-head. We could serve specialized drinks for the event. You could use your red wine to make a traditional sangria, and I could use my moonshine to make an apple-blueberry 'shine-ria. You could pour your rosé over crushed cubes made from the wine and call it a frozé, while I could make a cherry 'shine slush. I can add my Granddaddy's Ole-Timey Corn Liquor to regular grape juice and white grape juice and call the drinks red and white winey 'shine."

Her expression was intrigued, yet hesitant. I knew exactly what she was thinking and I addressed her concerns directly. "I'm sure you're wondering how it would benefit you to allow a competing product to be sold at your winery. Primarily, it's simply a new and interesting experience to offer your existing customers. I suspect many of them will stick with your wine. Most people have a preference for wine or hard liquor and tend to stay in their lane." I reviewed the statistics I'd accumulated, all showing that the majority of wine drinkers and purchasers were women. "My guess is your customer base is mostly female. Serving my moonshine could draw in a new crowd for you, attract more men."

The slight bobbing of her head told me she was giving my pitch serious consideration.

I continued. "I'd promote the Wine and 'Shine event to my customers. I'd provide all of the moonshine for the event, of course, and I'd also pay you twenty-five percent of my gross receipts for the night. Together, I think we could draw an even bigger crowd than you'd draw alone. What's more, with your winery hosting the Bootlegging Brothers, it seems only right to serve moonshine."

She had to chuckle at that. "You're quite convincing."

"If I haven't yet sold you on the idea, my moonshine will. I brought samples if you'd like to taste my flavors."

"I'd love to."

I reached down into my bag and retrieved the sampler set I'd prepared in miniature mason jars. Though each one held just under two ounces of liquor, collectively they'd pack quite a wallop. Realizing this, Pearl rounded up a wineglass and splashed just a dash of each flavor into it for her taste test. She savored each of my lighter-proof fruity flavors, but when the sample of Granddaddy's Ole-Timey Corn Liquor hit her tongue, she grimaced. "Whoa! That's some strong stuff!"

I gave her a coy smile. "If you lit a match, you could breathe fire like a dragon or a circus performer."

She laughed again before her eyes narrowed and she tapped her index finger against her cheek, all business now. "I suppose it can't hurt to try this Wine and 'Shine idea. But I'll need to run it by my husband, Darren, first, make sure he's on board." She stood. "Come out to the vineyard with me and meet him. He's harvesting grapes for our chardonnay."

I followed her outside. The steady sound of the winery's tractor carried across the field, along with the banging noises coming from the excavator as it dug at the rocky soil. The sun beat down on us as we made our way away from the barn, over the gravel parking lot, and onto the dirt. There, Pearl stopped by a large golf cart with nubby all-terrain tires. The cart had two bench seats facing front and a third seat at the rear that faced backward, along with a vinyl canopy in a blue-and-ivory stripe. "Take a seat and hang on," she said with a mischievous gleam in her eye. "I'm known to have a lead foot."

I climbed into the front passenger seat and took hold of the hanging bar overhead. Pearl hadn't been kidding. She took off at warp speed, throwing me back against the seat. We careened toward the vineyard, bouncing and jostling over the uneven ground, slowing down as we approached the first row of vines. As we rolled along the perimeter, Pearl pointed out the different varieties of grapes growing on the vines and told me about them, giving me a lesson in grapes to add to the lesson on pearls she'd already provided. She noted that each variety of grape ripened at a different rate and was ready to harvest at a different time, which enabled them to spread out their harvesting season.

"I wish we could grow muscadines," she said wistfully. "I love sweet muscadine wine, but it's too cold for muscadine grapes here. They do better along the coast."

I, too, appreciated muscadine wine. Granddaddy hated the stuff, said it tasted like Kool-Aid. Of course, his opinions were tainted by the fact that moonshine had long been the family business, even when it had been illegal.

As we drew closer to where Darren was driving the harvester, Pearl raised an arm and waved him down. He slowed and pulled to a stop a dozen feet away from our cart. A cloud of dust drifted and sparkled in the sunshine as he hopped down from the narrow cab. I surmised the equipment was specially made for vineyard work, to fit in the narrow lanes between the grapevines. Like his wife, Darren appeared to be in his mid to late fifties. He wore a pair of noise-canceling headphones over a bright-orange University of Tennessee ball cap. He removed them both as he walked toward us, revealing a mostly bald head with about three inches of salt-and-pepper hair forming a semi-circle around the back of his skull, connecting his ears.

As Pearl introduced me, Darren whipped a bandanna from his back pocket and mopped sweat from his brow. He gave me a nod as he tucked the bandanna back into his pocket. "Nice to meet you, Hattie."

He fanned himself with his cap as Pearl gave him the rundown on my proposal. "So? What do you think about hosting a Wine and 'Shine night?"

"Let's give it a go. Nothing ventured, nothing gained, right? Can't hurt to try and see what happens."

He gave me another nod in goodbye, plunked the ball cap back onto his head, and pulled it down tight. He leaned down and gave his wife a quick peck on the cheek before heading back to his tractor. *Sweet.*

Pearl turned to me. "Looks like we're on."

"Great!"

"Want to see a project we've got in the works before you go?" The gleam in her eye told me she was excited about the improvements they were making to the winery. Who wouldn't be happy to see their business expand and thrive?

"I'd love to."

She punched the gas on the golf cart once again and drove to the area where the crew was working. *Bang! Bam! Screeechh!* The bucket on the small excavator moved up and down as the clawlike edge dragged over the rocky soil, scraping up dirt, stones, and roots. The Caterpillar company's logo appeared along the excavator arm and across the back of the cab—the word *CAT* spelled out in white lettering outlined in black, with the letter *A* sitting atop a yellow triangle.

The man at the controls looked to be around thirty years old. He was tall, lean, and lanky, with short sandy hair and a full, boxy beard covered in part by a mask. To keep the dust out of his eyes, he also wore a pair of tinted protective goggles. I wouldn't mind a mask and goggles myself. The dust tickled my nose and had me blinking to clear particles from my eyes. The two men working with the shovels also wore goggles and dust masks. Although it was difficult to tell much about their faces with them being mostly covered, the streaks of gray in their hair, the leathery texture of their weathered skin, and the soft paunches around their waists told me they were middle-aged. Based on this fact, I surmised that Tate must be the one working the excavator.

The brushfire continued to burn not too far away. A pile of freshly cut logs stood near a stand of trees a hundred feet or so beyond the burning brush. This portion of the property must have had to be cleared in order to accommodate the Kemps' plans.

Pearl raised her voice to be heard over the noise of the heavy machinery. "The barn capacity is limited, even with the deck. Some days people spill over into the vineyard."

I cupped my hands around my mouth to amplify my voice. "Too many customers? Sounds like a good problem to have."

"It sure is." Rather than continue to shout, she drove us far enough away from the heavy equipment that we could speak at normal volume but still watch the men work. She stopped to resume our conversation. "We figured we'd make a nice outdoor space, put in a fire pit and add another bar out here so we can serve more customers." She held out her hand, moving her finger to indicate a meandering line of small marker flags on the ground nearby. "See those markers? The pool company is going to form a little river that will empty into the pond. It'll be lined with smooth river rocks. The water will recirculate, like a lazy river. The improvements will cost a small fortune, but we figured with the name of the winery being River Pearl, it ought to have a river."

The plans were solid. I could visualize the end result. I'd have to come back when the work was finished to see if the vision in my mind's eye had been accurate.

Pearl's gaze moved upward, locking on the old cock-eyed farmhouse on the other side of Racoon Mountain Road, the one I'd passed on my drive here. "We've been trying to buy that property across the road for years. It's got six hundred feet of actual riverfront. We've offered the woman who owns it an ungodly amount of money, but no matter how high we go she won't sell. Her name's Shirley Byrd. She says the land's been in the Byrd family for more than two centuries, since just after Tennessee became a state. She was born there and she said she plans to die there, too."

"Her death might come sooner than she planned," I said. "That house looks ready to collapse in on itself."

Pearl chuckled. "That old woman and her house will probably survive us all." Her smile faded slightly as she continued to stare across the road. "I worry about her sometimes. She seems a little off her rocker."

People might say the same thing about my grand-daddy. They might be right, too.

Pearl drove us back to the wine shop, parking the golf cart around the back of the building, where it had been before. We went inside, where I gathered up my things and thanked Pearl for agreeing to the event. "See you Saturday at four o'clock."

As I drove out of the winery, I passed the entrance to a dirt drive that led onto Shirley Byrd's property. Pearl had said the woman seemed off her rocker, but for the time being she was firmly seated on her rocking chair, slowly tilting forward and back.

I raised a hand in acknowledgment and she raised hers in reply. For a moment, I debated stopping to offer the woman a free jar of my moonshine. She looked to be about Granddaddy's age. She might enjoy a fruity splash in her iced tea like he did, and I always had a spare case or two in my van. But I thought better of it when my eyes spotted a long-barreled gun leaning against the wall next to her. Being unfamiliar with weapons, I wasn't sure if it was a rifle or a shotgun, but I guessed it was probably a shotgun. Shotguns didn't require good aim, which is why many people preferred them for self-defense. But, either way, the gun looked like it could do a great deal of damage. *Yikes.*

Chapter Five

On Saturday, Marlon planned to move from the apartment he'd been renting to the house he'd recently bought. His new home was a modest single-story redbrick ranch model, built in the 1960s and comprising three bedrooms and two bathrooms in twelve hundred square feet of space. Though the guacamole-green porcelain sinks, toilets, and tubs in the bathrooms were hopelessly outdated, the plumbing was solid and in good working order. His kitchen, like mine in my cabin, also reflected an earlier era, when automatic dishwashers were considered a luxury and thus not included. But the house had new carpet and a recently replaced roof. Plus, it sat on eight acres directly adjacent to the horse farm where he'd been living and boarding Charlotte. She'd be able to maintain her friendships with the other mares, even if they'd now have to gossip over a fence. Most of all, the property came with a mortgage that a public servant could afford.

I helped Marlon pack boxes in the morning, but it didn't take long. He was a typical bachelor, owning only a few dishes, a basic set of pots and pans, and a couple of dish towels. His bathroom contained only assorted toiletries and a few sets of bath towels. Although he was a mounted police officer, he was no clotheshorse. We packed up his bedroom and closet in record time. *How can men get by with only five pairs of shoes and a couple of sweaters?*

Marlon had borrowed my empty moonshine trailer to use as a moving van. He'd also hired two of the ranch hands to help him move his furniture from the apartment to his house next door. When they arrived, I took it as my cue to go. Besides, I needed to pack up myself, get ready for the evening's Wine and 'Shine event at the River Pearl Winery. Though I was disappointed Marlon wouldn't be able to come out to the vineyard, I hoped I'd be so busy tonight that I wouldn't have time for idle chatter anyway. If things went well, maybe the Wine and 'Shine night could become a regular event.

Marlon walked me out to my van. "Let's have dinner here next weekend. I should be settled by then. We can make popcorn and watch a movie, too. How's your Sunday night look?"

"Sunday's perfect." While my shop was open until nine most days, it closed at five on Sundays. "I'll bring a bottle of wine." The least I could do to repay Pearl and Darren Kemp for agreeing to host the Wine and 'Shine event was to buy a few bottles from their vineyard.

After leaving Marlon's apartment, I stopped at the florist to pick up fresh daisies. I drove to the Moonshine Shack, went inside, and quickly assembled some cute decorations for the evening's event. I gathered a dozen empty jugs of Grandaddy's Ole-Timey Corn Liquor, tied a blue-and-white gingham ribbon around the handle of each jug, and plunked three daisies into each of the open mouths. I stuck a tall wooden spoon into each jug, too. I'd clipped an old-fashioned wooden clothespin to the top of each spoon to hold discount coupons. Kiki had helped me devise the design. She wasn't just good at art, she was crafty, too. The pieces were folksy and charming.

Simone, one of the college students I'd recently hired to help out at the shop, arrived at a quarter to noon. Simone had light-brown skin, loose dark curls, and a girly-girl sense of style. She'd paired her neon-green store tee with a swishy pink miniskirt, strappy sandals with a three-inch heel, and lots of colorful jewelry and makeup. Her fun-loving look was deceptive. She was double-majoring in business finance and entrepreneurship and had made the dean's list every semester. That doesn't happen without hard work and tenacity. I should know. I'd made the dean's list every semester, too.

After Simone helped me load up my van for the Wine and 'Shine event, we opened the shop. Saturday afternoons were the busiest time in the store, and we spent the day tending to customer after customer. While I served samples to our patrons, Simone rang up and bagged their purchases and sent them on their way with a smile and a "Come back soon!"

Fortunately, Simone had a sorority sister who could use some cash and agreed to help her out at the shop for the evening. I trusted Simone to work hard but, for safety reasons, I didn't want to leave her by herself in the shop, especially at closing time. A young woman alone in a store could be seen as an easy target. The shop had come wired with a basic alarm system that would go off if a locked door was breached or a window broken. I'd later added security cameras as an additional deterrent, and bought a panic button device that could be carried in a pocket and would activate an audible alarm when pressed.

I handed the panic button over to Simone now. "Don't hesitate to use it if you feel even the slightest bit threatened."

"I won't." She slipped it into a pocket in her skirt, where it would be within quick reach.

I turned to her sorority sister. "Thanks for helping out. Take a jar of 'shine as a bonus."

"I will! Thanks."

I went out the back door to my van and climbed in. When I'd told Granddaddy about my plans, he'd asked if he could tag along. I knew he'd enjoy the music as well as a change of scenery. But the event would run into the late hours of the night and I worried whether he'd have the endurance to stay awake until it wound up. I decided if his energy petered out I could summon an Uber to take him back home.

When I rolled up in front of the Singing River Retirement Home, I found a small group gathered. Granddaddy sat on a bench, his cane resting across his knobby knees. Louetta sat beside him. Louetta's two friends stood nearby, as did two of my grandfather's buddies.

Granddaddy and Louetta stood as I pulled to a stop at the curb and unrolled my window. "Hey, Granddaddy. Hello, Louetta." I raised a hand in greeting to the rest of the group and gave them a general greeting. "Hey, y'all."

Louetta's eyebrows rose, disappearing under her snowy bangs. She pointed to herself. "You know my name?"

I fought a laugh. "It's been mentioned."

Granddaddy ambled to the passenger door. "Louetta

asked if she and her friends could come with us to the winery, but I told her your van only holds two people. My buddies asked about it, too."

Granddaddy had surrendered his driver's license a while back, but he appeared to be older than some of the others in the group. "None of them drive anymore?"

"A couple of them still drive," he said, "but not after dark. They could get themselves out to the winery, but not back home."

"How about I get them an Uber?" Heck, I could probably deduct the cost as a business expense since it would mean more customers for my moonshine.

Granddaddy turned back to address his friends. "Hattie says she'll call one of them private cabs to pick y'all up."

Louetta's face brightened even more. "You'd do that for us?"

"Sure," I said. "When will you be ready?"

"I'll need fifteen minutes to put on a fresh coat of lipstick and grab my handbag." Louetta turned to the rest of the gang. They murmured in agreement.

I worked my thumbs over my phone and arranged for a minivan to pick them up in a quarter hour. "It'll be a red Chrysler Pacifica." I gave them the license plate number and waved them over to look at the image of the vehicle and the driver. "Look for this car and driver."

The ladies giggled and the men whooped, excited about their outing. Louetta clutched her fists to her chin. "This is going to be so much fun!"

"See you soon!" I took off with my grandfather in my passenger seat and aimed for the winery. It took everything in me not to tease my grandfather about Louetta, but the last thing I wanted to do was make him feel guilty for seeking out female companionship. He'd been horribly lonely since Granny went on her way. I kept my thoughts to myself, even though I was happy for him.

Shirley Byrd was sitting on her porch across the road from the vineyard again today. The dog was again at her feet, and the long-barreled gun stood at the ready beside her. Though the gun made me nervous, I supposed the woman might feel like she needed protection living by herself out here. Other than the winery, there wasn't much else around. Just like a young woman alone at a store would make an easy target, so would an elderly woman alone in a rural house.

The parking lot was already half-full with patrons when we turned in. I found a spot near the end of the lot and climbed out of my van. It was a sunny day, not a cloud in the sky. After spending the first half of the day inside at my shop, I spared a brief moment to close my eyes, turn my face up to the sky, and bask in the glorious sunshine. It took only a few seconds of the pounding heat before I felt as though I were being shrink-wrapped in my own skin. *Maybe working indoors isn't so bad, after all.*

The thought had me opening my eyes and glancing across the vineyard to the area where the pond was under construction. The crew had made definite progress since Thursday morning. I could make out a large hole with well-defined edges. Looked like they'd finished digging the pond. It wasn't a perfect circle or oval. Rather, they'd made it an irregular shape to look more natural, contouring it to curve around several large oak trees sitting on the banks. The yellow Caterpillar excavator sat idle today on the near side of the pond. There was no construction crew in sight. Not a surprise given that it was Saturday, a day off from work for most people and probably the busiest day of the week at the winery. Even if the crew had been willing to work today, the noise and dust would have ruined the ambience for the winery's patrons.

While my grandfather carefully eased himself out of the passenger seat, I loaded several cases of moonshine onto a dolly to wheel them inside. As we entered the tasting barn, Pearl looked up from behind the counter. Just as before, she was dressed in all white, though her outfit today was dressier and more festive to fit the occasion. She wore a sleeveless knit maxi dress with faux pearls beaded along the waist and bustline. Rather than boots, she'd worn a pair of white wedges. The river pearl pendant hung around her neck, along with the earrings and bracelet she'd been wearing when I saw her on Thursday. I noticed all of the winery staff were dressed head to toe in white, a uniform of sorts, though each person put their own spin on the look. The solid-white outfits made them easy to spot among the crowd.

Pearl smiled in greeting. "Hi, Hattie. Who'd you bring with you today?"

I introduced her to my grandfather. "Five of his friends from the retirement home are on their way."

"Wonderful!" she said. "I'll get your group a nice table out on the deck." Turning back to me, she pointed to a spot at the end of the counter that she'd kept open for me. "You can set up there."

While she escorted my grandfather out to the deck, I proceeded to set up my 'shine station. I'd brought along a blender to mix the cherry 'shine slush, as well as the insulated beverage dispenser, which was currently filled with 'shine-ria—moonshine's answer to sangria. I'd add a small scoop of assorted fruit to the cups before filling them for an authentic sangria experience. I also had pitchers of regular grape juice and white grape juice to which I'd add unflavored moonshine to make winey 'shine.

Soft music played over the speakers while I set up my bar and scurried about the tasting room and deck, placing the jugs that contained the daisies, wooden spoons, and discount coupons on the tables and on either end of the stage. When I finished, I ran a slush out to my grandfather on the deck. Pearl confirmed that I was ready, picked up a microphone, and announced the kickoff of the Wine and 'Shine event. "River Pearl Vineyard is pleased to welcome Hattie Hayes of the Moonshine Shack to the winery tonight. We'll be engaging in some fun and friendly competition, folks. See what you think about her 'shine-ria and cherry 'shine slush. How do they compare to River Pearl's sangria and frozé? There are no wrong answers, just great drinks! Step on up to the counter and give her moonshine a try!"

In seconds, people began to wander over to my end of the bar to find out more about my offerings. Fortunately, one of the winery's staff had been assigned to process payments for the moonshine, probably to ensure customers didn't have to wait too long in line, but I suspected it was also to make sure I didn't try to stiff the winery for their share of my take. I took no offense. Pearl Kemp didn't truly know me, and it only made sense for her to protect her interests.

Louetta and the others came in the door and got in line at my station. When they reached the counter, she asked, "All of your drinks sound good. What would you recommend?"

With the day being warm, I suggested the cherry 'shine slush. I fixed five drinks for the group, as well as another for them to carry out to my grandfather, who'd no doubt be near the bottom of his cup by now. I pointed to the doors that led out to the deck. "He's got a table for y'all outside."

One of my grandfather's buddies responded with, "That's dope." He cut me a look, leaned in, and asked, "Did I use that term right? I heard it from my grandson."

"Yep," I said with a grin. "You sure did."

Drinks in hand, the group moved en masse toward the doors.

Shortly thereafter, I handed a 'shine-ria to a woman and thanked her. That's when I saw an arm moving back and forth in the air behind her. It was Garth Sheridan, waving to get my attention. I raised a hand, too, and returned his smile. When the line cleared a few minutes later and we experienced a momentary lull, I excused myself to give Garth a proper greeting. After all, he was the one who'd given me the idea to propose the Wine and 'Shine event. I grabbed the large manila envelope that contained a stack of the eleven-by-seventeen-inch posters of the Bootlegging Brothers I'd ordered along with the larger-sized posters I'd displayed in my shop. I also grabbed a prepared cup of my 'shine-ria. I found Garth with his brothers setting up at the stage on the outdoor deck.

Brody glanced my way and offered a quick "Hey" in greeting. Josh acknowledged me with a silent lift of his chin. As usual, Garth was friendlier than his brothers. "There's the shining star." He picked up one of the decorative jugs I'd placed on the stage and held it up. "These jugs your doing?"

"Yes. I thought they'd make fun stage decorations."

"I like them," Garth said. "Adds some folksy flair." He

returned the jug to the stage. "What were you doing behind the bar inside?"

"We're holding a Wine and 'Shine event tonight." I told him how I'd come up with the idea after he'd invited me out to hear the band at the winery. "Pearl and Darren thought it sounded fun, so here I am." I held out the cup. "I thought you might like to try my 'shine-ria."

Brody grunted. "Josh and I might like to try it, too."

I forced a smile at the surly strings player. "Coming right up. I'd planned to get you some, too, but I didn't think I could carry three cups and your posters without spilling on them."

Now that Garth had taken his cup from me, I unfastened the brad on the envelope and pulled out the full-color posters. "I ordered these for the band. I thought you could autograph them for your fans tonight."

Brody's scowl lessened and Garth's face brightened even more. "Wow! Thanks, Hattie. You're amazing!"

I wasn't sure the ability to upload a photo and a logo to a printing site qualified for amazement, but I'd take the compliment anyway. The posters had cost precious little, but I didn't point out how affordable they'd been. The greater value was in the idea that the band could offer them to their fans. That's where my business sense had come in. These brothers might know bluegrass, but they didn't have my background in marketing. I turned to Brody. "I'll be right back with drinks for you and Josh."

I scurried back to the bar, served two women waiting there a cup of white winey 'shine each, then filled cups of 'shine-ria for Brody and Josh. Hurrying back to the outdoor deck, I handed them over. As I turned to go, a family walked up. The father had the same physique, hair, and beard as the guy who'd been driving the excavator in the vineyard when I'd been here two days earlier. But in light of the fact that he'd been wearing a dust mask and goggles before, I couldn't be certain it was the same person. Beside the man stood a pretty woman with wheat-blond hair, cornflower blue eyes, and generous cleavage barely contained by the bloodred crossover top she'd paired with equally tight jeans. Other than a certain popular singer named Dolly, I'd never seen such an ample bosom. How the woman could draw breath was a mystery. On either side of the couple stood two adorable little girls. The girl holding the woman's hand appeared to be around kindergarten age, and had dark, glossy hair. The girl holding the man's hand was towheaded and tiptoeing out of toddlerhood, still chubby-faced and sucking her thumb, but steady on her feet. *Two years old, maybe?*

The older girl squealed and jumped up and down, clapping her hands together. "Uncle Garth! Uncle Garth!"

Garth scooped the girl up in his arms and proceeded to spin around with her squealing all the while. When he sat her down, the younger one stepped forward, her arms stretched up in request. Garth scooped her up and repeated the routine. Once he'd put her down, he made introductions. "Hattie, this is my sister-in-law, Camille, and her husband, Tate Hutchinson."

So, I had been right about the man's identity. He was the guy I'd seen driving the excavator, the one who'd gotten the Bootlegging Brothers the gig here at the winery, the one married to Brody's ex-wife.

Garth booped each of the girls on the nose as he introduced them. "These are my nieces, Imogene and Amelia." Imogene was the older girl, Amelia the younger.

Imogene turned to Josh. "Hey, Uncle Josh." Though

her voice was polite, it held less enthusiasm than it had when she'd greeted Garth. The enthusiasm diminished several more degrees when she greeted Brody with nothing more than, "Hey."

A look of hurt flitted across Brody's face at his daughter's lukewarm reception. He bent down to look her in the face. "Can I get a 'Hey, *Daddy*'?"

Imogene looked down at her shoes, but repeated the words he'd asked her to say. "Hey, Daddy."

"That's more like it." Brody gave his daughter an awkward pat on the head before standing and turning to Garth. "Why do I have to keep reminding you Camille isn't your sister-in-law anymore? Amelia's not your niece, neither. Never was. She doesn't share a drop of Sheridan blood."

Tate scoffed, Camille rolled her eyes, and Garth groaned and cut his brother a look of utter frustration. "Why you always gotta complicate things, bro?"

"I'm not complicating anything!" Brody snarled. "I'm just pointing out facts."

Garth shook his head and returned his attention to Camille and Tate. "Long as we're on the subject of facts, it's a fact that Hattie makes the best moonshine you'll ever drink."

When Camille and Tate looked my way, I said, "I'm serving shots inside. A cherry moonshine slush. 'Shineria, too. It's moonshine's answer to sangria. I'd be happy to make virgin drinks for your girls."

Camille said, "That's very nice of you, Hattie. Thank you."

I led the Hutchinson family to the bar inside and prepared drinks for them. "First round is on the house," I said as I handed them across the bar. So that the winery employee didn't think I was trying to stiff the Kemps on their share of my profits, I said, "They're with the band."

The girl lifted an unconcerned shoulder. She had no skin in this game. She'd get her paycheck regardless.

A few minutes later, the band was ready and Brody stepped to the microphone. "Howdy, folks. I'm Brody Sheridan. As always, I'll be playing strings tonight. These two guys up here with me are my little brothers, Josh and Garth. Josh'll be singing at ya, and Garth will be fooling around on his washboard and whatnot."

I watched through the open doors as Garth leaned over to speak into the mic and raised the new jug I'd given him. He held it so that the label that read GRANDADDY'S OLE-TIMEY CORN LIQUOR was clearly visible. "I'll be playing my new jug tonight, too, courtesy of Hattie Hayes from the Moonshine Shack. Hattie not only gave me this jug, she also gave us Bootlegging Brothers our first endorsement deal, got our band on the radio. Who's heard our jingle?"

The audience broke into applause and catcalls. Looked like many of them had heard our ad on the air. *Hooray!*

"For those of you who haven't heard it," Garth continued, "we're going to play it for you right now. Sing along if you know it."

He raised his jug into position as Brody launched into the banjo riff. Josh sang the jingle.

I met a moonshiner named Hattie,
Who learned to 'shine from her granddaddy.
Her liquor's the best, it outshines all the rest!
Get it at her Moonshine Shack!

I was thrilled to hear the crowd chant along to *She's a shining star! Get a jug! Get a jar!*

Garth grinned. "I can see our commercial has caught on." He pointed at me through the doorway. "That's Hattie at the bar serving moonshine. Y'all be sure to get yourselves one of her drinks."

The patrons turned to look at me, and I gave them a smile and a wave.

Not to be left out, Granddaddy stood from his table on the deck and waved his cane. "I'm the Granddaddy they sang about!" he called, beaming with pride. "I taught Hattie everything she knows about making moonshine!"

The audience applauded and whooped some more. Louetta smiled up at my grandfather.

As soon as the group quieted down and Granddaddy had retaken his seat, Garth gestured toward the jugs on the tables. "Y'all be sure to take those coupons with you tonight. The only thing better than Hattie's moonshine is getting it at a discount."

Garth glanced through the doors again and our gazes met. I put my palms together, dipped my head in a gesture of appreciation, and mouthed, *Thank you!*

His brother's sales pitch concluded, Brody raised his banjo and tapped his foot. "One! Two! Three! Four!" On the last count, the band broke into one of their bluegrass tunes.

As the band played their set, the patrons who'd been inside the barn shifted to the outdoor area and things slowed down at the counter. It was nice to get a breather. The letup continued into the band's first break, when the Bootlegging Brothers took seats at a table on the deck and autographed posters for the crowd. They took photos with their fans, too. Naturally, it was primarily the women who asked for the posters and snapped selfies with the band. What woman wouldn't want to have her picture taken with three attractive up-and-coming musicians? One woman leaned over and whispered in Brody's ear. A roguish grin played about his mouth as he pulled out his phone and appeared to be adding her to his contacts list. Shortly thereafter, another woman slipped him a napkin. No doubt her phone number was written on it. He tucked it into his pocket.

I took advantage of the respite to round up the jugs and mason jars from under the counter and return them to the empty cartons so they could be sanitized and used again. I'd sold far more moonshine than I'd planned for, a good problem to have, but my supply was running low and needed to be replenished. I prepared several cups that the winery employee could sell while I went out to my van to retrieve more product.

Brody's bright-blue Jeep and several dark-colored pickup trucks were parked near my van. They looked like the ones Garth and Josh had driven to the Moonshine Shack earlier in the week, but I couldn't be sure. All trucks looked alike to me, especially in the dim light of dusk. It was half past eight already. Soon, it would be fully dark.

I pulled open the back door on my van. Though the bay had a small overhead light, it may as well have been a firefly for all the use it was. I activated the flashlight app on my phone and leaned it against the inside of the bay so I could read the words on the boxes. I'd already used up the cartons of moonshine that had been placed near the rear of the cargo bay, and I had to climb inside to reach the cases farther up. I crawled backward, pulling the boxes across the metal floor to the back of the cargo bay and turned off my phone's flashlight. I was about to climb out of the bay when my ears detected voices I recognized as Garth's and Brody's. The night brought a gentle breeze into my van, carrying with it the smell of cigarette smoke.

Garth said, "Big crowd tonight."

Brody said, "That's because there's a good band playing."

Garth chuckled. "We can't claim all the credit. Some people came for the moonshine. They told me so. They didn't even realize we were playing tonight until they got here."

Good to hear. I'd noted the Wine and 'Shine event on the home page of my website. I'd mentioned the event to every customer who'd entered my store during the last two days and advertised it on the chalkboard sign in front of my shop. I'd sent an e-mail blast to the people who'd visited my website and signed up for my promotional newsletter. I'd also added the info to the outgoing message on the shop's landline voicemail. I felt glad my efforts had paid off.

From their vantage point, the band members must not be able to see that my cargo bay was open. Curious where their conversation would go, I hunkered down in the back of my van and leaned out just far enough that I could peek through the thin crack between the open cargo door and the van's frame. They stood about twenty feet away, near the front bumper of the pickup parked two spaces down.

Brody raised his hand to his mouth and an orange circle appeared, glowing in the darkening night. I'd noticed a NO SMOKING sign on the deck when I'd carried the drinks to the band. Looked like they'd come out here so Brody could take a cigarette break.

Garth went on. "Lot of people are saying they've heard

our commercial on the radio. Told you singing that jingle would be good for us."

"You were right," Brody conceded. "But you can't blame me for being cautious."

"I suppose not."

Headlights flashed behind my van. There was a crunching sound of a vehicle approaching on the gravel drive, and their conversation ceased for a moment. The motor turned off and a door slammed as the driver exited the vehicle.

Brody snapped, "What the hell is Hill Willie doing here? And why's he got his fiddle with him?"

Uh-oh. Although I needed to get back inside and tend to my customers, I was hesitant to exit the cargo bay right then. The Sheridan brothers clearly didn't realize I was back here and could overhear their conversation. I didn't want to make them feel uncomfortable. But, more important, I was more curious than ever how the conversation was going to play out. *Why had the arrival of this other guy gotten Brody so riled up?*

Garth said, "William is going to fill in with a song or two during our breaks. I talked to the winery folks about it. They said it was okay."

Brody nearly came unglued. "*I* didn't say it was okay! How much is he getting paid to be here? Whatever he's getting, it should've been ours!"

Garth held up his palms. "Calm down, bro! The winery's not paying William a dime. I figured inviting him to play would bring more folks out to see us, too. He's a damn fine fiddle player. Got his own following. Last I looked, he had over five thousand followers on Instagram and nearly that many on TikTok. We'll benefit from having him in the lineup."

There was a softer crunch of approaching footsteps on the gravel, and William stepped up. He wore old-fashioned round metal-framed spectacles and his brown beard hung down in a well-groomed point to the notch on the front of his neck. He wore a classic black western shirt with roses embroidered on the yoke. He greeted the others with a lift of his bearded chin. "Judging from all the cars in this parking lot, there must be a full house tonight."

"Yup," Garth confirmed. "The place is packed."

Brody flung his cigarette to the gravel, ground it out with the heel of his boot, and eyed William. "They came to hear the Bootlegging Brothers."

I heard more footsteps and saw Camille walk up with Tate and their girls. She had the younger one hoisted up on her hip, the toddler sucking her tiny thumb. Imogene stood beside her mother, holding her hand.

"Hey, William," Camille said. "Good to see you. You gonna play with the band tonight?"

Before William could respond, Brody snapped, "No! He's not! Our band is called the Bootlegging *Brothers* and we're staying true to our name. I don't care how good William plays the fiddle, he's not our brother, not our blood, and not welcome in the band!"

Chapter Six

Camille released Imogene's hand, pulled her daughter tightly against her side to muffle one ear, and covered the other ear with her hand, attempting to protect her daughter from the ugliness.

Garth groaned but, unlike Brody, managed to keep his cool. "I'm so tired of your bull, Brody. You're always bossing me and Josh around. William and I are closer than you and I have ever been. The term 'brother' can be metaphorical. I say we let him play with us and see what the crowd thinks. If they like him, we add him to the band. What do you think, Josh?"

Josh, as usual, was silent.

Garth said, "Quit being a wimp, Josh. Speak your mind."

Brody said, "It doesn't matter whose side Josh is on if you and I don't agree. All decisions have to be unanimous. Says so in our partnership agreement."

Tate jumped into the fray now. "Brody, you seem to have forgotten that I'm the one who talked up the band to the Kemps and got y'all this gig. You're getting awfully big for your britches for someone who needs a hand-up from his ex's husband."

"It's not much of a hand," Brody spat. "The band's only getting three hundred bucks for the whole night. That's just a hundred dollars apiece."

Tate chuckled mirthlessly. "Now that we know what you're earning tonight, you gonna pay child support on it?"

"You better watch your mouth!" Brody rose on his toes and stuck out his chest. "I'm a good father. I take care of my little girl. I've paid child support on every cent I've earned, from my barbering business and from the band, too."

Camille rolled her eyes. Tate hissed, "Like hell you have! You think we don't know you cut hair for cash under the table? Shoot, you'd be worth more dead to us than alive. Least then we could collect on the life insurance."

While Josh had remained silent, his face spoke for him. As I continued to peek through the crack between the cargo bay door and the frame of the van, I saw a discreet smirk tug at Josh's lips as he eyed Tate and Camille. He seemed to find the idea that Brody might have cheated them amusing for some reason. But when he turned to look at Brody, the smirk morphed into a thin, straight line of disapproval as his lips pressed tightly together. With everyone else focused on Brody, waiting to see how he'd respond, I seemed to be the only one who'd noticed Josh's face.

Brody gestured for Camille to remove her hand from Imogene's ear. After Camille reluctantly complied, he looked down at his daughter. "I'm going to give you the moon, sweetie. The stars, too. Just you wait and see." Lifting his gaze to Tate, he said, "Our music is about to take off and, when it does, Imogene will be living like a princess."

Tate barked a laugh. "That'll be the day! Garth and Josh carry the band. You're a no-talent wannabe."

Imogene looked up from Tate to Brody, her little face puckered in concern. Brody stepped closer and draped a hand over her shoulder, as if to reassure or protect her. Camille didn't appear to like it, but she didn't object. She probably felt caught in the middle.

Tate hadn't finished berating Brody yet. "You should let William take over on strings. He's ten times the player you are."

Apparently buoyed by Tate's support, Garth issued a threat. "You're always causing a ruckus and taking the fun out of things, Brody. You got me thinking maybe I should quit the Bootlegging Brothers and start a new bluegrass band with William."

For the second time tonight, a flicker of hurt passed over Brody's face. "You can't quit, Garth. We're brothers, remember? We've got to stick together. Besides, our partnership agreement says that if a member leaves the Bootlegging Brothers, he loses his interest in the music copyrights and won't receive any royalties. The copyright for all our music is in the band's name, remember? Only current members of the band get a percentage."

Garth hesitated before saying, "We're earning a little from our music, but it's not like any of us has been able to quit our day jobs. Maybe I'll just walk away."

"Go ahead. Walk." Brody lifted his shoulders and let them drop. He then negated the nonchalant gesture with a threat. "But if you start a band with William, or with anyone else in Tennessee, I'll get an injunction."

"A what now?" Garth asked.

"An injunction," Brody said, removing his hand from Imogene's shoulder. "It's a court order that says you can't do whatever it is you're trying to do. In your case, it would be starting a new band."

"You've got no grounds to get a court order!"

"I sure do! Our partnership agreement includes a non-compete clause. We all agreed to it for our mutual benefit, remember? You can't play music alone or with another band in the state of Tennessee for three years after you leave the Bootlegging Brothers."

Whoa. That term was harsh. The contract would render Garth as silent as his brother Josh.

Garth gaped and his eyes flamed with fury, but he didn't get a chance to respond before Imogene looked up at Tate, her little face wobbly with worry. "Can we go back to our table, Daddy?"

Brody whirled on Tate. "Imogene is my daughter! Not yours!" He beat his chest once like a gorilla. "*I'm* her daddy!" He looked from Tate to Camille. "You two need to remember that!"

"You want to be her daddy?" Camille cried, swiping an angry tear from her eye. "Then act like it!"

Brody stepped up to Tate, stopping just inches from him and glaring up at the guy with fury flaming in his eyes. Though Tate had about four inches on Brody, Brody had about twenty pounds on Tate. Which of the two would emerge victorious should things escalate to a fistfight was anyone's guess. I hoped we wouldn't find out, especially since the girls could get hurt in the fray.

I swallowed the lump that had formed in my throat. *Eeeep.* Things had gotten ugly. I really wished I'd just grabbed my moonshine and taken it inside. I felt trapped now.

Luckily, the doors to the winery burst open and Darren Kemp stormed outside. "Knock it off! All of you! I've got customers coming in, telling me there's about to be a fight out here. If y'all can't get along, just go home!" Like Brody had done only seconds before, Darren whirled on Tate, pointing a finger at the Sheridan brothers. "I thought you vouched for these guys!"

Tate raised conciliatory palms. "I did. I'm sorry about this." He took a deep calming breath and lowered his hands. "It's just some family stuff that got out of control."

Garth cut a look of disgust and contempt at Brody, who'd backed away but hadn't apologized. Garth had to do it for him. He turned to Darren. "Please accept our apologies. It won't happen again. We'll make sure of it. We'll get back to our set now." He cut Brody another look that said if he started anything else, it wouldn't be only Tate he'd be dealing with.

Darren shook his head and returned to the tasting room, closing the door behind him.

Muttering curses, Brody stalked off, also heading back into the winery.

Tate grunted. "Brody drinks too much mash and talks too much trash."

I felt my ire rise. My moonshine wasn't to blame for Brody's belligerent behavior. The guy had drunk only a single cup of 'shine-ria.

Camille looked up at her husband. "Let's go back to our table and finish off that bottle."

Tate nodded and the two headed back to the deck with their girls.

William said, "I think I'll just bow out, man, head on home."

Garth sighed. "That's probably for the best. Sorry you drove all the way out here for nothing."

"Hire a lawyer to look at that contract," William suggested. "See if there's a loophole."

Garth said, "Will do. First thing Monday morning."

Once Garth and Josh turned to head back inside the winery, I slid out of my van. William climbed into a chocolate-brown SUV a few spots away. A bumper sticker on the back read HAVE FIDDLE, WILL TRAVEL. A second read I'D RATHER BE FIDDLING. He backed out of his spot and eased his SUV past me as I loaded the moonshine onto the dolly. I wheeled my wares inside, resumed my place at the counter, and was serving a cherry slush to a customer when the Bootlegging Brothers retook the stage.

His fiddle and bow resting on his shoulder, Brody stepped up to the mic, putting back on his friendly, folksy persona. "We're back, folks! How bad did you miss us?" He made an upward motion with his palm, encouraging the crowd to make a lot of noise. He returned his hand to his instrument, grabbing the bow. "Y'all are in for a real treat now. My fiddle solo."

While Brody launched into his song, Pearl sidled over to me. She cast a glance toward the stage outside and pursed her lips. "Darren told me about their argument in the parking lot. I assume you heard what happened?"

I cringed. "Unfortunately."

"That Brody Sheridan sure thinks highly of himself."

He seemed to be alone in that regard, at least insofar as

those who knew him well. The female fans, on the other hand, gazed at Brody with eyes gleaming, starstruck by his musical abilities.

Luckily, the rest of the night went smoothly. I sold a lot of moonshine; the Kemps sold a lot of wine; and the visitors to the vineyard had a wonderful time enjoying the music, drink, and grounds. Some of them even got up to dance in front of the stage, including my grandfather and his friends. They may have lost some of their eyesight and hearing, but they'd lost none of their joie de vivre. Couples performed swing dance routines, while groups of young women improvised clogging routines and line dances. Things got a little out of hand when a woman who'd had a few too many climbed up on the stage, backed into an amplifier, and nearly knocked it over, but Garth managed to catch it in time and set it right.

Around ten, Granddaddy hobbled inside and came over to the counter. "We're plumb tuckered out. Can you call us an Oobie?"

"Sure," I said, not bothering to correct his mispronunciation. I whipped out my phone and arranged for an Uber to pick up his bunch. As before, I showed him the photo of the driver and the car. "It'll be here in ten minutes. You'll meet him out front."

"Thanks, Hattie. We've had a grand ole time tonight, thanks to you." Granddaddy reached over the counter to squeeze my hand.

I squeezed his hand back, softly so I wouldn't inflame his arthritis. "I'm so glad."

Among the last to leave at closing time were Camille, Tate, and their girls. Tate carried Amelia, who was now asleep on her daddy's shoulder. Imogene looked tired as well, rubbing one of her eyes with her fist. Surely, it was

way past her bedtime. I supposed her parents had considered the night a special occasion, a chance for Imogene
to see her father and uncles play with their band. The little
girl pointed to a daisy-filled jug on a table nearby and
looked up at her mother. "Can I take that jug so I can play
it like Uncle Garth?"

Camille turned to look my way.

"Sure, sweetie!" I called to Imogene. "You can take it
home with you." Maybe she'd become a bluegrass star one
day, too, and she could say it all started the day a moonshiner gave her a jug filled with flowers and decorated
with a bow. She might find a fun use for the wooden
spoon, too. Maybe she could use it in a tea party.

"Thank you so much!" The little girl reached out with
both hands, picked up the heavy jug, and cradled it to her
chest, carrying it carefully. Camille gave me a grateful
smile and thanked me, as well.

Just after the family had gone out the door, the four
members of Pearl's staff donned disposable cleaning
gloves. Two began to clean up inside, while the other two
staff headed out to the deck with plastic bussing bins to
gather up wineglasses, bottles, napkins, and trash. In the
tasting room, Darren picked up chairs and inverted them
atop the tables so the floor could be swept and mopped.
Meanwhile, Pearl joined me at the counter to complete a
tally. I pulled my cell phone out of the chest pocket of my
overalls. While her staff cleaned up around us, Pearl
called out the cash and card sales figures from the multiple registers, and I used the calculator app on my phone
to add up the total.

Garth ventured in from the deck to get a drink of water
from the cooler in the corner. He turned his twinkling
eyes on me as he filled his paper cup. "Don't you leave

without saying goodbye, Hattie." He drained the cup, dropped it in the trash, and put a hand to his chest. "It would break my heart."

I rolled my eyes good-naturedly at his melodrama. "Eh. Maybe I'll wave on my way out."

He clutched both hands to his chest in jest. "Ouch!"

Once he'd strolled back through the open French doors to the deck, Pearl leaned over and whispered, "He's cute. I bet he's going to ask you out on a date."

"I'd be tempted," I admitted, "if I wasn't already in a relationship." Garth's attempts to woo me were flattering, if futile.

When we finished reconciling the numbers, I settled with Pearl, sending her payment via Venmo. She issued me a receipt for my bookkeeping records.

"This was fun," she said. "Let's do it again sometime."

"I'd love to."

One of her staff walked past us with a bin full of wine-glasses. Pearl glanced at the bin and said, "I'd better get into the kitchen and get those glasses loaded in the dishwasher. Good night, Hattie."

"Good night, Pearl."

Laughter from outside drew my eyes to the deck doors. A glance outside told me that several groupies had stayed after the show to flirt with the band members. Brody seemed to be eating it up, chatting with the women, laughing and grinning. He paid particular attention to a blonde in a short denim skirt, heels, and a sequined tank top. Josh, as usual, said nothing, but he had a faint smile on his face, a sign that he, too, was enjoying the women's attention. Garth's demeanor was more professional. He listened to the three women who'd surrounded him and offered a polite nod or a short response in reply to their questions, but little in the way of encouragement.

I gathered up the jugs I'd decorated with the bows and daisies, starting with the ones inside the tasting room, before venturing out the doors to gather the ones I'd placed outside on the deck. I'd brought a dozen of the jugs with me, but could find only nine of them now. I'd given one to Imogene, of course, but the jugs that had been on either end of the stage were gone. So were the microphones and amplifiers.

Had the winery staff moved them when they'd cleared the stage? Could the two missing jugs have been broken and thrown out? Maybe a patron thought they'd make a cute decoration for their home and swiped them, or maybe a fan of the Bootlegging Brothers took them as a memento. Garth might have rounded them up in case he broke his improvised instrument again and needed a quick replacement. The jugs had added a fun look to the stage. Maybe the band planned to use them as stage decorations at later performances. Regardless, it didn't matter. The jugs weren't expensive. Neither were the wooden spoons or clothespins I'd used to display the coupons. I hoped only that they'd be put to good use.

I walked back into the tasting room and placed the decorative jugs in a cardboard case. After loading what remained of my moonshine back into cartons, I stacked all of the boxes on the dolly and wheeled it out from behind the counter. Darren was mopping the floor near the front door. No sense leaving footprints and undoing his work when I could exit via the deck doors.

I went outside, noting the last of the fans had finally departed. Josh was helping Garth pack up his instruments at the foot of the stage. As I rolled my wares across the deck, Garth called out to me. "Leaving, Hattie?"

"Yep," I said. "Heading home."

"Looks like you could use some help."

Though I prided myself on my independence, I'd been standing all day, and my feet and back were beyond sore. If Garth wanted to help, I wasn't about to say no.

He walked over, gestured to my dolly, and said, "Let me get that for you."

"Thanks." I released my grip on the handle and he took over, rolling it out to my van for me. Brody sat in his Jeep nearby. His door hung open, his left foot propped on the running board as his thumbs moved over his cell phone. He was probably posting a pic to social media, or maybe he was texting one of the women he'd met tonight. As I reached out to open my van's cargo bay, I cut a look at Garth. "How many women gave you their phone number tonight? A dozen? Two dozen? More?"

He chuckled. "I lost count, but they wasted their time on me. I don't go for the low-hanging fruit. When it comes to women, I like a chase."

I couldn't help but laugh at that. He bent over, grabbed the case of mixed moonshine from the dolly, and placed it into the cargo bay. I picked up the dolly and slid it in flat so it wouldn't roll around as I drove.

As I closed the cargo bay doors, he said, "You and I should grab dinner sometime."

"Sorry, Garth. I can't. I'm seeing someone."

He reached down, took my left hand, and held it up. "There's no ring on this finger yet."

"We've only been dating a few weeks. It's too soon to think about marriage."

He gently released my hand. "Then maybe you should

keep your options open." Easing away backward, he said, "If you change your mind, text me. Better yet, come back here and see me play. Assuming Brody doesn't get us fired, we'll be here the next three weekends. You can vie against the other women for my affections." He shot me a wink before turning away.

I had to admit the guy had a certain charm. Still, I'd made a commitment to Marlon and things were going well for us. Marlon had all the qualities I was looking for in a guy. He was handsome, reliable, honest, hardworking. He had a good sense of humor, too. I'd been darn lucky he'd ridden his way into my life. I wasn't about to throw all that away, even for a good-looking bluegrass musician.

I climbed into my van, pulled out of the parking lot, and aimed for the gate. The gate was still open but I slowed as I eased through, the jars of moonshine clinking in the cartons behind me. I pulled onto Racoon Mountain Road and passed the old farmhouse across the street. The windows were dark. Shirley Byrd must have already gone to bed. I wondered if the sound of the music and traffic from the winery ever kept her awake. I hoped not. Everyone deserved a good night's sleep.

It was nearly midnight and I was halfway home when I realized the front pocket of my overalls where I normally kept my cell phone felt unusually light. *Uh-oh.* I patted the denim. Sure enough, the pocket was empty. *Ugh!* I issued a loud groan. Including the time I'd spent at my shop today, I'd worked for thirteen hours straight. My feet ached from standing on them so long, and my eyelids felt like they weighed fifty pounds each. I'd been looking forward to arriving home and falling into bed. Instead, I'd have to turn around and head back to the winery to retrieve my phone. I had brunch plans with Kiki and Kate tomorrow, and we hadn't yet decided on a restaurant. We'd planned to text one another to finalize the details.

Sighing, I hooked a U-turn to head back to the winery. As I came around the last bend on Racoon Mountain Road before the entrance to the winery, I spotted the taillights of a vehicle ahead. The vehicle had turned off the main road onto the dirt drive that led onto Shirley Byrd's property. Looked like someone was paying the woman a visit. Or maybe the vehicle belonged to the woman. Maybe she'd been out somewhere and was returning home. It seemed awfully late for a woman her age to be out, though. I hoped the car wasn't a bad sign, that she was in trouble somehow, maybe suffering a medical issue and had called a family member for help.

I didn't see the vehicle as I drove past her property. Whoever was driving it must have pulled it into the shed or behind the farmhouse and turned off the engine.

I turned into the winery and pulled up to the closed gate. Unfortunately, without the security code, I couldn't open the gate to drive onto the property. I slid my gearshift into park, turned off the motor, and exited my van. Being as petite as I was, I managed to squeeze through the bars on the gate, but just barely. I had to turn my head sideways and suck in my tummy as hard as I could. Good thing I wore an A-cup bra or I might have been in trouble. Even as flat-chested as I was, I felt lucky I didn't get stuck.

There was only a sliver of moon that night, and I walked in near darkness, wishing I had a flashlight or a lantern. The barn was barely visible ahead, gleaming softly in the scant moonlight. The place that had been so open and festive only a few hours earlier now seemed eerie, closed, and quiet, as if trying to keep secrets. An owl hooted nearby, and something scurried in the brush.

Was it a field mouse? A snake? I didn't want to find out. I picked up my pace, moving as fast as I dared in the darkness.

When I reached the white barn, I was dismayed to discover that the French doors at the entry were now secured behind a pair of solid sliding barn doors. It was impossible for me to tell if there was anyone inside the building, but a dark-colored vehicle at the end of the lot told me someone should be around somewhere. The vehicle was backed into the parking space so I could see only the front. It appeared to be either a pickup or an SUV.

I raised a hand and knocked on the barn door. *Rap-rap-rap.* "Hello?" I called, cupping my hands around my mouth to amplify my voice. "It's Hattie Hayes! I forgot my cell phone!" When no one responded, I tried again, knocking harder and longer. *RAP-RAP-RAP-RAP-RAP!* It was a wonder I had any skin left on my knuckles when I was done. I called out again to no avail.

I circled around to the deck, tripping over the board at the threshold and stumbling forward a few steps until regaining my balance. The French doors on the deck were protected by sliding barn doors, too. I tried knocking at the deck doors and calling out, but I met with no more success than I had at the front door. I walked to the back of the deck and turned my head to look behind the barn. The golf cart Pearl and I had ridden in earlier in the week was gone. The Kemps must have used it to drive to their house across the vineyard.

I turned and ran my gaze over the dark vineyard. Sure enough, between trees in distance, I could see a light on in an upstairs room at the Kemps' private residence. The golf cart sat in their driveway. I supposed I could go knock on their door, but they wouldn't likely appreciate being interrupted while they were getting ready for bed. I didn't want to jeopardize our business relationship by being a pain in the neck.

I debated trying to find the person who drove the pickup or SUV. They could be an employee with a key to the barn. But I saw no sign of anyone on the property. No flashlight. No lights at the other barn off in the distance. Attempting to trek through the vineyard in the dark would be dangerous. What if I tripped again and sprained my ankle? I also thought about waiting to see if someone would come back to the vehicle, but I figured it might be a pointless endeavor. It was possible that whoever drove the SUV or truck was a patron who'd drunk too much tonight and had ridden home with a friend, intending to retrieve it the following day once they sobered up. Or maybe they'd come out of the winery only to discover that their vehicle had a dead battery or some other problem they didn't feel like dealing with at the moment. They could have called an Uber to take them home, just like I'd called one for my grandfather and his friends. *Who knows?* I supposed I should just come back the next afternoon to get my phone. I could e-mail Kiki and Kate and hope that they checked their messages in the morning.

I squeezed back through the gate, climbed into my van, and drove home. Before going to bed, I logged on to my laptop and sent off an e-mail to Kiki and Kate with a reference line typed in all caps: *LOST MY CELL PHONE!*

Chapter Seven

Luckily, Kiki checked her e-mails late Sunday morning, contacted Kate to let her know why I hadn't responded to the text chain they'd sent earlier, and informed me via a reply e-mail where to meet them for brunch.

Over mimosas and waffles topped with maple syrup and sweet blueberry goo, I told them what happened at the winery the night before, how the Bootlegging Brothers nearly became the Brawling Brothers. "Tate and Camille have had their fill of Brody, too. They seem to think he cheats on his child support, that he doesn't report all of his income so he can get away with paying them less than he really owes."

Kiki's nose quirked in disgust. "I could tell Brody was a self-centered jerk from the instant I met him."

Although my first impression had been much the same as Kiki's, my opinion had later softened a little after seeing the hurt looks on his face. He might be selfish, but he wasn't totally devoid of feelings. "Guess what." I leaned in over the table to share. "Garth asked me out."

Kate's jaw fell. "You are soooo lucky!"

I gave her a pointed look. "I'm lucky to have Marlon."

"Well, yeah," Kate said. "Marlon is ripped. Sweet, too. But he's not a celebrity."

The Bootlegging Brothers were only minor local celebrities, as of now. But they did seem to be on the rise. They could break out and became famous. *Who knows?*

Kiki said, "Your moonshine is like a love potion."

I scoffed. "You don't think I'm hot enough to attract guys like Marlon and Garth without putting some sort of spell on them?"

"It's not that," Kiki said. "It's just that you seem to be a very hot ticket right now."

I sighed. "That's how it always is. Dating a guy makes me happy and gives me confidence, which makes me more attractive to the guys who didn't pay attention to me before."

"It's a vicious circle." Kiki threw back the last of her drink and we all stood to go.

I convinced my friends we needed to keep this party going. After all, it wasn't every weekend that Kate could get a break from her baby or I had someone to cover my shop. We should make the most of our free time. We climbed into my van and drove out to the River Pearl Winery.

Shirley Byrd was again sitting on her porch, the dog at her feet and the gun nearby. She rocked slowly as we rolled past her place and fanned herself with a colorful, old-fashioned handheld fan.

Though the crowd at the winery was much smaller than the preceding night's crowd had been, there were still a respectable number of customers on-site, at least three-quarters of the indoor tables taken.

Pearl was working the counter. She smiled when she spotted me approaching. "Back so soon? Did you decide wine beats 'shine, after all?"

"Never!" I teased. "Actually, I forgot my cell phone here last night. Any chance you found it?"

She reached under the counter and pulled out a wicker basket containing two pairs of sunglasses, one pair of eyeglasses, a ball cap, a set of keys, a tube of lipstick, a single large hoop earring, and my cell phone. The basket must serve as their lost-and-found bin. She retrieved the phone and held it up. "This it?"

"Yep. Thanks."

After she handed the phone over to me, I introduced her to Kiki and Kate. I then turned to my friends. "What are y'all in the mood for? Red, white, or rosé?"

Pearl held up a half-empty bottle of sparkling wine that had been sitting in an ice bucket behind the counter. "Got the fizzy stuff on sale today, if you're interested. Five dollars a glass or just twelve dollars a bottle."

After a brief debate, we decided on a bottle of the bubbly wine. Pearl grabbed a fresh bottle from the cooler behind the counter, placed it on the counter along with three glasses, and rang us up. We took our bottle and glasses out onto the deck to enjoy the beautiful weather. We glanced around, looking for a place to sit. Every table on the deck was filled, but we got lucky. A couple rose from their seats, preparing to leave. We rushed over to claim the table as soon as they vacated it.

Kiki plopped down in her chair and proceeded to pour our first glasses. "This place sure is popular."

I took a sip of the wine and nodded as the fizz tickled my throat. I set my glass back down. "The winery was packed last night, too. The Kemps plan to expand their outdoor seating capacity. They're also installing a decorative pond. Over there." I pointed across the vineyard to where the excavator stood on the far side of the pond. *Wait.* Hadn't it been on the near side when I'd arrived at the winery yesterday afternoon? I was fairly certain it had been. Someone must have moved the machine in the interim. There was no crew in sight now, but maybe Tate and the other guys from the pond company had put in some time out here this morning, before the winery opened for the day.

Kiki glanced around. "Smart move to expand the outdoor area. This is where everyone wants to be."

For good reason. Children and dogs were permitted in the outdoor spaces, which meant people could relax and enjoy a nice glass of wine while giving their pets a change of scenery and without having to find a babysitter. Seeing the children made me think about Imogene Sheridan. Though she was biologically Brody's daughter, it was clear Tate Hutchinson was the man she looked to as her father. Though blended families were common and most ex-spouses found ways to get along, such didn't seem to be the case where Brody and Camille were concerned. Poor Imogene was caught in the middle. I could understand Brody being jealous that his own daughter had referred to her stepfather as *Daddy*, but he could've handled the whole situation better. Besides, given that she lived with her stepfather, it was a good thing she had a happy relationship with him.

With Dalton waking his parents up at night, Kate was perpetually tired and nearly nodded off after the morning's mimosa and a glass of wine. When her head bobbed for the third time in an hour and she nearly smacked her forehead on the table, we decided it was time to go.

Pearl was cleaning up on the deck as we left. "Bye, y'all!" she called. "Hope to see you again soon!"

Late Tuesday afternoon, I was restocking shelves, Smoky was lounging in the window, and Granddaddy was whittling in a rocking chair out front when the familiar *clop-clop-clop* of Charlotte's hooves drew my attention to the front window. After greeting my grandfather and tying Charlotte to the porch post, Marlon came inside. His expression was pensive. Before I could even ask what was wrong, he said, "Brody Sheridan is missing."

"Missing?" My jaw dropped. A million questions flooded my head at once and I stammered, "What . . . how . . . when . . . ?"

Marlon told me what he knew so far. "Garth called in a missing person report earlier today. Brody didn't show up for their band practice last night, and he's not answering calls. At first, Garth and Josh chalked it up to hard feelings from an argument they apparently had Saturday night at the winery."

I knew exactly what argument he was talking about.

He continued, "Brody didn't show up for his barbering job this morning. His appointment book was full, and he hadn't called in to say he was sick or that he'd be late. Brody's boss contacted Garth, looking for Brody. His Jeep is nowhere to be found, either. The neighbors at Brody's apartment complex say they haven't seen his car in the parking lot since Saturday afternoon."

I hadn't much liked the guy but, still, I didn't want to see harm come to him. "Could he have just gone off on his own for some reason? A vacation? Maybe to clear his head?"

"Seems unlikely. The bluegrass band's taking off. They had lots of gigs coming up. Also seems he would have told his boss if he planned to take some time off. Nothing seems to be missing from his apartment. His suitcase is still there. Phone charger. Computer. Toothbrush. Brody hasn't posted on social media since Saturday night, which is unusual for him. He usually makes two or three posts each day, promoting the band. Given the circumstances, foul play is suspected."

I was on social media frequently promoting my shop and products, and I, too, had noticed that Brody hadn't posted recently. Of the three Bootlegging Brothers, he was the one who'd been the most active online. I'd assumed that his recent lack of activity meant that he was either still annoyed with his brothers or simply busy with other matters. "Has anyone tried locating his phone?" I knew police had ways of pinpointing a cell phone's location by determining how strong the signal was when bounced off towers in the area.

"Our tech team tried to ping it. They got nothing."

I pulled out my cell phone and took a look at Brody's Instagram account. Sure enough, the last post included a photo of the band autographing posters on the deck at the winery. Had something gone awry after I'd left Saturday night? I told Marlon that Brody had been sitting in his Jeep, typing on his cell phone when I'd left the River Pearl Winery. "I'd driven halfway home when I realized I'd left my phone on the counter in the tasting room. I turned around and drove back to the winery. The automated gate was closed and I had to enter on foot. I went to the barn and knocked, but nobody answered. There was one vehicle still in the lot. A pickup truck or SUV. I'm not sure which. I only saw it from the front."

"What color was it?"

"I can't say for sure. There weren't any lights on out-side. But it was a dark color and it was parked at the far end of the lot near where the band members had parked their vehicles that night. It was backed in, though."

"I take it that Josh's and Garth's trucks weren't parked that way earlier?"

"No. They'd pulled in normally, front-first." I told him how I'd seen a dark truck with the Paradise Pools, Ponds & Patios logo on it at the winery on Thursday, and how I'd assumed it belonged to Tate since he'd been working out there that day.

"Could you tell if the vehicle you saw Saturday night had the logo on it?"

"I didn't see any logo," I said, "but it was on one of those removable magnetic signs. It would've been easy to take it off." I thought back to that night. "I don't know whether this is relevant, but I saw someone drive onto the riverfront property across the road from the winery. An old woman lives there, alone, I think, and her house was dark. It struck me as odd that someone would be turning into her driveway that late at night."

"What type of vehicle were they driving?"

"I don't know. I was too far away to tell. I only saw its lights."

Marlon mulled over what I'd told him. "Brody's Jeep isn't at the winery, so he must have left. It seems likely that the last person with Brody at the winery might know where he went next."

But who was that person and where had Brody gone?

Marlon pulled out his cell phone. "I'm gonna call Ace, see if she wants to come over here to talk to you."

Homicide Detective Candace "Ace" Pearce and I had

met on earlier investigations. She told Marlon that yes, she did want to speak with me. She arrived in her plain sedan shortly thereafter. Ace was a full-figured Black woman with stylish copper-colored hair and a no-nonsense demeanor. Slung over the shoulder of her blue blazer was an enormous tote bag that served as her mobile office. After greeting my grandfather outside my shop, she held the door for him as he used his cane to hobble into the store. He knew something was up if Ace had stopped by. Smoky seemed to sense that something was amiss, too. He stood from his perch in the window and watched us with his intent cat's curiosity.

After a curt greeting, Ace said, "Go through everything that happened Saturday night."

I reviewed the details once again. The arguments I'd overheard, between Brody and his brothers, as well as between Brody and his ex-wife and her husband. "Tate seems to think Brody has shorted them on child support by not reporting all of the cash he earns." I wondered if Brody had planned to report the cash I'd paid him for recording the jingle and for the photo shoot. I recalled the expressions on Josh's face during that part of the argument, how he'd first smirked, then appeared angry. I told her about William Hill, too. "Brody wasn't happy to see the guy. Things got loud and the winery's owner, Darren Kemp, came out of the building and told them to knock it off or go home." I told her how I'd inadvertently left my cell phone at the winery and that there'd been a single dark pickup or SUV in the lot when I'd returned. "I'm not sure which it was. Sorry."

"That's understandable," she said. "Most SUVs are built on a truck chassis. They're indistinguishable from the front."

I advised her of the vehicle I'd seen driving onto Shirley Byrd's property. "When I passed her house, I didn't see it anymore. It must have pulled behind her place or into the shed."

Ace glanced around the shop. "You got someone who can cover for you? I'd like you to come out to the winery with me."

Granddaddy said, "I can run the store. I'm not as useless as I look."

Marlon and I exchanged a glance, and I had to bite my lip to keep from laughing at my grandfather's unwitting self-deprecation.

"All right, then," Ace said. "You're in charge, Ben." She turned to Marlon and gave an almost imperceptible jerk of her head toward my grandfather, silently giving Marlon permission to stick around and help my grandfather if needed. After all, I was a potential witness to a major crime.

We left the shop, but not before I stopped at the front window to tell Smoky I'd be back soon. I gave him a kiss on the head, too. He gave me a low growl and an irritated tail swish in return. I loved my little furry guy with all my heart, but he could be a real brat sometimes.

I climbed into the passenger seat of Ace's unmarked white Chevy Impala, and directed her to the winery. Her radio was tuned to the same country-western station that had recorded my commercial. As we made our way out of the city and into the rural area, my jingle played and I sang along. I couldn't help myself. "She's a shining star! Get a jug! Get a jar!"

When the commercial ended, Ace looked my way with her brows raised. "The Bootlegging Brothers sang your commercial? You didn't happen to get crosswise with Brody, did you? Maybe off him yourself?"

I assumed she was joking, but with Ace one could never be sure. She had a way of putting a person off their game. "Brody was difficult during the recording session at the station," I said, "but we worked things out."

She returned her eyes to the road. "Difficult how?"

"He said I was getting the better end of the deal, not paying them enough even though he'd agreed to the amount in advance." I told her that I'd paid the band an additional fee for the photo shoot. "I offered him cash on the spot. I figured he'd be more likely to take the deal if he'd be walking away with money in his pocket."

She thought out loud. "He probably gets paid cash for some of his haircuts, too. I wonder if he keeps a lot of cash at his apartment, or maybe had some in his Jeep that he planned to deposit later."

She'd once told me that people generally kill for love or for money. Seemed she was thinking money might have been the motive in this case. If that was so, maybe someone had decided to go for more than the cash Brody had on hand. Maybe they'd also decided to cash in on his life insurance policy. "There's one more thing I remember. Tate said Brody would be worth more to him and Camille dead than alive, because then they could cash in on life insurance."

Her brows rose again, even higher this time. "Is that so?" She returned her attention to the road ahead of us. "I wonder just how much that policy is worth and when it was taken out."

I had no doubt she'd find out.

Chapter Eight

As we rounded the bend to approach the winery, I pointed to the old farmhouse up ahead. "See that old house? The Kemps have been trying to buy the land it sits on so they can expand the winery, but the owner won't sell. The car I saw Saturday night turned onto her property."

Ace glanced over as we drove past the house and headed for the driveway that connected with the road farther down. Shirley Byrd sat on her porch, as usual, along with her dog and gun. "That woman doesn't exactly look friendly." Ace activated her left blinker and turned onto the dirt driveway that led onto the Byrd property.

We were driving toward the house when Shirley Byrd rose from her rocker, grabbed what I could now see was a double-barreled shotgun, and aimed it at our windshield. Before I could even process the situation, Ace had slammed on the brakes, reached over to put a hand on the back of my neck, and shoved my head down between my legs. "Stay down!"

She grabbed the microphone from her dashboard and activated her public-address system. "Ms. Byrd! I'm Candace Pearce with the Chattanooga Police Department. May I speak with you for a moment?" The woman must have made an affirmative signal because Ace added, "I'm going to need you to put that gun down, please, ma'am." A few seconds passed and Ace said, "You can come up now, Hattie."

I raised my head to see that Ms. Byrd had put her gun down and sat back in her rocking chair, though the force with which she rocked back and forth said she was irritated by our arrival. Ace drove forward, parking the car near the porch. As the detective and I exited her plain cruiser, the dog pushed itself to an arthritic stand. Rather than barking or growling, he wagged his tail and opened his mouth, softly panting. We might not be sure yet about Shirley Byrd, but at least the dog didn't look like he'd give us any trouble.

The wind blew our way, bringing with it the sound of heavy equipment working at the vineyard across the street. The harvester moved through the vineyard, snatching grapes from the vines. Someone, presumably Tate, was working the excavator. The machine moved along the path marked with the small flags, digging the trench that would become the ornamental river. It was nearing four o'clock by that point, not long until quitting time.

Creak. Ace put a foot carefully on the first of the three steps that led up to the porch of the farmhouse. The wood was half-rotted and it was unclear whether it would hold our weight. She slowly stepped up. Luckily for her, the wood held. Unsure whether the steps could bear our combined bulk, I waited until Ace had climbed all three steps before following her up to the porch.

Before Ace could even offer her hand, Shirley snarled, "Why you here, interrupting my day?"

"I'm looking for a missing man," Ace said. "A guy named Brody Sheridan. His band played at the winery Saturday night."

Shirley snorted. "So, I've got him to thank for all that caterwauling I heard coming from over there."

Brody wasn't the band's primary vocalist. Josh was. But I saw no reason to fuel the woman's ire by pointing out that Brody played strings and sang only backup.

Ace said, "He was at the winery until at least eleven. Last we know, his two brothers were with him." She gestured to me. "Ms. Hayes was also at the winery, selling moonshine."

"Moonshine?" Ms. Byrd stopped her angry rocking and her face lit up. "Now you're talking. Those wine folks is snooty, but moonshine's for real people. Got any on you?"

"No. Sorry."

She sat back in her rocker, her face pinched in disappointment and disgust.

Ace reached down to pet the dog. "Hattie says she saw a vehicle drive onto your property late Saturday night, not long before midnight. Could it have been you? Or someone you know?"

"No chance," the woman said. "I went to bed shortly after sundown, like I always do. Had my box fan going to drown out the racket from the winery. But I saw the headlights when I got up to use my bathroom. I figured it was probably a couple looking for a romantic spot to neck."

A bluff overlooking the beautiful Tennessee River would certainly be romantic.

Ace asked, "Did you confront them?"

"Of course not," Shirley snapped. "I don't appreciate people traipsing all over my property without permission, but it was too late and too dark for me to go out there and shoo them away. I wasn't about to risk seeing their naked butts up in the air, neither."

"Understandable," Ace said. "Any chance you could tell what kind of car it was and who was in it?"

"Nope. Saw the headlights for a few seconds, that's all. When I came out of the bathroom, I didn't see nothing. I supposed they were turned off by then."

Ace cocked her head. "Did you call the sheriff's department to report the trespassers?"

"No."

Ace's posture and tone shifted just slightly. "Why not?"

"Because I've called them before and they don't do nothing other than tell the people to leave. They never charge 'em with trespassing. The deputies make excuses for 'em, say they didn't know they were on private property and that no harm was done. They act like I'm making a big fuss over nothing, and I just end up losing a night's sleep."

"I see," Ace said. "Would you mind if Hattie and I take a look around?"

"Do what you need to," Ms. Byrd said, flinging a hand. "Just leave me out of it."

Ace nodded. "Yes, ma'am."

The detective motioned for me to follow her. We picked our way gingerly down the steps and past the cruiser, heading back down the dirt drive on foot. The road was dotted with weeds and ruts filled with half-dried mud. Tall grass long overdue for a mowing filled the field and lined the drive.

When we neared the spot where the dirt driveway began at the paved asphalt, Ace pointed. "Look. The grass has been flattened there."

My gaze followed her finger. Sure enough, two swaths of grass had been laid flat by tires. Whoever had turned onto the property had taken off across the field.

Ace, too, turned off the dirt drive. Her loafers weren't exactly made for hiking through fields, but they'd do. As she followed the track, I followed her. We made our way across the shallow strip of land to the bluff above the river. The tracks didn't stop, though, even when they reached the edge of the bluff. I gasped. *Does that mean the car went over the cliff?*

Ace edged to the precipice. I did the same. The bluff stood a good ten to twelve feet over the river. The water moved lazily along below us, an occasional leaf or twig riding slowly along the current. About twenty feet from shore, a shiny substance floated atop the water, the shape irregular and iridescent. Thinner trails floated outward from it, all heading in the direction of the current. *An oil slick.*

In an instant, Ace whipped her radio from her belt to contact dispatch. "Get me a search and recovery team." She rattled off our location and returned the radio to her belt.

I looked from the river to her. "You think Brody drove off the cliff here?"

"I think it's best to let the facts and evidence tell us what to think. But we need to find out what's causing that slick." She glanced back at the farmhouse. "I better go tell Ms. Byrd she's about to have even more people traipsing over her property. Wait in the car."

Ace picked her way back through the field and down the drive to the farmhouse while I returned to her Impala. She walked back to her sedan a few minutes later. As we waited for the search team to assemble, we sat in the car, wondering what secrets the river hid beneath its surface.

Chapter Nine

An hour later, the three-person search team arrived via the river in a bright-red inflatable boat outfitted with a small outboard motor and a flashing yellow caution light. The two men and women appeared to be in their mid to late twenties, and all were extremely fit. They'd brought air tanks, buoys, lights, and ropes. The two divers were already suited up. Ace and I stood on the bluff as they donned their air tanks and prepared their safety ropes. While the current appeared to be moving slowly on the surface, it could be deceptively powerful. Without proper preparations, the divers could be swept downriver. The woman commanding the boat kept the motor running slowly, holding the boat in place as the divers went down. Bubbles rising to the surface marked their underwater trail.

They were under less than two minutes when their heads breached the surface. They swam over to hang on to the side of the boat. One of them removed the regulator from his mouth, turned, and called up to Ace. "There's a blue Jeep Wrangler down there!"

Though I'd anticipated as much, my gut nonetheless tightened into a hard ball on hearing the news. *It has to be Brody's Jeep, right?*

Ace cupped her hands around her mouth to amplify her voice over the whirr of the boat's motor. "Anyone inside?"

My gorge rose at the thought that Brody Sheridan's bloated corpse could be inside his car beneath the water. On reflex, I put my hand over my mouth. I kept my hand there until the second diver shook his head. He called out, "No body, but the driver's side door is open!"

Ace cupped her hands around her mouth again. "Got a license plate number?"

The diver recited the number.

I looked to the detective. "Is it Brody's?"

She nodded solemnly. "It's Brody's."

Ace continued to pelt the search team with questions. "Any damage? Dents? Broken glass?"

"Not that we could see."

What exactly happened here? Had Brody become disoriented in the dark and accidentally driven off the bluff? He'd had a couple of my moonshine drinks Saturday night, but nowhere near enough alcohol to be so impaired that he'd vector off the main road and drive off a cliff. Of course, he could have drunk more than I realized if he'd had the jug of moonshine I'd given him earlier in the week stashed in his Jeep. Or maybe he simply felt he needed to quiet his nerves after the arguments he'd had with his brothers, William Hill, and Tate and Camille. He could have driven over here to stare at the river and think things over. Water tended to have a calming effect. That's why so many dentist offices had fish tanks and spas featured faux waterfalls.

Maybe Brody been unable to see the bluff in the dark, or had been moving too fast to stop in time. Or maybe he'd accidentally hit the gas instead of the brake. Assuming Brody hadn't been buckled in when he went off the bluff, his body could have floated out of the Jeep and down the river. Or, if he'd survived the impact of his Jeep hitting the water, he might have opened the door himself and escaped. But if he'd made it safely to shore, why hadn't he shown up for work? It was possible he'd unfastened his seat belt and opened the door to escape his sunken car and then been swept downriver.

Ace must have had the same thoughts. She pulled her radio from her belt again to contact dispatch. "Get me a cadaver dog."

Though I'd just been speculating that Brody might have perished in the river, hearing the word *cadaver* made the situation hit home. My head went light and I took an involuntary step backward before steadying myself.

While we waited for the dog team, the divers went back under to take photographs with their waterproof camera, and to search for evidence in the vehicle and muck. They surfaced several times, bringing items up with them and placing them in the boat. Brody's fiddle in its case. Brody's guitar, banjo, mandolin, and mountain dulcimer. An earthenware jug of Granddaddy's Ole-Timey Corn Liquor with the cork removed. The jug was cracked, a thick line running from the bottom of the jug halfway up the side.

No. No! No! No! I gulped, involuntarily shaking my head and closing my eyes for a moment, imploring any and all higher powers to have mercy on me. *Please don't let my moonshine be involved in whatever happened to Brody!*

I opened my eyes to find Ace's pointed stare locked on my face. "Any idea why a jug of your moonshine would be in Brody's Jeep?"

"I gave the band members free moonshine as partial payment for the photo shoot. Maybe he'd left his jug in his car."

The divers went under the water once more. One came up a minute later with Brody's cell phone in his hand. The water must have ruined the battery. *That explains why the police had been unable to ping it from the cell phone towers*. The other brandished a wooden spoon. *Uh-oh*. My guts squirmed like a pile of snakes. *What was the spoon doing in Brody's Jeep?*

Ace had the same question. "Where'd you find that spoon?"

The diver said, "It was lying on the floorboard on the driver's side."

Ace angled her head and thought out loud. "Why would Brody have a wooden spoon in his car?"

"I think I can answer that." I told her about my centerpieces, how I'd put wooden spoons in each of the jugs and attached a clothespin to the spoons to display coupons. "Two of the centerpieces were missing when I went to collect them at the end of the night. They cost little to make, so I wasn't concerned." Though I'd originally thought the jug of moonshine the divers had found was the one I'd given Brody at my shop after the photo shoot, I now wondered if it was one of the missing centerpieces. I raised the issue with Ace, but said, "That jug doesn't have a ribbon, though."

"The ribbon could've been removed," Ace said, "or it could have come off in the water. Flowers and ribbon are lightweight, less likely to sink and stay put than something heavy. Either could have easily been washed downstream." Nevertheless, she called to the divers again, telling them to look for the ribbon and daisies on their next dive. If they happened to find either one, at least it would narrow down which of the jugs had been used. We'd know it was one that was taken from the winery. It would give us something to follow up on.

The divers went down again, but found neither the ribbon nor the daisies. *Hmm.*

As I pondered the situation, a thought surfaced in my mind. Might Brody have faked his death and skipped town for some reason? Brody could have jammed the wooden spoon under the dashboard to hold the accelerator down so that the Jeep would drive off the cliff unoccupied. I proposed the idea to Ace.

"That would only work if the Jeep had an automatic transmission," she said. "It would be darn near impossible with a manual transmission because the engine would stall if the clutch wasn't engaged." She waited for the divers to surface again and called, "Is the Jeep an automatic transmission or a stick shift?"

The divers exchanged glances. They were younger than me, either very young millennials or maybe even part of Gen Z, and my guess was neither of them was familiar with a stick shift. I was, though. My great-grandfather's old Ford flathead V8 had a manual transmission, as all cars did back in the early day of the automobile. When Granny was alive, she'd driven a 1978 Plymouth Volaré with a gearshift mounted on the steering wheel column, a system she referred to as *three on the tree.* She'd taught me how to drive the car when I was only twelve, but she let me drive it only around their yard. Even so, I'd had a blast circling their cabin over and over and over. I'd felt so grown-up.

Noting the men's confusion, Ace called, "Let me put this another way. How many pedals are on the driver's floorboard?"

One of them raised a finger in a *wait just a moment* gesture and disappeared under the surface again. When he came back up, he held up two fingers.

"Just two?" Ace called to be certain. "Brake and gas? No clutch?"

He shook his head and raised the two fingers again.

Returning to my theory, I said, "So Brody could have done it, then. Faked his death."

Ace angled her head one way then the other, still not convinced. "I'm not saying you're necessarily wrong, but a person's got to have a darn good reason for wanting to fake their death and disappear. It costs them everything. Their home. Property. Money. Relationships."

I couldn't imagine giving everything up like that, especially my relationships with my family and friends, let alone Smoky. I'd miss that furry critter something fierce if I couldn't see him every day, even if I did have to force my affection on him. "From what Tate said, Brody resented having to make child support payments to Camille."

"That may well be," Ace replied. "But is that enough reason to go through such an elaborate charade? Seems there'd have to be more. Besides, the theory doesn't jibe with the fact that Brody had plans for the band." She paused for a beat. "That said, your spoon-on-the-accelerator theory might have some merit."

"You mean—"

"Someone else could have jammed the spoon under

the dashboard," she said, finishing my sentence. "Maybe they killed Brody and figured dumping him and his truck in the river would be a good way to hide the evidence. Besides Brody, who might have got their hands on one of your centerpieces?"

"Anyone who was at the winery that night," I said, knowing that included a huge pool of potential suspects. "I gave one to Brody and Camille's daughter, Imogene, as they were leaving. She'd wanted a jug to play like her uncle Garth."

Ace angled her head toward the evidence in the inflatable boat. "That spoon could be from the centerpiece you gave to Imogene, then."

"As far as I know, Imogene took the jug and spoon home with her. She lives with Camille and Tate. She left with them Saturday night."

"Which means both Camille and Tate had immediate access to a spoon."

"They aren't the only ones," I said. "Two more of the decorative jugs went missing. They'd been on the stage during the show, but when I went to round them up at the end of the night they were gone. I figured they might have accidentally been broken and thrown out. There was a big crowd and some of them were dancing in front of the stage. They could have knocked them onto the floor. It's also possible a fan might have taken them as a memento, or that maybe one of the band members took them to use in a later show, as a stage decoration. Garth might have taken the jugs to play. He dropped one recently at a bluegrass festival and I gave him one of mine to replace it. He might have kept the two from the stage for backup."

"I'll follow up," Ace said, "see if anyone knows where they are."

When the divers seemed to have retrieved everything they could by hand, Ace thanked them for their time, arranged for an officer to meet them at a nearby boat launch to take custody of the evidence, and called her assistant at the police department to arrange for Brody's Jeep to be pulled out of the river. "Make sure a uniformed officer in a cruiser accompanies the recovery service. The woman who owns the property is armed and a little unhinged."

It dawned on me then that the noise of the heavy equipment at the winery had ceased. I glanced across the road to see the pickup with the Paradise Pools, Ponds & Patios logo on the door pulling out of the winery. Tate sat at the wheel, with the two crew members in the passenger seats. As surreptitiously as I could, I angled my head toward the road. "That's Tate Hutchinson," I said quietly.

Ace kept her face turned toward me, but her gaze slid sideways to the truck. "The driver?"

"Yeah. Is he looking over here?"

"Mm-hm," she said. "Driving awfully slow, too. He won't be able to see the rescue boat from the road. He could just be wondering what's going on over here, why two women would be standing on this bluff."

Or he could be guilty of harming his wife's ex-husband and be freaking out that we were standing precisely where he'd sent Brody's Jeep over the cliff.

Ace got a faraway look in her eyes for a moment before turning back to me. "You sure there was just one vehicle out here? Could there have been another one forcing the Jeep to drive this direction? Maybe more than one?"

"I saw only one set of headlights and taillights. If there was a second vehicle, its lights weren't turned on."

She issued a *hmph* as she pondered the information, and ran her gaze across the grass as if looking for additional sets of tire tracks. There was only the one. After a moment or two, she turned to me. "I could drive you back to your store, but that would slow me down. You mind staying put while the dog team takes a sniff around?"

"No problem."

A half hour after Ace had put in the request for a cadaver dog, a K-9 team arrived. The dog was a male black Labrador with a barely contained high-energy intensity evidenced by his anxious trembling. He was ready to go to work as soon as he received his cue. His handler was an athletic Latina woman in her midthirties. After brief introductions, Ace explained the situation. Jeep in river. Driver's door open. Owner of Jeep missing. "Mr. Sheridan's body could have washed downriver."

Holding her dog's leash tight, the woman stepped to the edge of the bluff and looked over. "I can take my dog along the cliff, but it's not going to be easy searching here. If a body was carried downriver, it probably got caught up somewhere where the water's shallower, maybe on a riverbank." She explained that, while it wasn't impossible for the dog to find a body in water, the river's moving current could make locating the body more difficult because the flow carried the scent downriver along with the water.

"Understood," Ace said. "Do what you can here, then we'll talk about next steps."

The woman and dog headed off, following the bluff in the direction of the current. The dog had its nose down, sniffing with concentration, its tail up and moving in a wag I suspected was unconscious. Unlike the Sheridan brothers, this dog did not appear in any hurry to quit his day job.

While we waited for the cadaver team to complete their task and return, I mused aloud. "If Brody was murdered, could the killer have disposed of his body somewhere else? Maybe the killer hoped that Brody's Jeep wouldn't be found in the river or, if it was, that law enforcement would assume Brody had accidentally driven off the bluff and that his body had been swept off somewhere downstream."

"That may well be what happened here," Ace said. "This could be nothing more than a tragic accident. Brody might have drunk too much wine or moonshine before he left the winery and got turned around in the dark, drove off the cliff before he realized what was happening. There's not much distance between the road and the bluff right here, not much room to make a correction."

"I hate to think he was drunk on my 'shine." If he was, he'd ignored the *Shine Smart* warning on my product label.

Ace said, "The medical examiner will run a toxicology report. Assuming we find a body, that is. Brody could have floated halfway to Kentucky by now."

I hadn't much liked Brody, but the idea of him becoming little more than flotsam on the river filled my heart with gloom. I engaged in a brief mental debate on the issue of whether Brody's disappearance was the result of an accident or something more ominous. An accident would certainly be preferable. I cast a glance over at the vineyard, the last place I'd seen Brody Sheridan alive. The excavator sat near the pond, its long arm hooked, the bucket resting on the ground. *It looks like an oversized bird digging for a worm . . .*

My heart skipped a beat. *Could the excavator in the vineyard have something to do with Brody's disappearance?* I turned to Ace. "There's something else I noticed." I told her about the excavator, how it had been on the near side of the pond when I'd arrived at the winery on

Saturday for the Wine and 'Shine event, but had been on the far side of the pond when I'd returned with my friends early the following afternoon. "It seems doubtful the pool company would expect their staff to work on a Sunday morning. Do you think the equipment could have something to do with what happened to Brody?"

She lifted noncommittal palms in a *who knows?* gesture. "I think it's something to follow up on."

By then, the K-9 handler and her dog were back from their search. "We didn't come across anything. I'll need to get a boat to better search this stretch of shoreline."

Ace said, "That might not be necessary. Follow me across the street."

While the K-9 handler returned to her cruiser, Ace and I walked back to her car. I waited by the passenger door while she continued on to the porch to address Shirley Byrd. "We're leaving now, Ms. Byrd. There will be some other folks coming here soon. Keep your gun put away and let them do their work, okay?"

The old woman heaved a sigh but said, "If I have to."

"Bye, now," Ace said, "and thanks for your cooperation."

The old woman said nothing more and just continued to rock. It seemed odd she didn't want to know what we'd discovered. *Shouldn't she be curious?* Seemed that most people would be. I raised the issue with Ace once we were seated in her car with the doors closed.

She lifted one shoulder in a half shrug. "It's a little odd, yeah. But maybe she'd rather just stay out of it."

Or maybe she already knew what we would find. Could she have witnessed more than she'd admitted? If so, could someone have paid her to keep quiet or, worse, threatened her life?

Chapter Ten

Ace pulled her cruiser out of Ms. Byrd's dirt driveway and turned onto Raccoon Mountain Road for the short drive to the Pearl River Winery. With it being midweek, only a handful of patrons were at the winery, as evidenced by the small number of cars.

She glanced my way. "Where'd you see the truck when you came back for your phone?"

I pointed. "There."

Ace pulled into a spot nearby, rolled down the windows, and turned off her car. Unlike before, no scent of smoke greeted us. Evidently, the winds were too high to burn brush today. The K-9 team pulled their cruiser in next to us.

Ace glanced around, doing a double take when she turned to look at the Kemps' house. I followed her line of sight. A dark pickup truck sat in their driveway.

She turned to me. "Could that truck be the vehicle you saw here when you came back Saturday night?"

I raised my palms. "I suppose it's possible. But the Kemps' golf cart was in their driveway. I assumed they'd ridden home in it together."

"Golf cart?"

"They use it to get around the vineyard." I told her how Pearl had driven me around the vineyard in it the week before, and that she'd parked it out of sight behind the retail barn.

Ace's head bobbed as she filed away the information, then she angled it to indicate the barn. "Let's go talk to Pearl. And by that, I mean I'll do the talking. You keep your mouth shut, okay?"

"Yes, ma'am."

We climbed out of her car and joined the K-9 team. As we made our way to the door, Ace glanced carefully around at the ground for any evidence that might be about. Spotting none, she headed into the winery with the K-9 team following. I trailed along after them.

A female staff member stood at the register, ringing up wine for a customer. She didn't look familiar. She hadn't been on duty Saturday night. Pearl stood in the walk-in cooler with her back to us, stocking white wine on the shelves. Dressed in a ruffly white prairie dress and her white wedge sandals, she looked like a trendy angel. She didn't turn around as we approached the counter. She must not have heard us come inside.

"Mrs. Kemp?" Ace called.

Pearl turned around inside the cooler. The smile on her face turned to confusion when she saw me with Ace, the uniformed cop, and the K-9. She thrust the bottle of wine she was holding into a slot on a shelf and rushed out. She looked from me to the dog handler to Ace, as if not sure whom to address. "Is everything okay?"

"No," Ace said. "Nobody's seen or heard from Brody Sheridan since he left here Saturday night."

"What?!" Pearl's face went slack in astonishment and she put a hand on the counter to steady herself. "Are you saying he's missing?"

Ace nodded. She slid one of her business cards across the counter and formally introduced herself. "Do you know where he went when he left here?"

"I have no idea," she said. "I'm not even sure exactly when he left." She said that after she and her husband finished cleaning up inside the barn, they exited through the rear door, set the alarm, and got into their golf cart to drive home. Because they went out the back way, they didn't notice who was still on-site, or what vehicles were in the parking lot. "We heard some voices, but we just figured it was taking the band members some time to get their things packed up and that they'd be leaving in another minute or two. We didn't pay the situation much mind. It was late, and there wasn't any reason for us to stick around." Pearl turned her attention from Ace to me, and her face darkened with suspicion. "Why are you here, Hattie?"

Having been told to keep my mouth shut, I cut a glance to Ace. The detective answered for me, "Hattie worked with the Bootlegging Brothers on a radio ad last week. That's how she knew they'd be playing here on Saturday. She was at the winery late that night. I thought she might be able to shed some light on things."

Pearl said, "I see." She cut me another suspicious glance. *Does she think I have something to do with Brody's disappearance?* I could see why she might suspect me. After all, I'd suggested the Wine and 'Shine event only after learning the band would be performing at River Pearl. Maybe she thought I'd purposely put myself in a position to have easy access to Brody.

Ace circled a finger in the air. "Okay if we take a look around?"

"Of course," Pearl said. "Let me know if I can do anything to help."

I followed Ace and the K-9 team out the deck doors. We headed across the vineyard, aiming for the still-empty pond. As we approached, I pointed out the general spot where the excavator had been parked on Sunday. "It was parked somewhere around there."

Ace and I stopped and stood back to give the K-9 team room to work. The officer bent down to release the dog from his leash. He looked up at her expectantly, fully focused, waiting for direction. Once she'd issued the order for him to scent, he put his nose down and got right to work. I found myself thinking about both the K-9 and Charlotte, how both dogs and horses were instrumental in police work. Cats seemed fairly useless in comparison, though I supposed a feline could help out if a police station suffered a rodent infestation.

I watched in fascination as the dog snuffled along the pond liner for a dozen feet, then turned back the way he'd come. He extended his snout and tried to lift the liner with his nose, as if to get a better scent. Then he sat down on his haunches and looked up at his handler expectantly. *Has he gotten a hit on something?*

"Good boy!" The handler reached down to scratch his ears in reward for his work. He wagged his tail, happy to have been of service. Smoky never did anything helpful. With him, it was always *me-me-me-meow.*

Ace pulled her phone from her pocket and placed a call to Pearl Kemp. "Could you come out to your pond, please?"

Pearl emerged from the winery a moment later. She climbed into the golf cart and drove fast in our direction, bouncing over the uneven ground. She rolled to a stop next to us, anxiety lighting up her eyes.

"We'll need to do some digging." Ace pointed down at the dog, who sat dutifully next to the liner. "He's issued an alert. Something's under that liner."

Pearl raised a hand to her chest and folded slightly over the steering well. "Oh, no. Oh, God, no! Not here!"

I knew how she felt. I'd experienced the same horror when the divers brought the cracked jug of moonshine up from the depths of the river.

Having abandoned the harvester in the vineyard, Darren emerged on foot from a row of grapevines and jogged in our direction. If he hadn't been entirely sorry Saturday night that they'd hired the Bootlegging Brothers to play at the winery, he would be now. He'd traded the bright-orange University of Tennessee ball cap he'd been wearing when we'd met last week for a brown nylon sun hat. The sun hat had a flap that hung down on the sides and back to keep his neck from getting sunburned. A smarter choice, since it would better protect him from the sun's unrelenting rays.

He panted as he reached us, bending over to put his hands on his knees. He looked up at Ace. "Pearl texted me. What's going on?"

The detective repeated what she'd told Pearl. "The cadaver dog alerted on your pond liner. We're going to have to remove it and dig."

Darren shook his head and slumped farther, as if the weight of the news threatened to pull him down into the ground, too. When he straightened, he looked from Ace to the handler, a hint of hope replacing some of the angst on his face. "Any chance the dog could be wrong?"

The handler sighed. "It's not likely."

Ace ran her gaze over the white barn, squinting. "Does your barn have security cameras?"

"No," Darren replied. "We've got an alarm system, but we don't have any cameras on the property. We didn't see any reason to install them. There are usually people around the winery, workers or customers, so that's a natural deterrent for thieves. We've got vaults for storing most of the wine inventory, and the cooler has a lock and a security screen built into the door. Plus, the winery is off the beaten path. Robbers wouldn't likely want to come here, where there's only one road out. They could be easily intercepted if a deputy were in the area."

The explanation made sense. Until the murder happened on the steps of my shop, I hadn't had security cameras at the Moonshine Shack, either. It was unfortunate, though. Video footage could have provided critical information about what happened to Brody.

Ace pulled a roll of cordon tape from the pocket of her blazer. "I'll need to establish a perimeter here." She turned to the Kemps. "Y'all can go on about your business for now. I'll let you know if we need anything else. But don't say anything to anyone, not even your employees. Tell them I said you had to keep mum."

Pearl nodded, biting her lip. Darren dipped his head in acknowledgment, too. He draped an arm around his wife's shoulders and escorted her over to the golf cart. As the two set off for the barn, Ace turned to me. "I'll call an officer to come and drive you back to your shop. You can wait there."

I turned my head and looked after the golf cart. "You couldn't have told me this sooner so I could catch a ride back with the Kemps?"

Ace chuckled. "The exercise will be good for you." Before finally dismissing me, she sent me an intent look. "Keep your lips zipped, okay? I don't want rumors to start flying until I can get a handle on things."

"Can I at least tell Marlon?" Ace and Marlon had worked together for years and were close. She kept very little from him. What would it hurt if I beat her to the punch?

She grunted and rolled her eyes, but acquiesced. "Okay, but *only* Marlon." She reached out to put her hands on my shoulders, giving me a pointed, yet appreciative, look. "Thanks for the information you gave me today, Hattie. If you hadn't seen Brody's Jeep drive across Ms. Byrd's land, and hadn't noticed that the equipment had been moved, I might still be at square one."

I felt proud that my observations had led to evidence. "Glad I could help."

When she released me, I turned, strode back across the vineyard, and stood in front of the barn. As I waited for my ride, I pondered over what had happened at the pond. It seemed clear that someone had used the excavator to dig a hole and then buried Brody's body in it sometime Saturday night or early Sunday morning. But the excavator wasn't quiet. *Wouldn't the Kemps have heard the noise and come out of their house to investigate?*

I turned to look at what I could see of their house between the trees. Their home sat well beyond the vineyard, and it was quite some distance from the pond to the house. If they'd had their television or a fan on, or if they were already asleep, maybe they wouldn't have heard the machinery. Shirley Byrd hadn't mentioned hearing the equipment when Ace spoke with her earlier, and her house sat about the same distance from the pond as the Kemps' house. Whoever had buried Brody must've worked quickly. It was also possible that whoever had buried Brody didn't use the excavator. Maybe they'd dug the hole with a shovel or some other tool, or even their hands. The dirt in the pond would have been freshly dug and likely loose, so maybe it had been easy to move. The excavator could have been moved from the near side to the far side of the pond for reasons other than digging Brody's grave.

A few minutes later, a police cruiser pulled into the lot and stopped behind Ace's car, the engine idling. I walked over and opened the passenger door. The male officer at the wheel leaned across the console to address me. "You might want to sit in back. My Dr Pepper spilled all over the passenger seat when I had to floor the gas pedal to go after a speeder."

I looked down at the seat. A wet, brown stain spread across it. Brown liquid sat on the floorboard, too. "But if I ride in the back, people will think I'm a criminal."

"Would you rather be thought a criminal or have wet and sticky pants?"

Some choice, huh? Sighing, I shut the front door, opened the back door, and climbed in. A panel of metal mesh separated me from the officer. The back of the cruiser smelled of body odor, but I supposed that was to be expected. People probably broke out in a nervous sweat when they were being hauled in for booking. There were no door handles back here, no way to escape. I felt trapped in a cage. It was unnerving.

The officer circled around in the parking lot and drove me back into the city. Every time a car passed us or we stopped at a traffic light, the people in the other cars looked over at me. Their expressions ranged from curious to disgusted. A middle-aged woman looked over and did a double take before her mouth fell open. *Crap!* It was one of the women from my mother's bunko group. My "arrest" would be fodder for their rumor mill, but what could I do? Ace said I had to keep quiet.

The officer pulled to a stop in front of the Moonshine Shack, climbed out, and opened the back door for me as if he were a chauffeur and his patrol car were a limousine. Though the gesture seemed chivalrous, it was born of necessity since I had no way of opening the door myself.

I took the hand he held out and used it to lever myself out of the backseat. "Thanks. Come back sometime when you're off duty and try my moonshine."

"I'll do that."

I went into the store. Granddaddy rang up a customer while Marlon bagged their jars. The two made an odd, but adorable, sales team.

I reached out to run a hand over Smoky's head before meeting Marlon's gaze. "Where's Charlotte?" I asked.

Marlon said, "I moved her out back. Figured it was safer. She's left some droppings in your lot, but I'll clean them up now that you're back."

"I'll come with you." I turned to my granddad. "I'll be right back."

"Okey doke."

Marlon and I walked through my stock room and exited

through the back door into my rear parking lot, where he retrieved a small shovel and trash bag from Charlotte's saddlebag. While he scooped up Charlotte's droppings, I gave him the proverbial poop. "The search team found Brody's Jeep in the Tennessee River just across the road from the winery. All of his instruments were still in the car, but he wasn't."

"Anything else?" Marlon asked. "Maybe something that could provide a clue?"

I grimaced. "Yeah. A wooden spoon and a cracked jug of my moonshine."

He closed his eyes before scrubbing a hand down his face. "Your moonshine seems to make trouble wherever it goes."

I was tempted to argue the point, but he wasn't wrong. My moonshine had been implicated before in suspicious deaths. I hoped this time would be the last. I continued to fill him in. "The driver's door was open on Brody's Jeep. At first, we'd thought he'd been swept downstream, but then I remembered that the excavator I'd seen at the winery had been moved between Saturday evening and Sunday afternoon. I mentioned it to Ace, and she had the K-9 team take a look at the pond. The dog indicated that there was something under the pond liner. That's when Ace sent me back here and told me to keep my mouth shut until they figure things out."

He eyed me, one brow cocked. "Can you do that? Keep your mouth shut?"

"I can," I said, "with the help of some duct tape."

Marlon chuckled. He knew as well as I did that, hard as it would be, I'd keep the news to myself until Ace gave me the go-ahead to share it. The last thing I wanted to do was jeopardize a murder investigation, especially one that could implicate my moonshine.

Marlon leaned down and gave me a peck on the cheek before swinging himself up into the saddle. I ran a hand over Charlotte's neck in goodbye, and she stomped her foot once, telling both me and Marlon that she was ready to get moving. Marlon issued a *click*ing sound, gave her sides a gentle squeeze with his thighs, and off they went, *clop-clop-clop.*

Chapter Eleven

On Wednesday, just after I'd opened my shop at noon, the same *clop-clop-clop* greeted me. Leaving Nora to handle a customer, I grabbed two green apples from the mini fridge and stepped out front to speak to Marlon. His face was grave, even more so than I would have expected. *Uh-oh.*

"Bad news?" I handed one apple to him for a snack. I cupped the other in my hands and held it out for Charlotte. Her whiskers tickled my palms as she used her lips and teeth to grab the treat.

"Bad news?" he repeated. "Yeah. You could say that. Brody's body was found buried in the pond at the vineyard, like we expected. The condition of his corpse indicates he was probably killed on Saturday night or Sunday. He was buried deep."

"My initial guess was right, then? The excavator was used to dig his grave?"

"Looks that way." He took a bite of the apple and ran the back of his hand over his lips to remove the errant juice.

"The killer had to be Tate, then, right?" After all, the excavator belonged to the pool company he worked for, and he'd been the one using it to dig the pond at the winery. He'd have the key to the machine. Though I wasn't certain, the vehicle I saw parked at the winery when I went back for my phone could have very well been his truck. After all, the gate had still been open when I left. Though he'd left with his wife and their girls earlier, he could have driven back onto the property before the gate was later closed for the night. My heart constricted at the thought of Amelia losing her daddy to prison. Seeing as Imogene lived with Camille and Tate, he'd been her daddy, too, even if by her mother's marriage rather than blood. Camille would be heartbroken, too—assuming she wasn't in on it, that is.

Marlon finished chewing, slid down from Charlotte's back, and gave her the rest of his apple, as well. "Ace is questioning Tate and Camille at the station as we speak. I went with her to round them up this morning. She wanted to catch them before they left for work."

"How'd they react when she told them Brody's body had been found?"

"About like you'd expect," Marlon said. "Neither of them broke down. Camille shed a few quiet tears and Tate shook his head quite a bit, but that's all. They both said they'd figured something bad had happened to Brody and that they'd prepared themselves for the worst. They'd prepared Imogene, too."

I couldn't even imagine how hard it would be to have to tell your child that they might have lost a parent. "Did

Ace ask them about the life insurance policy Camille had on Brody?"

"She did."

"How much is it worth?" I asked.

"A quarter-million dollars."

"Is that all?" While 250 grand was certainly nothing to sneeze at, it wasn't exactly a huge windfall, either. It represented only a few years' earnings for most American families these days. *Would that sum be worth killing for?* I supposed it might if the victim was also a source of grief and frustration. Heck, the money might simply be a bonus. "When was the policy taken out?"

"Right after Camille and Brody's divorce," Marlon said.

"She bought life insurance *after* their marriage was over? That seems strange."

"I thought so, too, at first, but Ace says that's not necessarily unusual. Camille said it replaced a policy she and Brody had while they were married. She couldn't count on him to keep the insurance current, even though the divorce decree required it. It was a way to ensure support for Imogene in the event something happened to Brody."

"Makes sense, I guess." I looked up into Marlon's face again. The tension that remained in his neck and jaw told me he hadn't gotten to the worst part yet. "Go ahead," I said. "Spill the tea."

He took a deep breath before continuing. "Ace told me Brody's head was bloody. We won't have an official cause of death until the medical examiner's office takes a look at him, but Ace suspects he died of blunt force trauma. The lab found traces of blood on the moonshine jug that was recovered from Brody's Jeep. A strand of his hair was stuck in the crack, too."

"Oh, no!" I struggled to wrap my mind around this new evidence. Brody Sheridan was killed with a jug of my moonshine only a few days after recording a jingle that sung its praises. I no longer felt like a shining star. I felt like a weapons supplier, a dealer in death. I groaned and put my face in my hands. Having just fed Charlotte, they smelled like fresh apple and horse. It was bad enough that one of my wooden spoons had possibly been used to hold down the accelerator on Brody Sheridan's Jeep, but knowing one of my hard, heavy jugs had been used to crush the musician's skull made me feel sick. I hoped word wouldn't get out that the Hayes family's moonshine was good for more than just drinking. What would happen to my brand and my shop if the public learned that a jug of my 'shine had been a device of death?

I lifted my head. "Could the jug found in Brody's Jeep be the one I gave Imogene?"

"No. Imogene's jug was sitting in their living room this morning. Still has the ribbon on it, but they'd put the daisies in a small vase with some water and added the wooden spoon to their kitchen collection. Camille said Imogene's been blowing on that jug all day long since you gave it to her."

It was a small solace to know that at least one of my jugs was being used for a positive purpose. But I wondered where Tate had gotten the jug used in the crime. Had he taken one of the decorative jugs from the stage? Or had Camille been in on the plan to kill Brody and swiped a jug herself? Maybe they'd planned the crime in advance and bought a jug at a local liquor store after hearing about the Wine and 'Shine event and realizing I'd be selling my moonshine at the winery. Maybe they'd hoped

Garth would be fingered for the murder since he played my jug. But framing their brother-in-law—or whatever he was to them—would be a lousy thing to do. What's more, the three seemed to be on good terms.

Of course, I could be jumping to conclusions. Hard evidence, like fingerprints, could tell us for certain whether Tate was the actual killer, as I suspected. "What about fingerprints?" I asked. "Were there any on the jug in Brody's Jeep or did the water wash them off?"

"There were plenty of prints," Marlon said. "With the jug having been in the water, it made them harder to lift, but water alone doesn't always wash away the skin oils that come from people's fingers. To fully remove the prints, they'd have to be wiped. Fortunately, it was a warm night Saturday. People were probably sweating a little, especially any of them who were out on the deck."

Marlon was right about that. I remembered seeing my grandfather pull a bandanna from his back pocket and mop his brow when he and Louetta were dancing. Having learned that suspects did not have to voluntarily give their prints unless and until they were arrested, I wondered whether Tate had cooperated with Ace and Marlon. "Did Tate willingly give his fingerprints?"

"He did. So did Camille. Ace even took prints from Imogene, just so the lab would be able to identify them if they were on the jug. Garth and Josh had given theirs earlier, when Ace gathered the family to give them the news. Everyone was remarkably cooperative."

"And? Whose prints were on the jugs?"

"The only identifiable prints on the jug were Brody's, Garth's, Camille's, Imogene's, and yours. We don't know who the others belong to."

"None were Tate's?"

"No."

That fact surprised me. I'd felt pretty sure Tate was the guilty party. "Does that mean Tate didn't do it? That he's not Brody's killer?"

"The lack of prints doesn't clear him. He could have easily gotten the jug from Camille and used it to clobber Brody. He could have worn a pair of his work gloves or wrapped a napkin or cloth or even a shirtsleeve around the handle of the jug so he wouldn't leave prints. Of course, the fact that Garth's prints were on the jug raises the question of how they got there."

"That's a question I can answer," I said. "Garth picked up one of the jugs when I went out on the deck at the winery to talk to him. He asked if I was the one who'd put the jugs on the stage, said he liked the folksy touch."

"Oh, yeah? I'll pass that information on to Ace."

Surely, we'd soon know what had taken place. The fingerprint evidence might be inconclusive, but Ace was an expert interrogator, and if Tate and Camille were guilty, she'd find a way to get it out of them. "If Camille's and Imogene's prints were on the jug, that means it was definitely one I'd displayed at the winery, not the jug I'd given Brody after the photo shoot, right? Camille and Imogene have never been in my store, at least not as far as I know."

"I suspect you're right. In fact, we found a nearly full jug of moonshine in Brody's apartment. It's got your prints on it and his, but none of the other prints could be ID'd. Given those circumstances, it must be the jug you gave him in your shop last week."

We wrapped up our discussion. I didn't even realize that I was staring at the floor, trying to come to terms with this news, until Marlon reached out a hand and gently lifted my chin. He looked me in the eye, his amber eyes filled with concern. "None of this is your fault, Hattie. If your jug hadn't been readily accessible, the killer would have found something else to kill Brody with."

I appreciated his attempt to comfort me, even if it wasn't entirely effective. I gave him a soft smile and he released my chin.

"See you soon," he said. With that, he swung himself up into the saddle.

As Marlon rode off, I turned back to my shop. The poster of the Bootlegging Brothers still hung in my window. *Should I take the posters down? Should I ask the radio station to pull the commercial?*

After mulling things over for a moment, I decided neither would feel right. Removing the posters or pulling the commercial would be like pretending Brody had never existed, as if I were erasing him somehow. I couldn't do it. I felt bad enough knowing he'd been killed with one of my moonshine jugs. Besides, Garth had been kind to me, and pulling the commercial could be detrimental to his music career. Josh's, too. Nope, for better or worse, my moonshine and the Bootlegging Brothers were in this mess together.

Marlon came by again on Thursday with an update. My grandfather was sitting and whittling in a rocking chair out front when Marlon rode up. Smoky was lying in the front window. He made an odd chirping noise and stood to stare out the window, fluffing out his fur so that he looked larger.

Nora glanced over at my cat. "If I didn't know better, I'd think your cat is trying to impress that horse."

"He's got a hopeless crush on her." It was true. Smoky came to life each time Charlotte strode up. I walked over and gave my cat a scratch behind the ears. "She's too much woman for you, little guy."

As if he'd understood me, he hissed and swiped at my hand.

I walked out the door. "Hey, Marlon. Got an update for me?"

"I do."

"Tate's in custody, right?" I asked, assuming Ace had broken him down. "What about Camille? Was she in on it?"

"Tate and Camille had been cleared, at least for now."

My eyes narrowed of their own accord. *How could Tate have been cleared when his excavator had been used to dig Brody Sheridan's grave?*

Marlon filled me in. "Tate and Camille claim they went straight home after they left the winery, put their girls to bed, then went to bed themselves. Tate says he left the excavator parked on the near side of the pond at the end of the workday last Friday, and that he has no idea who had moved it to the other side of the empty pond over the weekend."

No idea? Tate's claim seemed absurd. "Whoever moved the excavator had to be someone who worked for the pool company, right? They'd be the only ones with access to the key."

"That's the thing," Marlon said, frowning. "Whoever moved the excavator wouldn't need the pool company's key."

"Why not?"

"Because the keys are universal. Heavy equipment manufacturers make only one key for all of their equipment. Anyone with a Caterpillar key could have moved the excavator."

Had I heard him right? "Are you saying the keys aren't unique to each machine?"

"That's exactly what I'm saying." When my mouth went agape, Marlon said, "It was news to me, too. Tate said the equipment manufacturers provide universal keys because it makes things easier for the crews. Each crew member can have their own key if they need to use a piece of equipment or move it. It keeps them from having to go hunting down the correct key. Apparently, you can even buy sets of master keys for construction equipment. They're sold at some building supply stores and online."

"Doesn't seem very secure."

"It's not," Marlon agreed. "In fact, it's fairly common for construction equipment to be stolen."

Thinking aloud, I pointed out the obvious. "Whoever moved the excavator must've had a key to that particular brand of equipment."

"Exactly. And guess who does?"

Darren Kemp was the first name that came to mind, probably because I'd seen him driving the tractor in the vineyard. But then I remembered that his tractor was not yellow but green, a John Deere rather than Caterpillar. "Who?"

"Someone close to Brody," Marlon said. "Someone in his band of brothers."

Please don't say it's Garth. I swallowed hard and again asked, "Who?"

"Garth."

I said please*! Well, I'd thought it anyway.* "Why would Garth have a key to Caterpillar equipment?"

"He's employed by the city of Chattanooga, in the public works department. The city uses Caterpillar brand equipment, same as Tate's pool company."

Now that Marlon said this, I recalled Garth having mentioned his job with the city when he was talking about wanting to quit his day job. *He'd said something about Josh working for the highway department, too, hadn't he?* "What about Josh? Does he have a Caterpillar key, too?"

"Not in his possession. Not that he'll own up to, anyway. He said he's got keys to Kubota, Hitachi, and Komatsu equipment, but that the crew chiefs always have copies of any other keys they might need. Ace looked into it. TDOT uses a variety of brands of equipment. Caterpillar is one of them."

I wondered if Josh could have pocketed a Caterpillar key when working on a job. Heck, maybe he'd thrown the key in the river after sending Brody's Jeep over the bluff. I pondered another alternative. "Could Josh have borrowed Garth's key?"

"Doesn't seem likely," Marlon said. "Garth said he keeps his equipment key in a pocket on his safety vest. He keeps the vest in his truck. Josh doesn't have a key to Garth's truck."

"Has Garth been arrested, then?"

"No," Marlon said. "The key is only circumstantial evidence, and it's not enough by itself to support an arrest, especially in light of the fact that the keys are universal and readily available. But Ace is going to keep digging."

Digging. The word made me wince.

Marlon noticed my reaction. "Sorry. Poor choice of words."

Changing to a happier subject, I said, "What's on the menu for our dinner date Sunday?"

Marlon wagged his brows. "How about I surprise you?"

"That means you haven't given the meal any thought or shopped for groceries yet, doesn't it?"

Marlon put a hand to his heart and gave me a roguish grin. "I feel so seen."

On Friday morning, Smoky batted his jingle ball around our cabin while I took care of some long-neglected domestic duties. I washed the pile of dishes that had been sitting in my sink for days, scoured the bathroom, and ran three loads of laundry. I vacuumed the dust bunnies from under the bed, ran a cloth over the furniture, and tossed out the old food in my fridge, some of which was so fuzzy it was no longer identifiable. The one downside to running a retail business that was open seven days a week was that my home life suffered. Then again, maybe my business was just a convenient excuse. Even before I'd started making moonshine, my cabin hadn't exactly been immaculate. A woman's got to make her priorities, after all, and housework was pretty far down on my list.

After cleaning the inside of the cabin, I swept the front porch. Movement caught my eye as a little birdie alit on the top of the shed behind my home. Leaving the broom on the porch, I walked to the shed and pulled the doors open. Inside sat the 1932 Ford flathead V8 that my great-grandfather had used in his moonshine business. With all the rust covering it now, you'd never know that the car had outrun law enforcement hundreds of times during the Prohibition era, including Marlon's great-grandfather on multiple occasions. If not for a tire blowing out, Sheriff Landers might have never caught Eustatius Hayes. My granddaddy might still lament the capture of his father, but I was glad that the sheriff's great-grandson had chosen to pursue me. Admittedly, I'd been much easier to capture. Marlon hadn't needed a weapon. He'd disarmed me with his sexy smile and Southern charm.

I stepped inside the shed and circled the ancient car, carefully looking things over. *Hmm.* I blew a layer of dust off the hood and bent over to take a closer look. While much of the hood had succumbed to oxidation, a few spots of the original shiny black paint remained. I wondered whether the car could be restored—assuming the cost wouldn't be prohibitive. I also wondered whether it was something I could do on my own. After all, Kiki and I had fixed up the horse trailer and transformed it into a mobile moonshine bar. After some thought, I realized that, while she and I were perfectly capable of completing a simple, whimsical project like the trailer, it would take someone more skilled to properly restore and repaint the vintage automobile. I also decided it was worth looking into.

Early Friday evening, Kiki was hanging out at the shop with me when a group of men in their thirties and forties came into the store. All wore boots, jeans, and either western-style shirts or tees. They glanced around for a moment before the one in the lead selected a jug from a display of Granddaddy's Ole-Timey Corn Liquor. He held up the jug. "This the murder moonshine?"

Murder moonshine? Though Ace had surely sworn the Kemps, the winery employees, and Brody's family to secrecy when they were questioned about the two missing decorative jugs, someone clearly had loose lips. Still, I'd been instructed to stay silent on the subject and I wasn't about to validate their supposition, even if I knew it to be true. "I don't know anything about that," I said, "but it's good stuff. You'll enjoy it."

Another man pointed to the poster of the Bootlegging Brothers that hung on the wall. "How much for one of them posters?"

Although I had several copies of the full-sized poster in my stock room, it seemed in poor taste to profit from Brody's death. Rather than debate the matter with the man, I simply said, "I don't have any for sale."

"Shame," he said. "I would've paid good money for it."

Kiki cut me a look that said *Sure you don't want to make some easy cash?* I gave her a look back that said *It wouldn't feel right.* The two of us were close enough that we could hold entire conversations without saying a word.

The men grabbed jugs of moonshine and brought them to the cash register. Some bought just one jug, while others bought all they could carry. All told, they purchased twenty jugs among them. Kiki bagged them in heavy-duty bags as I processed the credit card payments or made change for cash.

"Thanks!" I called after them as they went out the door. "Come back soon!"

As soon as the door swung closed behind them, Kiki pounced, holding me by the shoulders and looking me directly in the eye. "What did they mean by 'murder moonshine'?"

I bit my lip. "I'm sorry, Kiki. The detective said I'm not allowed to say anything."

Her eyes narrowed and she released me. "You don't have to. I'll consult the source that knows all, tells all."

She stepped behind the counter and wiggled her fingers and circled her arms over the computer keyboard as if it were a crystal ball. She tapped a few keys, then looked at the screen. "According to @PurtyCowgurl on Instagram, Brody Sheridan was beaten to death with a jug of your Granddaddy's Ole-Timey Corn Liquor and his body was dumped in the vineyard at the River Pearl Winery."

The Internet trolls hadn't exactly gotten things right, but it was close enough.

Kiki sucked air through her teeth. "Sorry, Hattie. You don't deserve this."

Surly or not, Brody hadn't deserved what happened to him, either.

Shortly after the men left the store, a group of young women entered. The first one through the door had pink highlights in her blond hair and wore a T-shirt from my alma mater, the University of Tennessee at Chattanooga. She stopped in her tracks and threw her arms out to her sides, forcing the others to glom together behind her. "There it is." She slowly raised a pointed finger with all the drama of a Broadway actress. "The 'shine that put out Brody Sheridan's light."

Kiki issued a soft groan beside me. "Let me guess," she called to the coed. "Theater major?"

The girl tossed her head and spread her lips in a thousand-watt smile. "How'd you know?"

"Lucky guess."

The night continued in the same fashion. Customers coming in to take home a jug of the 'shine that took Brody Sheridan out of this world. I'd hoped my store would be busy, but not for such a macabre reason.

After closing, I ran a tally on the register, took a look

at the bottom line on the tape, and sighed. "This was one of my most profitable days ever."

Kiki said, "You shouldn't be sighing. You should be shouting *Yippee!* And promising to take your two best friends on a Caribbean cruise."

"It wasn't *that* much money," I said. "But I could take you kayaking sometime soon."

"You're on."

Kiki's boyfriend, Max, swung by to pick her up just after closing. Like Kiki, Max was of Japanese descent, though his family had immigrated three generations ago. Also, like Kiki, Max considered himself to be a living piece of art, his body a canvas. He didn't only work in various metals as a sculptor, he wore crazy amounts of metal, too. Seven metal hoops adorned the shell of one ear, while a single hoop adorned the lobe of the other. He had two hoops through his right brow and one through his nose, as well as thick rings on each finger, including his thumbs. He'd cut the sleeves out of his ironic ballet slipper–pink Dolly Parton concert tee, revealing the sleeve tattoos composed of his own artwork. Images of cartoon robots, planets, and even Kiki's cats made their way up and down the skin of his arms.

Max greeted us with "Yo, shop wenches." Smoky had climbed onto the counter, and Max ran a hand over his back. "Yo to you, too, cool cat." Max grabbed the remaining blue-and-white ribbon from the counter, unspooled it, and dragged the ribbon across the floor. Smoky hopped down from the counter and chased after him, pouncing on the ribbon and trying to catch it, enjoying the game.

"Hey, Max," I said. "Any chance you know how to get rust off old metal?"

Max jerked the ribbon in the air now and Smoky jumped up, claws out, to try to snatch it. "I know how to do everything that pertains to metal. Why?"

"My great-grandfather's old Ford is sitting in a shed behind my cabin. I've been thinking about having it restored—the exterior anyway. I thought it would be fun to put it in front of my shop so people could sit in it for a photo op. Hashtag Moonshine Shack."

"Think no more," Max said. "I'll do it. Fifty bucks an hour plus expenses. Automobile paint ain't cheap."

"Deal." We shook on it. I mused aloud. "Maybe I'll put out some old-fashioned hats so people can dress up to look like they were from that era. You know, like those period photos people have taken in tourist traps. It would be an organic way to spread the word about my products."

Kiki added, "And spread lice."

Though she was right, I ignored her. *Party pooper.* I gave Max my address and a cash advance of three hundred dollars to buy materials. "Keep this project between us," I said. "I don't want my grandfather to find out. I want to surprise him." Granddaddy would be thrilled to see his father's old rattletrap looking sharp again, even if it didn't run.

With that, Kiki and Max left my shop. I rounded up Smoky and headed home to our cabin, wondering all the while who had dug Brody Sheridan's grave. All we knew was that it was someone with a Caterpillar key, a jug, and a reason to want the guy dead. Unfortunately, that included a wide pool of people.

On Saturday, Simone and her friend covered the store so that I could attend Brody's funeral. Word of the service had spread like wildfire and, by the time I arrived at the church for the service, it was standing room only. I gave a nod to Marlon, who stood just inside the door to the sanctuary, wearing a suit rather than his uniform and looking quite handsome in it. I squeezed into a spot along the back wall on the other side of the door.

I caught only a glimpse of Josh and Garth, who sat in the left front row with a middle-aged couple I assumed were their parents. William Hill sat in the second row behind the immediate family. Though Brody had insisted that Camille and Tate were not his family, they were nonetheless seated on the front row on the right, along with Brody's daughter, Imogene, whose little head barely reached the top of the pew. I didn't see Camille and Tate's daughter, Amelia. Looked like they'd left the toddler at home. Good call. Toddlers could be unpredictable and disruptive.

Ace sat near the back, casting occasional glances about as if assessing those in attendance. Rather than her usual pants and blazer, she wore a charcoal gray dress today. I wondered whether those around her realized she was the detective working Brody's murder case.

Not long after I arrived, Darren and Pearl Kemp stepped through the doors. Their faces appeared stricken. It was no wonder. Their winery would be forever tainted as the site of a notorious murder. Like me, they were likely torn between wanting people to forget this violent, tragic event as soon as possible, and guilt for wanting Brody to be forgotten quickly so they could move on. They glanced around for a seat. Seeing none, they sought a space to stand along the perimeter. They ended up in a corner and soon disappeared from sight as people filed in and filled in the space in front of them.

The service was somber and solemn, as expected. It was strange, too, in light of the fact that Brody's killer had yet to be identified and could even be sitting among the crowd. I wasn't the only one to have this thought. The crowd whispered and glanced around, apparently speculating who might be guilty. The pastor prayed for swift justice for the fallen fiddler.

In honor of their lost brother, Josh and Garth ascended the steps to stand next to the altar. Garth played his guitar and Josh led the mourners in singing the country gospel classic "I Saw the Light," though they slowed the song's usual quick pace significantly. To my surprise, William Hill joined them with his fiddle for a second song. The three launched into a slow, somber version of "I'll Fly Away."

Having zero vocal talent, I sang softly, not much more than lip-synching the words. As I sang, I pondered the trio at the altar. It seemed a little odd, maybe even disrespectful, that Garth and Josh would invite William to play with them at Brody's funeral. Brody had expressed such outrage when Garth proposed that William play with the Bootlegging Brothers at the winery. Then again, Brody hadn't exactly been reasonable, about William or much else. Maybe his brothers didn't take his protestations seriously since he seemed to always be complaining about one thing or another, and often acted in his own self-interest. I wondered if Garth and Josh would invite William to take Brody's place playing strings for the band. From what I heard right now, he was indeed a fine fiddle player, better even than Brody, *may he rest in peace*.

When the service wrapped up, Brody and Garth formed a receiving line of sorts outside the church. Evidently unable to face the huge crowd in their moment of grief, their parents had gone ahead, driving to the cemetery for what would be a private burial. I wondered if the family regretted not making the memorial service private as well. With the enormous crowd milling about, as well as the TV camera crews and reporters outside the church, the service had the feel of a strange, somber circus.

I was swept along in the line as people left the church, and soon found myself face-to-face with Garth and Josh. Not knowing them well, I felt awkward. I kept my condolences short and simple. "I'm so sorry, you two. I hope you can find peace soon."

As usual, Josh stayed silent, an almost imperceptible lift of his chin the only sign he'd heard me. Meanwhile, Garth's shoulders were slumped, as if he carried an enormous, unseen burden. Was he feeling guilty? If so, was it only because he'd argued with Brody Saturday evening, or was it because he'd ended his brother's life?

Garth cleared his throat and said, "Thanks, Hattie." His voice was raw and gravelly, as if he hadn't slept. The bags under his eyes and his sagging face were more evidence of the effect Brody's death had on him.

Josh, who'd sung perfectly, appeared unaffected. I didn't know what to make of that. In light of the fact that he was normally so calm and expressionless, maybe it didn't mean anything. Still, you'd think losing his brother would have him looking more upset.

My musings were interrupted when Garth reached out and took my hands in his. "You made Brody's last night special. Our fans loved those posters you had made for us. We signed so many we felt like superstars." He managed a weak smile.

"I'm glad." I gave him a small smile and squeezed his hands gently in return. Over his shoulder, I could see Camille, Tate, and Imogene. A reporter approached the family, but Tate held up his hand and shook his head, letting the journalist know they would not be speaking to the media. William Hill stood with them, tugging at his necktie as if it were strangling him and shifting anxiously from foot to foot as if eager to get away from the church and the crowd. *Hmm*.

When Garth released me, I turned to walk away. I noticed Marlon standing a few feet farther down, frowning slightly. He didn't seem to like the attention Garth had given me, but what could I do? I wasn't about to refuse to take the guy's hands when he'd just lost his brother. It would be cruel.

I stepped over and spoke briefly with Marlon. "Glean anything at the service?"

His gaze shifted to Josh. "Josh Sheridan doesn't seem too broken up about his brother's murder."

"I thought the same thing." Still, Josh was characteristically cool, so maybe his behavior was nothing out of the ordinary. Then again, maybe he'd borrowed Garth's Caterpillar key and one of my jugs, and used them to kill Brody and hide both the evidence and his brother's body. But what reason would Josh have had to end Brody's life? None he'd ever directly expressed, as far as I knew. Then again, how much did I really know about these people? Precious little. *Maybe I should do something to change that.*

Chapter Twelve

The Moonshine Shack was so busy on Sunday I didn't get a chance to take a break. Customers circled in and out in a constant stream, everyone eager to take home a jug of Granddaddy's Ole-Timey Corn Liquor. Some who came in groups even pretended to hit one another over the heads with the jugs, their jokes in extremely poor taste. The posters of the Bootlegging Brothers disappeared from my windows and walls, surreptitious thieves absconding with them after I'd again refused to sell them. The bustling crowd had made it easy for them to get away with their petty crimes. Lest someone decide Smoky would make a good souvenir, too, I locked my furry feline in the stock room, where he'd be safe.

Granddaddy leaned against the back of the counter to steady himself as he bagged the jugs. "I've never seen nothing like this!" he said. "I didn't know this shop could hold so many people. How many you think are in here?"

I glanced around. It was impossible to get an accurate count with everyone milling around. "Enough to violate the fire code," I concluded.

Although the macabre obsession with the jugs was making money hand over fist for my Moonshine Shack, Granddaddy and I didn't want to profit off Brody's death, nor did we want the reputation of our family's moonshine to be tarnished. Once the murder was solved, things would settle down. I knew Ace was working hard to gather information, and I hoped she'd be able to piece everything together soon. I also wanted the murder solved for Garth's sake. I simply couldn't believe the affable guy was guilty. Knowing his brother's killer still walked free must be eating him alive. Garth had done me a big favor convincing his brothers to sing the jingle for my shop. I wanted to return the favor by helping Ace identify Brody's killer.

Though plenty of people came to the Moonshine Shack to buy my wares, it wasn't just customers circling in and out of the store. Three reporters came by to question me. One was with a local newspaper. One wrote for an online news source. The third was a raven-haired field reporter from a local television station. She wore a solid-blue sheath dress and a determined look on her face. She was the same reporter who'd shown up at my shop after a man was poisoned at the recent model train convention. He'd drunk some of my moonshine, and I'd been forced to close the Moonshine Shack until my inventory had been analyzed for safety. Looked like the reporter was eager to pounce on me again.

She entered the door and sashayed her way through the crowd. "Ms. Hayes? May I have a word? On camera?"

"I don't know anything," I said, though it wasn't exactly

true. I just didn't know anything I was allowed to share with anyone other than Marlon. "Plus, I've got a lot of customers to take care of." I gestured around at the bustling crowd in my shop.

"I see." She cocked her head. "The fact that Brody Sheridan was killed by one of your moonshine jugs has been a tremendous boon for your shop, hasn't it?"

Ugh. I knew she was only looking for an angle, but if she went with that story I'd look like a heartless, money-grubbing monster. I shrugged. "The store's always busy on weekends."

"Is that so?" She looked around at the customers before grabbing a jug of 'shine, holding it up, and calling out, "Who's here because they heard Brody Sheridan was killed with one of these jugs?"

Nearly every customer in the store raised their hand. The reporter looked at me and arched her brows. She then turned and looked around, as if searching for the best person to interview for her story. She approached an attractive fortyish man. "Would you be willing to be interviewed on camera out on the street?"

He agreed and the two headed toward the door. She carried the jug of moonshine with her.

"Excuse me!" I called to her. "You can't take unpaid merchandise out the door."

"Don't worry," she said. "I'll bring it right back when we're done." With that, she flounced out the door.

Sheesh. That woman's got nerve. The least she could have done is buy the jug of moonshine.

She performed a quick interview at the curb and then stepped back into the shop. She lifted the jug into the air and called to me, "I'm putting this jug back now. See?"

She made a show of returning the crock to the display, then turned and again flounced out of my shop.

Sigh.

I pulled into Marlon's gravel driveway promptly at six o'clock Sunday evening. Charlotte stood at the fence on the side of Marlon's acreage, one leg cocked sassily up behind her. On the other side of the fence were three mares—one gray, one black, and one paint. All four looked my way as I drove up. *Looks like I've interrupted their gossip session.*

I'd brought Smoky along with me. I knew he'd have fun exploring Marlon's new home. I'd also brought along two spider plants and a bottle of wine, a white blend from River Pearl Winery that we could enjoy with dinner and while watching the movie.

Marlon must've seen me through the front window. He stepped out onto the porch and greeted me with a smile before coming down the steps to relieve me of my heavy cat.

I followed Marlon into his new home. The house looked fairly austere with only his meager furnishings inside. Good thing I'd brought him the pretty pair of plants as a housewarming gift. The foliage would fill things out and soften the look. The spider plants were also nontoxic to cats, so there'd be no risk to Smoky if the stinker decided to chew on them.

Marlon set the carrier down on the carpet and turned to take the pots from me. He glanced around his living room. "Where should I put the plants?"

I pointed to the brick hearth. "Put one by the fireplace," I suggested. "The other can go on the coffee table."

As he arranged the pots, I prepared a water bowl and litter box for Smoky, then knelt down and released my furry pet from his carrier. The cat paraded out and looked around, as if deciding which part of the room to explore first. He chose the brown faux-leather sofa, sashaying over and lifting his paws to the side to sharpen his claws on it. "Smoky! No!" I rushed over to pull his claws out of the thick synthetic fabric. He growled and gave me a look of disgust before skittering off down the hall.

Marlon's television was tuned to the evening news. The reporter who'd been at my shop earlier appeared on the screen, the front of the Moonshine Shack in the background. She proceeded to question my customer about why he'd come to my shop. *"I wanted to see the jug that killed Brody Sheridan,"* he said. *"I couldn't imagine such a thing was possible, but these jugs are hard as a rock and heavy, too. I can see why Brody's killer chose it as a weapon."*

Marlon caught me scowling at the screen. "Don't worry, Hattie. This will blow over."

But when?

Marlon motioned for me to follow him into the kitchen.

I raised my nose and breathed in the aromas. "What smells so good?"

"Corn bread and beans," he said. "My grandmother's recipe. She made it with a secret ingredient so it would be extra moist."

I glanced down into the open garbage can and, noting the contents, said, "Was that secret ingredient yellow squash?"

Marlon looked from me to the can. "Uh-oh. Don't tell her I spilled the beans."

"Speaking of beans, they smell great, too." A huge pot of butter beans simmered on the stove, releasing a savory scent.

We fixed our plates, poured the wine, and settled on the two stools at his butcher-block island. As we ate, he filled me in on the status of Ace's investigation.

"Garth and Josh both told Ace that they left the winery at the same time. Garth pulled out in his truck with Josh right behind him. They headed in opposite directions once they reached Raccoon Mountain Road. Josh headed north, and Garth drove south. They both claim that, last they knew, Brody was sitting in his Jeep in the winery's parking lot, texting a woman who'd slipped her phone number to him on the down-low. They both said they warned Brody not to contact her. She'd come to the winery with her boyfriend, and he was a big guy."

There was only one reason why a guy would be texting a woman that late at night. He was looking to make a booty call. Unfortunately, with Brody's phone being destroyed by the river water, there'd be no way to get the woman's name and number from his phone. "Has Ace contacted Brody's cell phone provider?"

Marlon nodded as he swallowed a bite of corn bread, then wiped his mouth. "She's put in a request for his records. If the woman responded to the text, it's possible her boyfriend tailed her back to the winery, realized she was meeting up with Brody, and put a quick end to him. Or maybe the boyfriend intercepted the text, responded as if he were her, and then deleted it so his girlfriend wouldn't be aware. The boyfriend might have shown up and gotten into things with Brody. But it's also possible either Josh or Garth turned around and returned to the winery. Since the two of them drove off in opposite directions, either could've gone back to the winery without the other knowing."

I tried to make sense of the information, but it felt as if my brain might break. Tate still seemed like the most viable suspect to me, only because he normally worked the excavator that was used to bury Brody. But I'd seen him and Camille leave the winery with their children. He had an alibi for the rest of the night. She did, as well. Of course, the two provided alibis for each other and could be lying. Maybe one of them had returned to the winery later, or maybe they'd even worked together to end Brody's life so that they could collect on his life insurance policy.

It was also possible that William had lain in wait nearby after Brody had thrown his hissy fit about William playing his fiddle at the winery. Maybe William had planned to follow Brody and confront him, but seized the opportunity to attack Brody at the winery when Brody remained there alone after his brothers left. Even so, this possibility seemed far-fetched. William would need a key to the excavator to bury Brody's body and, as far as I knew, he didn't have access to a key. Then again, like any of the other potential suspects, he could have ordered one online or bought one from a builder's supply outlet. But would he even know that the Caterpillar equipment keys were universal? It wasn't exactly common knowledge.

"What about the jugs that went missing from the stage?" I asked. "Did Ace find out where they'd gone?"

"No luck there," Marlon said. He scooped up a forkful of beans. "Ace questioned Tate, Camille, Garth, Josh, and the Kemps about them. All of the winery staff who were working Saturday night, too. Nobody seems to know where they went. Ace said unless and until they're accounted for, she's going to assume any and all suspects had access to them."

When we finished our dinner and sat down to watch a movie, I set my thoughts aside. I didn't want to waste any more of my time with Marlon thinking about Brody Sheridan's murder. I'd rather enjoy Marlon's company.

Marlon turned on his big-screen TV and logged into a streaming service. "What are you in the mood for? Action? Adventure? Fantasy? Comedy? Drama? Horror? Thriller?"

"Rom-com," I said. "The funnier and sweeter, the better." I'd had enough drama, horror, and thrills in my real life lately.

"All right," he said with a mischievous gleam in his eyes. "But just know that if I catch you admiring Channing Tatum's abs, what we have is over."

I teased him right back. "I'll have to make sure you don't catch me, then."

He clicked the button to start the movie and draped his arm around me. Smoky hopped up and settled himself on the back of the sofa behind us, a furry chaperone. I snuggled up to Marlon, glad to set aside my worries and woes, if only for a while.

Chapter Thirteen

On Monday morning, I puttered around the cabin. While I continued to ponder the murder case, Max worked out back in the shed with his electric sander, grinding rust off the old Ford. The sander filled the air with a high-pitched squeal and tiny particles of rust. Good thing Max wore noise-canceling headphones and a full face mask to protect his eyes and lungs.

All four tires were hopelessly flat when we'd opened the shed earlier that morning. They'd been that way for decades. Max had jacked up the car, removed the wheels, and stashed them in the back of my van so that I could take them to an auto shop to determine whether they could be repaired. I hoped they weren't too far gone.

Smoky watched Max work from the window, intrigued, the swish of his tail indicating he had a lot of unanswered questions. I stepped over, gave Smoky a scratch behind the ears, and explained the situation.

"We're fixing up Great-Granddaddy's old car for the Moonshine Shack. But don't worry, boy. I'll let you check it out before we allow any humans to sit in it."

I stepped outside to leave and noted that Max had already made quite a bit of headway. The hood was rust-free for the first time in decades. I raised a hand to wave goodbye to him. Holding the heavy sander, he couldn't return the gesture, but he lifted one of his legs and made a waving motion with his foot.

I climbed into my van and wound my way down the mountainside. I carried the first tire into the auto repair shop and laid it on the counter. "Think you can repair this tire?"

The mechanics gathered around and burst into guffaws.

"Is that tire from a bicycle?" one joked.

The tire was indeed much narrower than modern car tires. I whipped my phone from the chest pocket of my overalls, pulled up photos of the car, and showed the pics to the mechanics.

One gaped. "Is that an original Ford flathead V8?"

"Sure is."

Their demeanor immediately shifted.

"Sweet ride!" one of them said. "Any chance you're looking to sell it?"

"Sorry, but no," I said. "My granddaddy would never let that car out of the family." I told them I planned to put the car in front of my Moonshine Shack shop so people could take photos in it.

"Moonshine Shack? Wait. Are you the girl who makes that murder moonshine?" The guy took a step back as if to put more distance between us.

As if I were going to whip out a jug and clobber him with it for no reason. Sheesh.

Before I could respond, one of the other men turned to him. "What are you talking about?"

The first guy pointed an accusing finger at me. "One of her jugs killed Brody Sheridan."

"No," I said, "some *person* killed Brody Sheridan." It's not like the jug had come alive and committed homicide on its own.

The second guy said, "The bluegrass singer?"

"Yep," said the first. "It's been all over the news. They found him buried in a vineyard west of the city."

The second guy eyed me warily.

"*I* didn't kill him," I said. "Why would I? His band sang the jingle for my shop."

The second guy's face broke into a grin as he broke out in song. "She's a shining star! Get a jug! Get a jar!"

The first one said, "It's a catchy tune. I'll give you that."

I tried to steer the conversation back to what I'd come here for. "About the tires. You think you can repair them so they'll hold air?"

He bent over and took a closer look. "These are well beyond repair. But if you're looking to replace them, I can make some calls, try to find some for you."

"That would be great. Thanks so much."

He pulled a bandanna from his pocket and wiped some grease from his hands. "I restore old cars as a hobby. Matter of fact, I've restored a flathead before. Had a fun time doing it, too. If you want to get the car running, I could take a look at the engine for you."

"I hadn't planned on restoring the engine. I assumed it

would be a hassle to find parts and cost a fortune to get the car into condition to pass an inspection."

The mechanic disavowed me of these notions. "A flat-head V8 is an antique automobile. There's all kinds of exceptions for classic cars like that, to let the owners keep them authentic. Cars didn't even have seat belts or turn signals back then. In fact, if you only drive the car on weekends and federal holidays, you don't have to renew the registration every year."

"Really?"

"Yup. It's a special rule for folks who only drive their old cars to car shows, or in parades and such, and don't use them for general transportation."

I'd never thought of driving the car in a parade, but that would be a great way to advertise my moonshine. I could order plastic shot glasses and toss them out to the crowd. "Would I need to have the car towed here for you to look at?"

"I'd have to do the work here," he said, "but I can run by your place tonight to take a look at it and prepare an estimate."

"Thanks! It's in the shed out back." I gave him my ad-dress and phone number, left the auto repair shop, and aimed for the winery.

Ace had shared some information with Marlon, which he'd then shared with me, but I wanted to see what else I might discern for myself. Maybe I'd stumble across some-thing she hadn't, or maybe a suspect would be less intimi-dated by a short woman in overalls than a seasoned detective in a business suit, and be more likely to let something slip. Because Camille had vouched for her hus-band's whereabouts Saturday night, and vice versa, nei-ther had been taken into custody. Even so, it seemed to me that Tate was still the most likely person to have killed Brody Sheridan. He had a motive and, if he'd swiped one of my missing decorative jugs, he could have had the means. He also knew that the excavator was on-site and readily available to dig a grave.

I slowed as I approached Shirley Byrd's property. As always, she sat on her porch, her dog at her feet, her long gun within easy reach. She'd struck me as a gun nut before, but the weapon was more understandable now that a murder had been committed so close to her property. I stopped on the road and unrolled my window. "Hi, Ms. Byrd!" I called. I put my left foot on the brake and hovered my right foot over the gas pedal in case she reached for her gun and I needed to floor the pedal to get out of range quick. "I'm the moonshine girl! I've got some for you, if you'd like!"

She put her hands on the arms of her rocking chair and pushed herself to a stand. Her dog hobbled along beside her as she ambled in my direction. She moved slowly. Good thing it wasn't far from her porch to the road.

When she stepped up to my window, I asked, "Would you like a jug of pure moonshine, or a fruit-flavored jar?" I started to rattle off the varieties I offered. "I've got peach, blackberry, app—"

She flung a hand dismissively. "Don't give me none of that sissy stuff. I want a jar of the real thing."

A jug of Granddaddy's Ole-Timey Corn Liquor it is. I fished one out of the cargo bay and handed it out the window to her. *Too bad I can't drive around neighborhoods and sell 'shine from my van like an ice cream vendor.* "Enjoy!"

"I will." She raised the jug in salute. "Thank you."

I drove on and arrived at the winery a quarter hour

before the tasting room opened. Once again, the gate was closed. I didn't know the code to open it, so I pulled over, parked along the side of the drive, and squeezed through the bars again. I raised a hand to shield my eyes from the sun and looked across the winery. Tate and his two-man crew were working at the pond, though they were using hand tools today rather than heavy machinery.

I bypassed the tasting barn, noting the golf cart sitting behind it. Pearl must already be inside, getting ready to open the shop. I continued on until I drew near the pond. Tate and the other men were installing flat, off-white limestone pavers around the edge of the water feature. My guess was that the stones served a dual purpose, holding the liner in place and creating a decorative border. The yellow Caterpillar excavator sat well off to the side now, evidently having served its purpose here.

Tate glanced up as I approached. He appeared slightly wary, but not unfriendly. While the other two men continued to prepare the soil and install the paving stones, Tate stopped working, stood his shovel up next to him, and rested his hand on the handle. It crossed my mind that a shovel to the head could be as deadly as a moonshine crock. *Such a lovely thought, huh?*

"Hi, Tate," I said. "Do you remember me? We met Saturday night."

"Sure," he said. "Hattie something-or-other, right? You're the one who sells the moonshine."

"That's right." I hiked a thumb over my shoulder to indicate the barn. "I came out to buy some wine, but I didn't realize the shop wouldn't be open yet."

"Should open soon," he said. "Noon, I think? I know I've seen people on the deck around the time we take our lunch breaks."

"How's Imogene enjoying her jug?" I asked, though I already knew the answer.

"She's played it a bunch," he said. "Been using the jug in her tea parties, too."

"A dash of moonshine would definitely make a tea party more fun. For the adults only, of course."

He chuckled. "You got that right."

I decided to prod him a bit. "The detective asked me who had access to jugs of my 'shine. I didn't like having to mention that Imogene took one home, but I had to tell her the truth. I'm sorry if it implicated you. It must have been frustrating to be wrongfully accused."

"Don't worry about it," Tate said. "You only did what you had to do. Besides, they cleared me right quick. Camille, too. That detective's got her work cut out for her. There's no shortage of people who'd want to put an end to Brody Sheridan. The guy wasn't exactly easy to get along with. Pretty much anyone who'd ever met Brody had considered cracking him upside the skull at one point or another." He shook his head. "I can't imagine how Garth and Josh put up with Brody all these years."

Is he trying to throw suspicion off himself and onto Garth and Josh? Or was that an innocent comment? I hardly knew Tate, certainly not well enough to read him. "I understand that Brody was found here in the pond." I gestured at the empty pond next to us.

"He was," Tate said. "Looked like he was buried sometime during the night on Saturday. When me and the crew got here Monday morning, we noticed that the pond wasn't as smooth as we'd left it on Friday. There were some rocks and dirt clods and grass clippings lying inside it. We just figured maybe they'd fallen into the hole from the piles we'd left along the edge, that maybe the dirt had been blown around when the vineyard's crew mowed over the weekend, or that some of the winery's customers had come out here and caused it, stood on the loose dirt or kicked it or whatever. We just smoothed it out again and started installing the liner. We'd planned to start at the other end of the pond first, but the winery's crew had left their mower on that side, so we started over here instead. We had no idea we were covering Brody up."

Is he telling the truth? If only I could know for certain. "I hope I don't sound insensitive," I said, "but having my moonshine associated with Brody's death has tarnished my brand. People are calling it 'murder moonshine.' I'm hoping this case gets solved soon so things can get back to normal and I can restore my brand's reputation. I'd like to see it solved for Garth's and Josh's sakes, too. Garth's been nothing but nice to me. He convinced his brothers to sing my jingle. It's brought me a lot of new business."

"Garth's a good guy," Tate agreed. "He and I have always gotten along."

I cocked my head. "You got any theories on who killed Brody?"

He snorted. "Like I said, Brody rubbed a lot of people the wrong way. He had a big ego and he was hard to get along with. Always wanted things his way. I suspect the detective thinks it's a Cain-and-Abel situation, that Brody was killed by one of his brothers, but I'm not sure I agree. I've known Garth and Josh for years, and they don't seem like the killing type to me. But if I had to say it was one of Brody's brothers or the other, my money would be on Josh. Still waters run deep, you know? That said, I think it's much more likely William Hill could have had something to do with it. He's got the most to gain from getting Brody out of the picture. The band was starting to make a name for themselves. With Brody gone, William can step right into his shoes, finish what Brody started."

Though Tate had a point, I wasn't convinced he was being entirely honest. After all, Tate had commented that Brody would be worth more to him and Camille dead than alive. His statement said he'd clearly contemplated the value of the life insurance proceeds in comparison to Brody's life. Surely, it would be a huge relief for Camille not to have to deal with a difficult ex-husband, too. Tate could have killed Brody because he was tired of the guy giving Camille grief. Imogene, too. Brody had pitched a fit and put the poor little girl in the middle of the fray Saturday night after she'd innocently referred to Tate as "Daddy." Maybe Tate's protective instincts had overtaken him, like when Will Smith assaulted Chris Rock at the Oscars.

Having gathered what little I could from Tate, I bade him goodbye and headed to the winery's shop. By then, the tasting barn was open for business. I found Pearl inside and bought a couple of bottles of the red blend she'd used to make her sangria Saturday night. "It was absolutely delicious."

She leaned in over the counter and whispered, "The secret is to marinate the fruit in the wine for twenty-four hours beforehand." Grinning, she put a finger to her lips. "Don't tell anyone. I sell lots of the sangria here in the tasting room. I don't earn as much if people take the wine home and make it themselves."

Smiling, too, I whispered back, "Your secret is safe with me." Like her, I earned a higher profit percentage selling my moonshine drinks at the Bluegrass Festival than I earned selling a jar or jug of moonshine. Turning to more grim matters, I asked, "What do you think happened?"

"To Brody?" She shook her head and stared past me for a moment, as if the answer were outside the windows, before returning her gaze to me. "I wish I knew, Hattie. I've been thinking it over ever since they found him buried in the pond, but I don't have any answers."

"You think it could have been Garth or Josh? They use heavy equipment on their jobs. They'd know how to operate the excavator."

"I suppose it could have been one of them, or even both of them together, but I just can't see it. They came out here together and asked to see where Brody had been found. When I showed them, Garth broke down. Josh kept trying not to cry, squeezing his eyes shut as hard as he could. They were pretty torn up about it."

"What about William Hill?"

"Their new fiddle player?" She raised her palms. "I don't know what to tell you. They all seem like stand-up guys to me."

"Did you notice any of the female fans fawning over Brody?"

She offered a mirthless chuckle. "I saw lots of female fans fawning over all the boys in the band."

"Any with a beefcake boyfriend who might not have appreciated the attention Brody was showing her?"

"Hmm." She looked up for a few seconds, as if trying to picture the deck late that Saturday night when we'd been cleaning and closing things up. When she looked to me again, her expression was sour. "Now that you mention it, I do remember a big guy skulking in a corner. A white guy with brown hair and a beard. Don't think I'd be able to identify him, though. I don't recall anything unusual about him, other than his size."

She rang me up, processed my credit card, and handed

me a bag containing the two bottles I'd purchased. "It was nice seeing you again, Hattie."

"Same here, Pearl. Take care."

As I drove away from the winery, I saw Shirley Byrd still sitting on the lopsided porch of her farmhouse. The dog was back at her feet, and she held a huge plastic tumbler in her hand. Judging from the cubes and the color of the liquid inside the cup, she'd filled it with iced tea. When she raised the cup in toast as I passed, I realized she'd likely spiked her cup with the moonshine. I hoped it would help settle her nerves.

I drove to the Moonshine Shack. Nora had already opened the store for the day. She went about her usual routine, stocking shelves, dusting, wiping fingerprints from the door and jars. Meanwhile, I worked online, adding posts to the Moonshine Shack's social media accounts to generate interest in my products. I posted a photo of the drinks I'd served at the Bluegrass Festival, along with the recipes, and invited everyone down to the shop to buy a jug or jar so they could make the recipes for themselves.

Busy as I was, I had a hard time concentrating on my work. My mind kept returning to Tate. Had he told me the truth? Was there more to his story? He and Camille must have given Ace consistent stories or she would have held one or both of them in custody. But had they fabricated their story? Maybe even practiced it? Had one or the other of them actually returned to the winery the night Brody was killed? If the gate had been closed already, they could have waited for it to open to let a patron out, and then quickly driven in before the gate swung closed again.

Curious, I snooped on Camille Hutchinson's social media accounts. She'd posted approximately eight million pics of her two adorable girls, but who could blame her?

My feeds were filled with images of Smoky. He might not be my flesh and blood, but I loved my furry guy with every fiber of my being. Several of Camille's posts were of her daughters playing with their playgroup. I started down a rabbit trail from there and learned that the playgroup planned to meet up at Coolidge Park on Wednesday. The park was located on the Northshore waterfront. With an antique carousel and play fountains, it was the perfect place to take a group of energetic children on a hot summer's day. But I couldn't just show up there alone. It would look like I was stalking Camille, which would be true, but I preferred to make my intercepting her appear to be a mere coincidence.

I whipped out my phone and texted Kate. I'd filled both her and Kiki in on what details of the case I could share, and they knew I was eager to resolve the case so that my brand would no longer be besmirched by the murder and so I could help Garth put the matter behind him. *Snoop op Wednesday Coolidge Park. Camille H. will be there with playgroup. You and Dalton available?*

A few minutes later, she sent an affirmative reply. *Dibs on Black Beauty.* That was fine with me. When we rode the carousel, I'd look for a horse that resembled Charlotte.

I could hardly wait to question Camille, to see if her story was the same as Tate's. If I could poke a hole in it, maybe she'd spring a leak—a leak that would allow us all to put Brody's murder investigation to rest.

Chapter Fourteen

My phone pinged with a text Tuesday morning. The mechanic sent a detailed estimate for restoring the engine. The total would be $4,200. Not cheap, but with the recent increase in moonshine sales I could afford it. Besides, because I'd be using the car in my moonshine business, the expense would be tax-deductible. I texted him back. *Let's do it.* I sent him half of the amount via Venmo so he could start tracking down the rare parts he'd need.

Little progress had been made in the murder case over the last twenty-four hours and things seemed to be stalled. Marlon stopped by the Moonshine Shack late Tuesday afternoon to tell me that Ace had finished interviewing everybody who'd been at the winery that fateful Saturday night, but that no one had slipped up and incriminated themselves.

"Could the killer have been someone who wasn't at the

winery?" I asked. "At least, not while it was open? What about the girl Brody was allegedly trying to get in touch with?"

"Ace obtained records from Brody's cell phone carrier," Marlon said. "He sent a text to one of the groupies, saying he was about to leave the winery and would love to go by and see her." He didn't have to explain. It was clear exactly what Brody had in mind. A hookup.

"Did she respond?"

"Not until the following morning. She'd put her phone on silent and gone to bed. She texted him back saying she hadn't expected to hear from him so soon and that she was free that day if he wanted to get together. Ace has spoken to her."

"Was she the one with the jacked boyfriend?"

"No, she's single."

"Nobody to fly into a jealous rage, then."

"Not unless she's lying. She said she was wondering why Brody didn't get back to her. When she heard that he'd disappeared it all made sense."

Of course, Brody couldn't respond to the woman. By the next morning he was dead and his phone was destroyed by the river water.

I mulled things over. Even though this particular young woman didn't have a boyfriend, there were still plenty of other people who might have been jealous of the attention Brody had given her—his other fans. I wondered if he'd added more than one phone number to his contacts that night. I asked Marlon if that were the case. It was.

"He'd added three other women's names. He hadn't contacted any of them, though."

"What if one of them hung around the winery, but out

of sight somewhere? Maybe she saw him get the other phone numbers and became upset. Maybe she waited for him in her car so she could confront him after the show."

Marlon raised one shoulder. "Ace considered the crazed-fan theory, too, but neither Garth nor Josh noticed any cars around when they left the winery. I suppose it's possible a woman might have stayed in the shadows until she realized Brody was alone, but it seems unlikely."

With Ace's investigation stalled, I hoped I could get some new intel tomorrow, when Kate, Dalton, and I would intercept Camille at Coolidge Park.

Simone and Nora covered the shop on Wednesday while I drove to meet Kate at the park. I hadn't told my employees what I was up to. If Ace or Marlon happened to come by looking for me, they wouldn't be happy to learn that I was insinuating myself in the investigation. But I simply couldn't help myself. I wanted this puzzle solved. I'd fibbed and told my staff that I needed to run by the bottling company to check on things.

Kate and I met in the parking lot. It was a warm, sunny day, but the partly cloudy sky provided occasional, brief respite from the rays. Kate wore a tank top and a pair of shorts that appeared ready to come apart at the seams. She tugged at the waistband. "Ugh. These shorts are so tight. I've still got fifteen pounds of baby weight to lose."

"You look great," I told her, and I meant it, too. "There's no shame in moving up a size."

"I might have to," she said. "I take Dalton for a long walk in his stroller every day, but the scale won't budge."

Dalton lolled in his stroller, still too young to sit up

straight. He sucked on a pacifier, cute and cuddly and content. I reached in and tickled him with both hands. He giggled up at me in that hiccupy way babies do and my heart swelled with tenderness. "I could just eat you up." I put my face down near his. "Nom-nom-nom."

He giggled again, an easy audience for my comedy shtick.

I stood back up and we made our way into the park.

As we walked, Kate glanced my way. "Any chance you need any more help at the Moonshine Shack?"

"I could always use help," I said. "Are you thinking of going back to work?" I knew she'd struggled with the decision of whether to return to her full-time job after giving birth to Dalton. She'd eventually decided to be a stay-at-home mother, at least for the time being, subject to reassessment later.

"To tell you the truth," she said, "I feel isolated. I miss adult conversation and the camaraderie. I don't want the stress and responsibility of a full-time job, but if you could use me, I'd love to come maybe two or three afternoons a week."

"You're hired!" I grabbed my friend in a bear hug and squeezed her for a few seconds before releasing her. "I could definitely use the help." Simone's college class schedule left her available only a couple of days a week and weekends. Nora normally worked Monday through Friday during the school year, but she had to leave when school let out in the afternoons. Kate could stay until five o'clock. Kiki already helped me out on occasion, and it would be fun to have our other close friend working with us. Plus, having Kate at the store to take care of the daily details would free me up to focus on big-picture matters, like promoting my products. "You can bring Dalton with you, if you'd like."

Her face brightened even more. "Really?"

"Really." After all, I didn't even leave Smoky at home, and I knew Kate would miss her precious son while she was at my shop. Besides, part-time childcare was not only difficult to find, but could also make working at my store not cost-effective for her. "We can set up one of those portable playpens in the stock room for his naps. When he gets bigger, you can put it behind the sales counter so he can play while you're working."

"Thanks, Hattie," Kate said. "I hope this will be good for both of us."

"I *know* it will. When do you want to start?"

"Tomorrow?"

"Perfect."

I glanced around. Lots of mothers and children milled around, with an occasional father or nanny interspersed among them. Kids in bathing suits shrieked in glee as streams of water shot up from the ground at the interactive fountain, falling back to the concrete with rhythmic splats. The children jumped and danced and put their hands and feet over the spigots, then moved to release a torrent, having an absolute blast playing in the water. Meanwhile, the women stood nearby, chatting amiably as they kept a close eye on their kiddos.

My gaze roamed the mothers, but I didn't see Camille among them. "Let's see if she's at the carousel."

Kate walked along beside me, pushing Dalton in his stroller over to the carousel. Lively music greeted us, growing louder as we drew closer. Unlike most carousels, which primarily featured horses, this carousel included other animals, as well. Among them were an ostrich, a tiger, a lion, a giraffe, a zebra, a frog, a goat, a dog, and a cat.

I stood and watched as the animals circled past, trying

desperately to identify Camille or Imogene among the riders. Not an easy feat with everyone in motion. Once the carousel had made a complete revolution and I hadn't spotted them, I turned to look at the people waiting in line. They weren't there, either. "Maybe they're running late." Or maybe they wouldn't come at all. It had been only a little over a week since Camille's ex-husband and Imogene's father had died. Maybe they weren't up to facing the playgroup yet.

Dalton turned his head toward the carousel, spit out his pacifier, and made a cooing sound. *Ooo-ooo.* Kate said, "I think that means he wants to go for a ride."

A few minutes later, Kate bypassed the beautiful black horse she'd have preferred and sat on one of the bench seats, carefully cradling Dalton in her arms. The horse that most resembled Charlotte was already taken by a gap-toothed girl of about eight, so I sat nearby on the cute black-and-white cat. Once the carousel was fully loaded, the operator started the motor. The ride took off slowly, gradually gaining speed until leveling off, keeping pace with the music. It had been years since I'd ridden a carousel. It was just the lighthearted break I needed right now. Dalton enjoyed it, too, his little mouth forming smiles and issuing coos as we went around and around and around. His head turned, too, taking in all the sounds and sights.

After a couple of minutes, the ride slowed to a stop and we climbed off.

Kate strapped her son back into his stroller. Leaning over him, she said, "What did you think, Dalton? Was that fun?"

He issued another coo.

"I think that means 'yes,'" I said.

Kate beamed down at her baby boy. "Or maybe it means 'I love you, Mama.'"

"It could be that, too." Now that Dalton was settled, I suggested we walk the perimeter of the park. We set off in search of Camille once again. *We're certainly getting our steps in today.*

We circumnavigated the park and came around the carousel for the second time. *There she is!* Camille wore denim shorts and a pink bikini top. Her cleavage spilled out of the tiny swimsuit. She stood with her hip cocked, not unlike how Charlotte had been standing when chatting with her mare friends. Amelia was propped on her mother's hip. Camille appeared relaxed and happy, not at all like someone who'd recently lost their ex and their daughter's father to a violent murder. *Hmm.* Even if she no longer had romantic feelings for Brody, it seemed she should be at least a little affected, didn't it? After all, the guy had once meant enough to her that she'd married him, and they shared a child.

Camille chatted with another woman whose son bounced up and down in front of her as she attempted to apply sunscreen to the moving target.

"Be still!" the woman admonished her impatient son. "It'll only take a second."

I nudged Kate and used my eyes to indicate Camille. "That's her," I said softly. "In the pink bikini and jean shorts."

Imogene frolicked in the spray nearby, giggling and looking like she didn't have a care in the world. It was a small consolation to realize the little girl wouldn't miss her father much. Had he been a better parent, his death would have been much harder on her. Still, I remembered the hurt look on his face when Imogene had greeted him at the winery with very little enthusiasm. Clearly, he loved his daughter. Maybe he just didn't know how to be a good father. Maybe Tate had an easier time winning Imogene over since the two spent much more time together. These realizations made me sad for everyone involved.

Kate and I continued in their direction. As we approached the play fountain, the breeze carried a soft mist that cooled our skin and left shiny droplets in our hair. My curls would frizz out soon, but that was okay. The cool water was a welcome respite from the heat. The kids continued to shriek in joy, and the spigots continued to spit out bursts of water in irregular patterns. *Splat. Splat-splat.*

As we passed Camille, I stopped in my tracks, feigning surprise. "Camille? Is that you?"

She turned to look my way. Her skin had a sheen and my nose detected the fragrance of coconut suntan oil, the quintessential scent of summer. Her eyes narrowed as she tried to place me. A few seconds later, they flickered with recognition. "Oh. Hi. You're the moonshiner. Maddie, right?"

"Actually, it's Hattie," I said. "Hattie Hayes."

I introduced her to Kate and Dalton. In return, she introduced me to her friend, whose son finally stopped wiggling long enough that she could finish slathering the sunscreen on him.

"Go play!" Camille's friend called, giving her son an affectionate swat on his little rear as he went. The woman turned back to us. "You're so lucky you have girls, Camille. Boys are exhausting. So much energy!" She looked down at Dalton in his blue stroller before turning her eyes on Kate. "Just you wait," she told Kate. "Once your son

starts walking, you won't be able to keep up with him."
The woman's smile belied her complaints. It was clear she
loved being a mother to a rambunctious boy.

"Mommy!" called the boy, standing in the spray and
waving his hand. "Come in with me!"

The woman pulled off her T-shirt to reveal a ruffled
one-piece bathing suit underneath. She tossed the tee into
a beach bag and tiptoed into the water, laughing and
splashing her son.

A telltale sound came from the stroller. Kate groaned.
"Someone's going to need their diaper changed." She gestured to a nearby bench. "I'll be right back." With that,
she rolled the stroller over to the bench and pulled out a
pad to lay atop it.

Now that we were alone, I turned back to Camille.
"This must be such a hard time for you and Imogene. I'm
so sorry for your loss."

"Our *loss*?" Camille snorted, her expression sour.
"There wasn't much to lose."

"Oh. I knew you and Brody were divorced"—I
cringed—"but were things that bad?"

Her chest heaved as she took in a deep breath. "My
relationship with Brody was a whirlwind romance and,
like a whirlwind, it ended in damage and disaster. All
Brody cared about was becoming famous, and he'd step
on anyone to get there."

"That's unfortunate." I glanced over at her daughter,
frolicking in the fountain. "Good thing you and Imogene
have Tate now."

Camille's sour puss transformed into a smile. "We're
so lucky. Tate's a great guy, and a wonderful father. He
and Brody are like night and day. Brody would hardly lift
a finger for us, but Tate would do anything."

Including kill? "If nothing else," I said, "he was a talented musician. Maybe Imogene will follow in his footsteps."

She released a long breath. "Maybe. Brody did take her to music lessons. He didn't like handing money over to me, but he didn't mind paying the instructors. The lessons weren't cheap, either. Imogene was learning violin, piano, even the harmonica. I thought she was too young, but he disagreed. I suppose he was right. She's starting to catch on and she enjoys the lessons. She even practices without having to be reminded."

Brody may have failed in many ways as a father, but at least he'd given his daughter the opportunity to explore her natural talents. "That's wonderful. Maybe Imogene and Amelia will have their own band one day. They could call themselves the Speakeasy Sisters and give the Bootlegging Brothers a run for their money."

Camille's lips curled up in a half smile at that thought.

I paused for a moment, then said, "I wonder what happened to Brody. Who killed him."

"Whoever it was," Camille said, crossing her arms over her bosom, "they did the world a favor."

Whoa! That was a crass thing to say, even if she had no love for the man any longer. "You're not worried?" I asked Camille. "I mean, it's scary to think a murderer is on the loose. What if the killer decides to go after someone else?"

She quirked her shoulders in a dismissive shrug that caused her breasts to bounce like beach balls. "Brody must've pissed someone off. I'm sure his death was personal."

The fact that she didn't feel threatened made me curious. Could her lack of concern stem from the fact that she knew who the killer was and could be certain they posed no risk to her or her children? "Personal?" I repeated. "You mean you think whoever killed Brody was someone close to him?" *Your husband, perhaps? One of his brothers?*

"I know that it wasn't Josh or Garth. They've always been good to me and Imogene. Even after the divorce, they still treated me like family. They didn't take sides. I suppose they knew it was Brody's fault our marriage failed. His music came first. He wasn't an easy person to get along with."

"I can vouch for that," I said. "He gave me a hard time when we were recording the jingle for my moonshine and doing the photo shoot at my Moonshine Shack."

Her eyes narrowed and she cocked her head slightly. She assessed my face, as if she were trying to determine if *I* might be the killer. But was she just putting on an act, or did she truly think I could be the culprit?

I asked, "What about William? Any chance the killer could be him?"

"Who knows?" Camille said. "I've met him a few times before, but I don't know him well. He might have seen getting rid of Brody as a way to get into the band. With that contract Brody manipulated his brothers into signing, there was no way William would be able to join without Brody's permission—or his elimination." She raised her arms from her chest and splayed hands tipped in bright-red polish, as if holding something at bay. "I'm not pointing fingers, though, okay? I'm just stating facts. I'd hate to see anyone spend the rest of their life in prison for doing away with someone who didn't give two licks about anyone but himself."

While she'd mentioned Garth and Josh, she hadn't directly mentioned her husband. At the risk of upsetting her,

I broached the subject. "I was getting moonshine out of my van Saturday night when Tate and Brody got into that argument in the winery's parking lot. I heard Tate say something about y'all having life insurance on Brody. Will you be getting a large sum? Have y'all filed for it yet?"

A cloud passed over Camille's face. Her brows formed a deep V and she skewered me with a look. "That question's a little out of line, don't you think? I mean, I hardly know you."

I raised my palms in contrition. "You're right. I'm so sorry. I could've phrased that much better. All I meant was that I hope it will be a lot, given that Brody died in such a tragic way and that Imogene is still so young. It would be nice if something good could come out of this. From what you and Tate have said, Brody wasn't reliable about paying the child support he owed you. At least now you won't have to worry about getting support for Imogene. With the life insurance money, you can even afford for her to continue her music lessons."

Camille's shoulders relaxed a little, but not entirely. "I guess."

My mind went back to the discreet smirk on Josh's face when Tate had brought up the child support. I still didn't quite understand what Josh had been thinking, why he'd seemed at first to find their dilemma amusing, but when his focus had shifted to Brody his expression had changed to one of disapproval. "I could be wrong, but I thought I saw a grin cross Josh's face when Tate and Brody were arguing about the child support."

Camille cut her eyes away for a moment before turning back. She said nothing.

I prodded her again. "Any idea why Josh would find it funny that Tate and Brody were arguing like that?"

Just as Pearl Kemp had gotten a faraway look for a moment at the winery, Camille stared past me at something on the horizon for a beat or two. Her face took on a pained look. *Does that mean something?* It was impossible to know. She shifted her gaze back to my face, but said nothing. She just shook her head softly.

I told Camille how people had been coming into my store to buy jugs of 'shine as if they were a souvenir. "They're referring to my Granddaddy's Ole-Timey Corn Liquor as 'murder moonshine.' It's disturbing. I hope the case will be solved soon."

"Me, too," she said, but her voice lacked conviction. "Of course, a lot of murder cases go cold . . ."

Is she hoping Brody's suspicious death will go unsolved, too? I wished I could read the woman's mind. Unfortunately, while her body was on display for all to see today, her mind seemed to be closed. The discussion of the murder had reached a natural end, but I hadn't learned anything new and wasn't quite done feeling Camille out yet. I decided to raise the matter of Garth, how he'd asked me out. "Garth asked me out when he came to my shop to write the jingle."

The brows that had recently formed a V now rose toward her hairline. "He did? You said 'yes,' right? You'd be crazy not to."

"I'm definitely tempted." Leaning in a little, I said, "Woman to woman, what can you tell me about him?"

"Only good things," she said, matter-of-factly. "He's attractive, obviously. All the Sheridan brothers are."

"Obviously," I agreed with a big grin.

Amelia pushed against her mother, wanting down. Camille set Amelia down on the concrete and admonished her to be careful. After Amelia toddled into the fountain,

Camille kept an eye on her while continuing to sing Garth's praises. "He's a great guy. Good sense of humor. Responsible. He wouldn't run around on you, either."

I took it the same couldn't be said for the Sheridan brother she'd once been married to, the one who was now buried—for the second time—in the dirt.

I'd raised the subject of Garth's proposed date only to buy myself more time to talk to Camille, but it dawned on me then that actually going on a date with Garth could provide me the opportunity to learn more about him and determine whether he might have been Brody's killer. I also realized the date could put me in danger, so I'd have to be careful. It wouldn't be a real date, of course, only an intelligence-gathering mission. I was in a unique position to get closer to the guy. I had to take advantage of any opportunity to solve the case.

As Kate and Dalton rolled back up beside me, Amelia darted farther into the fountain, slipped on the slick cement, and fell backward, landing on her itty-bitty bottom in the shallow water with a soft *splash*. While her diaper had cushioned her bottom, the little girl's hands were scraped. She looked at her palms, raised her face to the sky, and sent up a wail as if imploring all of heaven to help her.

Kate put a hand to her chest. "Poor thing!"

Camille rushed into the spray to help her younger daughter. While Camille was righting Amelia and assessing her minor injuries, Imogene wandered back over. She stood outside the perimeter of the fountain, looking into the spray, searching for her mother among the teeming crowd.

"Hi, Imogene." When the girl looked up at me, I said. "I'm Hattie. The lady who gave you the jug with the ribbon, remember?"

She smiled. "I remember. I've been practicing every day. Uncle Garth says I'm getting real good, too!"

"That's wonderful, honey." I pointed into the fountain. "Your sister fell. Your mom's tending to her." Realizing the situation provided me the opportunity to confirm whether Tate and Camille had been telling the truth about their alibi, I seized the moment. "You sure stayed up late that night I met you and your parents. When your father and uncle's band was playing at the white barn?"

Imogene beamed, seemingly proud of herself. "I took a nap that day so I wouldn't get sleepy."

"Wow," I said. "You didn't even fall asleep on the drive home?" A moving car was like a rocking cradle to a child, luring them into la-la land. Heck, even as an adult I found it hard to stay awake in a moving car at night.

Her face fell slightly. "I fell asleep in the car. I couldn't help it."

I noticed she'd said "car," not *truck*. "You were in your mommy's car?"

She nodded. "Mommy woke me up when we got home." She stood a little taller before adding, "But I walked up to bed all by myself."

"What a big girl you are!"

The beam came back. "I'm too big for Mommy to carry now."

"But not too big for your daddy? Your daddy still carries you sometimes?"

She nodded again.

If her daddy still carried her sometimes, and if he was with them that night . . . "Why didn't he carry you up to bed that night?"

"I wanted him to, but Mommy said he went to get the

garbage cans from the curb and that I should be a big girl and put myself to bed."

Was it true? Had Tate really gone to get the garbage cans, or had Camille made an excuse for him? Had Tate actually returned to the winery, instead? "You didn't see your daddy at all after you got home that night?"

Imogene shook her head. Kate and I exchanged a glance. The surprise in my friend's eyes told me she understood the significance of what Imogene had just revealed. Even Dalton seemed to sense something big had just been exposed. He issued an elongated *ooooh*.

"What about your daddy's truck?" I asked Imogene. "Was it parked at your house?"

She shrugged.

"You don't know? Didn't you see it?"

"Daddy's truck doesn't fit in the garage. Only Mommy's car does. Mommy says that's because the garage is messy and we need to clean it out."

I laughed. "My shed is messy, too. Cleaning's no fun, is it?"

She grinned. "No!"

"Was the garage door closed when your Mommy woke you up and you went inside?"

She nodded. "Mm-hm."

In other words, it was possible that Camille and Tate had lied to Ace when they told her they'd both remained at their house after driving home from the winery. Tate could have driven his truck back to the vineyard to finish his argument with Brody. After all, they hadn't resolved anything. The only reason they'd stopped arguing was because Darren Kemp came outside and told them to keep it down.

Had Tate returned to the winery and put Brody out of

their lives permanently? Maybe Brody had one or both of the missing jugs in his possession. Maybe he'd taken them to use as props for the band, as stage decorations. Brody could've assumed I wouldn't mind since they weren't valuable. If he'd happened to have asked, I would've gladly allowed the band to keep the jugs. They advertised my moonshine, after all. Maybe Tate had used one of the jugs to whack Brody's skull and the spoon to hold down the accelerator on Brody's Jeep as it careened off the cliff and into the Tennessee River.

Maybe adorable, innocent little Imogene had just provided the evidence that would solve the case.

Chapter Fifteen

Knowing that Ace would be annoyed if she realized I'd intentionally stalked Camille to the park, I decided to run my revelations through Marlon. It wouldn't be the first time he'd served as a buffer or intermediary between me and Ace. He and Charlotte *clop-clop-clopped* up to my shop later that afternoon. He tied his horse to the post and stepped inside, the open door letting in the warm outside air and the sounds of traffic. Things quieted down as he closed the door behind him. "Hey, Hattie."

"Hey." I motioned for him to follow me into the stock room. "Come on back. We'll get some water and a carrot for Charlotte."

The two of us walked to the back room. Marlon used the utility sink to fill the clean bucket I kept on hand for his horse, and I grabbed a carrot from my mini fridge. We carried the items out front. Marlon placed the bucket on the curb in front of Charlotte. She swished her tail and nickered as if in thanks, then lowered her head to take a drink.

I put a hand on the horse's flank and gave her a pat. She was warm to the touch and slightly damp with sweat. She'd enjoy this respite in the shade of my porch. Turning from the horse to her rider, I said, "I have news."

"About the case?" Marlon asked.

"Yeah. I went with Kate to the park earlier today. We ran into Camille Hutchinson there. She'd taken her girls to play in the fountain with their playgroup. What a coincidence, huh?"

Marlon's eyes narrowed. "Sure," he said. "Coincidence."

Clearly, he wasn't buying my story. But he wasn't chastising me, either. *Thank goodness.* "Camille didn't tell me anything interesting, but Imogene did."

"Imogene?" Marlon cocked his head. "Camille and Tate's daughter?"

"Yes."

His expression became incredulous, his jaw going slack. *"You interrogated a child?"*

Charlotte lifted her head, her muzzle dripping, and eyed me as if she, too, thought I'd gone too far. She stomped a foot and whinnied.

"I only spoke to Imogene briefly while her mother was tending to her little sister."

Marlon still didn't look pleased, but now he was curious. "What did she tell you?"

"That she fell asleep in her mother's car on the drive home from the winery the night Brody disappeared. Her mother woke her up to go inside. Their car was in the garage with the door closed and Tate wasn't around. Imogene said she asked Camille where Tate was because she was tired and wanted him to carry her upstairs to bed.

Camille told her that she'd have to walk inside on her own because he'd gone out front to round up the garbage cans. Seems to me that he might've taken Imogene up to bed first if he was still around. Also seems the garage door should have been open so he could bring the cans inside."

"Maybe," Marlon said, rubbing his chin in thought, "or maybe they keep their garbage cans somewhere other than the garage. Some people keep them on the side of their house, or behind their fences so they're not an eyesore."

"Even so, wouldn't you think he'd enter the house through the garage after Camille and the girls rather than going through a different door?"

Marlon said, "That would be typical, probably. But he might have had a reason for not going in that way."

My ire rose. I was tempted to stomp my foot like Charlotte. Here I thought I'd stumbled onto an important clue, and Marlon was summarily dismissing it. I continued to argue the point. "Imogene said Tate parked his truck in the driveway because it wouldn't fit in the garage. She said she didn't see his truck after they arrived back home. Tate could have climbed into his truck and driven back to the winery to finish what he and Brody had started earlier."

Seeming to sense my irritation, Marlon met me halfway. "That could be, too." He angled his head to better look me in the eye. "I'm not saying you're not onto something, Hattie. I'm just trying to think things through, determine if there's another explanation for his behavior. Because if there is, you can be damn sure that's what he's going to tell Ace."

"You'll pass this information along to her, then?"

"I will. I think it's significant enough that she'll

question Tate again, nail him down on the particulars of that night. Of course, there's always the chance that Imogene might have told her mother what you two talked about. Camille and Tate could be formulating a story as we speak."

"I don't think Camille even noticed me talking to Imogene."

"Let's hope that's the case."

Kate and Dalton arrived at the Moonshine Shack a few minutes before noon on Thursday. I'd given her the security code for the back door, and she rolled her son inside in his stroller.

"Oh, good!" Granddaddy cried. "I've got me a buddy now."

He played peekaboo with Dalton as we set up the portable crib/playpen combo in the storeroom next to the recliner I'd bought for my grandfather to take his naps in. I showed Kate the shelf space I'd cleared for her to store diapers, wipes, spare clothes, and other items her baby boy might need. I rounded up a firefly-green T-shirt with my store logo on it, and held it out to her. "Here's your uniform."

She changed her top in the powder room, emerged, and buckled her baby carrier over her shoulders.

Granddaddy circled a gnarled finger in front of her. "What's that contraption you're putting on?"

"It's a baby carrier," Kate said. "It makes the baby feel secure, but keeps your hands free." She held out her hands and shook them, jazz hands style. She picked up Dalton from his stroller and slid him into his pouch, facing inward. The next thing we heard was a wet *urp*. Kate cried out and reflexively backed up. It was a futile gesture, given that the source of the goo was strapped to her chest.

I fished another size medium tee off the stack. "Here's a fresh uniform."

While my grandfather used his cane to amble from the storeroom into the shop, I lifted Dalton from the carrier. Kate unbuckled it, used a burp cloth to wipe the goo off the carrier and herself, and returned to the powder room to put on the clean shirt.

Ready now, Kate, Dalton, and I went into the shop. My grandfather sat out front in a rocking chair. He turned and used his cane to tap on the window. "Bring that boy to me!" he called. "I'll tend to him."

Kate bit her lip, forever the nervous mother.

"You have nothing to worry about," I told her. "That man raised five children and a dozen grandchildren. He's a pro with babies."

I followed along as Kate carried Dalton out front and carefully handed him to my grandfather.

Granddaddy situated the baby in the crook of his arm and looked down at Dalton. "We fellas got to stick together." He began to rock. "I've got some stories to tell you, son. How about we start with the one where my daddy got arrested for running moonshine?"

Kate smiled and turned to me. Her look said *You're right. My baby's in good hands.*

We went back inside. Nora had arrived by then and was thrilled to learn I'd hired another staff member as it meant she'd be free to take an afternoon off now and then. She showed Kate the ropes. How to work the cash register. How to run credit cards through the machine. How to apply a discount if someone had one of the many coupons I passed out willy-nilly. Nora then showed Kate where we kept the inventory of each flavor, and where she could stack the folded cartons to be reused. Kate caught on quickly and, a mere half hour later, was handling customers like she'd been working here for years.

While my employees trained and worked, I sat at my computer, devising a simple video that told my shop's story, much like my jingle did. I'd had the task on my to-do list for weeks, but hadn't found the time to complete it. I planned to upload it to YouTube and post it on the Moonshine Shack's website and social media accounts. I'd heard dynamic content got more attention than static photos, and figured I'd give the theory a test.

I started with a photo of the newspaper article detailing my great-grandfather's arrest by Marlon's ancestor, the Hamilton County sheriff. I went on to add photos of the exterior and interior of the Moonshine Shack. I ended with a photo of me holding Smoky in my arms with my grandfather standing at my side. I added captions to each image, telling potential customers where they could find my wares and inviting them to the shop to sample my 'shine. I set the commercial to music, adding the jingle to play on repeat as the images transitioned.

When I was done, I showed the video to Nora, Kate, Granddaddy, and Dalton. Dalton gave it an *ooh-ooh*, while Kate and Nora made a few suggestions on the timing and transitions.

Granddaddy grinned. "A television commercial? We're going big-time!"

"We are!" No sense spoiling his excitement by explaining the difference between TV and online video sources, or telling him how easy it was to create this type of content and make it available. After making the tweaks Kate and Nora had recommended, I uploaded the commercial to

YouTube and added a link on the Moonshine Shack's website. *Amazing what you can do online these days.*

The rest of the day went quickly. The mechanic from the auto repair shop called to let me know they'd tracked down a set of tires for the old Ford. *Yay!* The tires would arrive sometime the following week. Nora, Kate, and Dalton left at five o'clock. After babysitting all afternoon, my grandfather was tuckered out. Granddaddy took a short nap in the storeroom, then shared a takeout sub sandwich with me for dinner and kept me company until closing time. He grabbed a jar of my fruity blueberry moonshine on our way out the door.

I fought a smile. "Is that a gift for Louetta?"

He didn't even try to deny it. "I'm gonna make her some of your Blueberry Bluegrass Tea. I think she'd like it."

"I bet she will, too."

M arlon didn't get back to me on Thursday. When the workday ended, I dropped Granddaddy at the Singing River Retirement Home. Curious and impatient, I decided that, rather than wait for answers, I'd see if I could get them myself. I searched for Camille and Tate's address online, and found it in the county's property tax data, which was public record. I decided to drive past their house and see what, if anything, I might note. Luckily, it was dark by nine thirty and they should be inside, putting their kids to bed or doing chores or watching television, so I didn't have to worry too much about being spotted as I cruised by.

As I approached their modest white colonial, I looked for their garbage cans. *Nothing on this side.* The garage door was closed and the porch light was on. Tate's truck sat in the driveway, the magnetic PARADISE POOLS, PONDS & PATIOS signs attached to both doors. I rolled by, noting that a wreath of artificial flowers in the shape of a heart adorned their front door. A birdbath stood in their front flower bed. The pink petunias underneath it drooped, in need of watering. As I eased past, I spotted an L-shaped latticework fence on the side of their house, open to the back. It stood just in front of a side door that likely led into the kitchen. Behind it I could make out two large plastic garbage cans.

Ugh. Looked like Marlon's theory might have some merit. If Tate went to round up the garbage cans from the curb the night Brody was killed, it would be logical to assume he'd placed them behind the fence and entered the house via the side door. It still didn't explain why he hadn't carried sleepy little Imogene up to bed first, though, especially if he was as loving a stepfather as Camille made him out to be. Then again, maybe the couple was trying to encourage Imogene to take responsibility for herself. After all, teaching a child self-sufficiency was something good parents did.

I circled the block and headed home. I had a little more information, but still no definitive answers. Would Brody's murder ever be solved?

Marlon had been assigned to work an evening shift on Saturday. Simone and her sorority sister covered the Moonshine Shack while Kiki, Max, and I drove out to the winery to hear the new Bootlegging Brothers, now with William Hill playing strings. We arrived early and were lucky enough to score a table on the deck not far from the stage. The band's sound was even better than before, and the trio interacted with a casual ease. If I didn't know different, I'd think the three of them had been playing together for years.

Tate, Camille, and their girls were back to hear the band. I raised a hand in greeting when my gaze met Camille's across the deck. While Camille raised only a tentative hand, Imogene grinned ear to ear and waved like her life depended on it. Her enthusiasm on seeing me warmed my heart. Who'd have known that giving a child a simple, inexpensive jug would bring them so much joy?

Garth spotted me in the crowd and sent a smile and a wink my way. I sent a smile back, but no wink. The band wrapped up one song and prepared to start another. To my surprise, Garth stepped up to the microphone. "Folks, you're in for a real treat tonight. My niece, Imogene, is going to play with us on this next song. She's been practicing her jug real hard. This will be her debut performance but, believe me, she's going to be a big star one day. I only hope she won't forget the guy who taught her how to play." He turned his wink on his niece and she giggled, bringing her shoulders to her ears. "Please join me in giving her a warm welcome!"

Garth, Josh, and William applauded and the audience joined in. Smiling bright, Imogene clutched her jug tight in both hands as she walked to the stage. The jug still bore the blue-and-white gingham ribbon that had been on it when I'd given it to her. She was dressed just like a miniature Bootlegging Brother in boots, jeans, a plaid shirt under a dark-blue vest, and a tweed newsboy-style cap. *Adorable.*

She carefully climbed the three steps up to the stage. Garth scooped his niece up in his arms and plunked her down on a tall stool so everyone would be able to see her. He looked down at her. "You ready, Imogene?" When she nodded vigorously, Garth said, "All righty then. Let's play!"

Josh counted out, "And a one, and a two, and a three," and the band launched into "Turkey in the Straw," a cute and lively, kid-friendly song. Each time Imogene blew into her jug, her eyes went wide with effort. The little girl gave it her all, and the crowd ate it up, cheering and whistling to encourage her. She smiled big between blows. Garth bent down so the two were ear to ear, blowing into their jugs side by side. It was about the cutest thing I'd ever seen and, to my delight, many in the crowd were recording the performance to share on social media. With the adorable Imogene blowing into a jug clearly marked with GRANDADDY'S OLE-TIMEY CORN LIQUOR I was sure to get a bump in sales, this time for a good reason rather than a creepy one.

When the song ended, Garth and Imogene engaged in a dueling jug duet. He'd blow a series of short and long toots on his jug, and she'd repeat the pattern. Then she'd challenge him to repeat a pattern she'd created. If that back-and-forth didn't win Garth an uncle-of-the-year award, I didn't know what would. When Imogene left the stage, the crowd rose in a standing ovation for the tiny troubadour.

During the band's next break, Garth ventured over to our table, where I introduced him to Kiki and Max.

Garth shook both of their hands. He eyed their piercings, tattoos, and punk attire and good-naturedly said, "Let me guess. Coming to hear a folksy bluegrass band was not your idea."

Kiki laughed but said, "Don't sell your music short.

Bluegrass has broad appeal these days. We came willingly. Of course, it didn't hurt that there'd be wine."

Garth gestured to the empty chair at our table for four. "Mind if I take a seat?" When we unanimously replied in the affirmative, he plopped himself down.

"How are things going?" I asked gently. "Is it hard to play without Brody?"

"A little," he admitted. "It's got a different feel. But, if I'm being honest, it's a lot more fun. Brody had a way of sucking the joy out of things." He paused for a beat, a dark look passing over his face, before he looked at me imploringly. "I probably shouldn't have said that, should I? Even if it's true, it's not very nice."

"Don't be hard on yourself. Family relationships can be difficult. It's normal to have mixed feelings." I leaned toward him. "Truth be told, as much as I love my granddaddy, I also think he can be a stubborn old coot. Doesn't mean I love him any less."

Garth gave me a grateful, if feeble, smile. "William already knew all our songs, so it's been an easy transition. He even put out some feelers and got us a weekend gig in Gatlinburg in early October, and another in Atlanta right after."

"That's wonderful, Garth! Word of the Bootlegging Brothers must have spread."

"William's made connections," Garth said. "He's good at the business side of things. Brody never really was, even though he insisted on being in charge." Garth seemed to go vacant for a beat before giving his head a hard shake, as if to throw off the bad vibe brought about by talking about his deceased brother. "William, Josh, and I have tossed around the idea of relocating to

Nashville. We're not sure whether it's better to be big fish in a small pond or small fish in a big pond."

The only thing I knew about ponds is that it was better not to be dead and buried in one like Brody Sheridan had been. "Well, I hope you stick around Chattanooga long enough to take me out on a date."

He cocked his head, a grin playing about his lips. "Change your mind, did ya?"

"I realized I wasn't ready to be fully committed. I was afraid if I didn't go out with you at least once, I might look back one day and realize I'd missed out."

Kiki and Max were in on my game and didn't betray me.

"I'm glad you came to your senses," Garth teased. He pulled his phone out of his pocket and slid it across the table to me. "Put your name and digits in there for me."

I entered my name and phone number into his contacts and returned the phone to him. A part of me wondered whether I'd just given my personal cell number to a killer. The thought made my innards wriggle.

He pointed to my nearly empty glass. "What're you drinking?"

"The Riesling."

He stood. "Save my seat. I'll be right back with another glass for you." He walked into the tasting room.

I turned to Kiki and Max. "I feel a little icky about this."

"Why?" Kiki said. "He's damn cute. His eyes are totally dreamy."

Max scowled and waved a hand in her face. "Boyfriend. Right here."

She leaned over and gave him a noisy smooch on the cheek. "Just because Garth is cute and dreamy doesn't mean you aren't, too. I wouldn't be sitting next to you otherwise. My standards are high. I know what I deserve."

Max sat up straight and nodded. "All right, then."

Kiki cut me a discreet grin and mouthed, *Men. So easy.*

Garth returned a minute later with two glasses of wine. After handing my wine to me, he took a seat and raised his glass. "To new friends. And maybe more."

He sent me another wink, this one at point-blank range. *What a flirt.*

The rest of us raised our glasses and clinked them against his. "To new friends."

Over the next few minutes, Kiki and Max told Garth about their various art projects. Garth listened attentively, asking detailed questions that said he'd been truly paying attention, not just going through the motions.

Max told him about my great-grandfather's old car. "I'm restoring it," he said. "The exterior anyway. I've got all the rust off now. It's ready for paint."

"And new tires," I said. "A mechanic at an auto repair shop tracked some down for me. They should arrive soon. He's going to get it running again. I'm going to put the car in front of the Moonshine Shack and let people take pictures in it, maybe take it to auto shows or drive it in parades, too."

Kiki took a sip of her wine, set her glass down, and addressed Garth. "Once the car's ready, you should let me shoot new photos of the band." She left it unsaid that the new photos would reflect the Bootlegging Brothers' current makeup, which no longer included Brody Sheridan. "Y'all could pose on the car with your instruments."

I added, "And some jugs and jars of my moonshine."

As soon as I'd made the suggestion, I realized it might

have been in poor taste, given how Brody had been killed. But Garth didn't seem to take offense where none was intended.

Instead, he said, "That's a great idea, Hattie. We can order more of the small posters to sign at events, too."

"What about T-shirts with the image printed on them?" I suggested. "We could split the cost. I could sell some at my shop, and y'all could sell them at your appearances. It would give both of us a new revenue stream."

"I'd be up for it," Garth said, "but we need to run it by Josh and William. Can't imagine they'd have any objection. Josh and I are useless with numbers, so William will be handling the bookkeeping for the band. He could front you the funds for the shirts."

I slid my phone across the table to Garth this time. "Can you put William's number in my phone?"

"Sure." He picked up my phone and added William Hill to my contacts.

Our conversation was cut short when Josh and William took the stage, the break over. Garth glanced over at them, tossed back his remaining wine, and set the glass on the table. "I've got to get back to the stage. Been nice hanging with all y'all." He turned to me. "You'll be hearing from me. Soon. Before you have a chance to change your mind again." He gave me a roguish grin and stood.

Garth returned to the stage. The band launched into another original crowd-pleasing tune, "Hip-Hop Hillbilly," an amusing mash-up of bluegrass, rap, and utter nonsense that William and Garth had written only a couple of days prior. Not only did Garth play the washboard, jug, and spoons in the song, he also beatboxed. At Josh's invitation, the crowd sang along loudly to the lyrics, which rhymed the word *hip-hop* with *pig slop*, *bull plop*, *soda pop*, and Tennessee's most famous peak, *Rocky Top*.

When the song ended, the crowd cheered and whooped. *Looks like the Bootlegging Brothers might have their first big hit on their hands.*

Kiki, Max, and I continued to listen to the music, sip our wine, and enjoy the beautiful sunset. Once the sun disappeared behind the trees, the sky gradually became dark, a crescent moon providing scant light. It was then I spotted an angelic apparition in white venturing out from the back door of the barn and heading across the vineyard, barely visible in the darkness. *Pearl Kemp.*

I set my wineglass on the table. "I'll be back in a bit."

I crossed the deck, stepped off the back side of it, and trailed after Pearl, calling out to her as I carefully picked my way across the ground. "Pearl! Wait up!"

She turned and stopped, waiting for me at the edge of the dark vineyard.

When I caught up to her, I asked, "Is everything okay?"

She sighed. "I suppose so. We've got a big crowd tonight, which is good, but . . . Well, when I hear everyone singing and having a great time, I can't help but feel a little guilty. We had a huge crowd here after Brody Sheridan's funeral, too. Most of them had attended the church service. They bought bottle after bottle to toast him, nearly cleaned us out of our inventory. It's the same tonight. We've sold record amounts of wine. We're profiting off his death. It just feels . . . wrong." She reached up to wipe an errant tear from her cheek.

I grimaced. "Tell me about it." I told her how the murder had increased traffic at my shop. "I feel guilty about that, too. I suppose the best we can do is donate some of the profits to charity."

Her face brightened. "That's a great idea, Hattie. We'll do that." She turned from me to look out across their land. "I was going to take a short break to stretch my legs and clear my head. Some company would be nice. Want to walk out to the pond with me?"

"I'd love to."

We continued on to the pond, able to walk faster once our eyes adjusted to the darkness and we could see the subtle contours of the land. We stopped at the edge of the pond and stared across it. The water feature had come along nicely in the few days since the cadaver dog had sniffed out Brody's body buried in it. The moon reflected off the surface. My mind toyed with thoughts of blood and water. Brody had valued blood, wanting only his blood brothers to play in the band, and for his daughter to recognize only him as her true daddy. His own blood had been tragically spilled in a place now filled with water. *Such irony.*

Pearl stepped over to the white wooden bridge that spanned the pond and lifted the small cover that concealed a series of switches. "What do you think of this?" She flipped the switches and a circle of lights appeared in the water on either side of the bridge. The lights shone upward, illuminating the spray of the twin fountains. The droplets and mist sparkled in the lights.

"Wow," I said. "It's beautiful."

"I think so, too. Tate and his crew did a great job out here. They've still got the patio to install, but that shouldn't take too much longer. We're hoping to have this space open in two or three weeks."

"Does it concern you?" I asked. "Having Tate working out here?"

"Why would it?" Pearl asked.

"As far as I know, he's still on the list of potential murder suspects."

"Oh. That." Pearl's lips pursed as she seemed to consider the possibility for the first time. "No, it doesn't concern me, not really. From what I gather, everyone thinks Brody was killed because of something he did or said, that he brought it on himself. I'd never considered that the killer might come after me or Darren. What reason would they have?"

"None, I hope." Pearl had been very gracious to allow me to sell my moonshine at her winery. I'd hate to see anything bad happen to her or her husband.

The breeze carried a fine mist our way. It cooled my skin and reflected like fairy dust in the air. Once again, I thought back to Brody's words about William not being blood to the Sheridan brothers. If blood is truly thicker than water, it stood to reason that William Hill might have been Brody's killer. He wouldn't have a family tie holding him back. He was good friends with Garth. He might have somehow been able to surreptitiously slip Garth's Caterpillar key out of the pocket on his yellow safety vest, use it to operate the excavator, and then return it with Garth being none the wiser. Or, if he'd planned ahead, he could have obtained his own Caterpillar equipment key. I didn't know what William did for a living, but maybe he worked with heavy equipment, too, like Garth and Josh. I also recalled what Garth had just told me, that William already knew how to play all of the Bootlegging Brothers' songs. Had William prepared himself to step into Brody's place? It seemed coincidental that he was also taking over managing the band's business and finances. Had he realized the band had good moneymaking potential, and that Brody's mismanagement was holding them back from earning the income they could? He might have seen Brody as standing in the way of a good financial opportunity.

I bent down to trail my fingers through the cool water. "Who do you think could have killed Brody? Do you think it could have been Tate?"

Pearl mused for a moment. "I don't think so. Other than his argument with Brody in the parking lot, Tate's been no trouble. He shows up on time, works hard, does a good job. I just can't imagine someone so reliable and responsible could be a killer. Same for Garth and Josh. I just can't see any of the Bootlegging Brothers as killers. Since their brother's been out of the picture, they've been perfect gentlemen and a great attraction for the winery. William seems like a good guy, too. Truth be told, I foresee the band soon becoming too popular to play a small venue like our winery. Darren and I feel lucky to have them perform here while they're still willing."

Of course, the killer could had been on their best behavior to avoid suspicion. It was only natural to assume someone polite and industrious couldn't do something so dastardly. Maybe all of the men had conspired together to get rid of Brody, each for their own reasons. They could have each played a part, carefully choreographed the evening so that no single one of them would be the obvious culprit. It was an intriguing theory, if not a likely one.

I stood and turned to face Pearl. "I'm not sure if Ace told you this, but I returned to the winery the night Brody was killed. I saw his Jeep's lights when it drove across Ms. Byrd's land. I saw a pickup or SUV in your parking lot, too."

Her eyes flashed and she stood straighter. "You did? Did you get a license plate or at least a make and model?"

She clasped her hands to her chest. "Oh, please, tell me you did! Then the police could track down Brody's killer and we can all put this behind us."

"I'm sorry," I said. "I didn't realize the vehicle was important, so I didn't pay much attention. I was more concerned with trying to get my cell phone back."

She tilted her head, her eyes narrowing slightly. "How'd you get onto the winery property? The gate would have been closed."

"It was," I said. "I entered on foot."

"Did you climb over the gate?"

"No. I squeezed through it."

"Must be nice to be so thin. I used to be thin, too, before middle age caught up to me. If I tried to squeeze through that gate now, I'd get stuck like Winnie the Pooh in that honey tree." She chuckled, but then her demeanor became more serious. "You didn't see anyone around when you came back?"

"No. I only saw the truck or SUV."

"Good thing," Pearl said. "If whoever killed Brody was still around, they might have hurt you, too, if they'd spotted you."

The thought gave me goose bumps. "Remember when I came to the winery that Sunday? With my two friends?"

"I do," Pearl said. "You picked up your phone and y'all had some sparkling wine."

"That's not all," I said. "I don't know if Ace told you or not, but I'm the one who noticed the excavator had been moved. Of course, I didn't realize that the killer had run Brody's Jeep off the cliff and buried Brody's body in your pond here. But now that I know it, I'm a little surprised you and Darren didn't hear the noise of the machinery at your house."

"Ace Pearce asked us about that, too," Pearl said. "We heard nothing, but that didn't surprise us. We've got storm windows. They don't just insulate, they filter out noise, too. Our bedroom is at the back of our house, and we had the late news on while we were getting ready for bed. Even if any of the noise got through the windows, the television would have drowned out the sound of the machinery." She sighed. "If only we'd heard. We would have gone out to investigate. We could have caught the killer red-handed."

Chapter Sixteen

S peaking of sounds," Pearl said, "I'm not hearing the band. They must be taking another break. I'd better get back to the counter. It's always busiest between sets."

She reached down and turned off the lights on the fountains. Once again, I found myself in the dark, actually as well as metaphorically. Our eyes adjusted after a moment or two, and we strode as fast as we dared back across the dark vineyard. We both shrieked when something bounded across our path, and dissolved into laughter when we realized it was only a jackrabbit, its white tail bouncing up and down as it hopped away.

At the end of the night, groupies gathered around the Bootlegging Brothers, just like before. Josh and William grinned like fools, enjoying the attention lavished on them by the young, pretty women, as well as a handful of wannabe bluegrass stars looking for advice.

As before, Garth remained professional. He answered

questions, was polite and pleasant, but deflected the female fans' attempts to force phone numbers and e-mail
addresses on him. "Sorry," he said, more than once. "If I
take a phone number or e-mail, I'll end up in the dog-
house."

Although the women's faces drooped in disappointment, at least none seemed to take it personally. He wasn't
rejecting them. Another woman had simply beat them to
the prize. I knew he was fabricating things, pretending to
be in a relationship when he actually was not, but Garth
knew better than to insult the people who made up a big
part of his fan base. The white lie was harmless. Still, I had
to wonder if he'd told other lies, bigger lies, lies to save his
skin.

I gave Garth a wave goodbye as Kiki, Max, and I departed. He was in the middle of signing an autograph and
could offer only a soft smile and a twinkle of his eye. My
heart might have melted if not for the fact that a certain
mounted Chattanooga police officer had already laid
claim to my affections.

On Sunday morning, Max finished painting my great-
grandfather's old Ford. He'd done a fabulous job. The
black paint was smooth, flawless, and so shiny we could
see our reflections in it. The windshield was still cracked,
but I figured that flaw added some character and authen-
ticity to the vehicle.

"Thanks so much, Max! It looks perfect!"

He scoffed in jest. "You didn't expect anything less
than perfection from me, did you?"

"Of course not."

He held out his hands and waggled his fingers. "Better

pay up, Hattie. Before I send my goons to break your kneecaps."

"By 'goons,' do you mean Kiki?"

"Of course. She's the toughest person I know."

"You're scared of her, aren't you?" I teased.

"Little bit," he said. "It's oddly sexy."

"Say no more!" I cried, grimacing. I handed over an envelope filled with the remaining cash I owed him, and added a heartfelt hug. "My granddaddy is going to be so excited to see this car!"

'd just opened the Moonshine Shack later that day when my cell phone vibrated against my ribs and the text tone blurted from the chest pocket of my overalls. I pulled out my phone. Garth had sent me a flirty text. It read:

Who? You and me.

Why? Winky-face emoji.

When, where, and how? You tell me.

Both Kiki and Kate were at the store with me. Kate's husband had taken their baby to visit his parents and my friend was enjoying a rare moment of independence.

I held up my phone so my friends could read the screen. "What do I do?"

Kiki said, "You want the murder resolved ASAP, right? Text him back and tell him you want to meet up right now."

"Here?" I asked.

"No." She looked up in thought. In light of the fact that Kiki was an artist, her suggestion was no surprise. "Tell him it would be fun to take a walk through the sculpture garden at the Hunter Museum of Art. It's within walking distance and it's a public, outdoor space. You should be safe there and you won't have to get into a car with him."

"Good idea."

Kate pointed out the front window of my shop to the Tipperary Tavern, the Irish pub across the street. "Have him meet you for drinks first. You can ply him with alcohol. Loosen his lips with liquor."

"Another good idea." *What would I do without my two best friends?* I responded to Garth, telling him I was at my shop but had enough staff on duty that I could step out for a couple of hours for drinks and fresh air. I told him I'd be waiting at the tavern.

His reply came quick. *On my way.*

I winced and looked up at my friends. "Is this cruel? I'm leading him on."

"For good reason," Kate said.

"Yeah," Kiki said. "All's fair in love, war, and murder investigations."

"That's not how the saying goes."

Undeterred, Kiki said, "The murder part is implied. Besides, he already knows he's not the only guy vying for your affections, right? It's his choice to risk heartbreak."

Kiki could find a way to justify just about any behavior. It was one of her strong suits, if one that had gotten us into some mild trouble in high school. She'd convinced me to toilet-paper the trees at the home of our algebra teacher. We'd couldn't stop giggling and had been caught by a neighbor who'd taken his dog out for a late-night potty break. I only hoped I wouldn't be so obvious today when I interrogated Garth.

I freshened up, brushing my hair and adding a coat of soft-pink lipstick to my lips. I headed across the street to

the Tipperary Tavern. Miranda, the honey-haired propri-
etor, was tending bar this afternoon. She and I had met
months earlier, and I'd subsequently mentored her in business when she'd taken over the bar. Judging from the consistent traffic flowing in and out of the pub most days, she
was doing quite well for herself. A half-dozen men sat at
the bar now, most of them wearing jerseys and all of them
staring up at a television screen broadcasting a soccer
game. Miranda stood behind the counter, a bar towel in
her hands.

"Hey, Miranda." I sat down at a small round table with
two chairs.

"Hey, Hattie." She ran the towel over the bar to wipe
up a spill, and placed a small bowl of cocktail peanuts in
front of a customer. "What can I get you?"

I ordered one of the moonshine drinks she and I had
concocted. "Make it a triple."

"*A triple?*" she said. "Someone's tired of thinking."

"It's for a friend." I didn't tell her that I'd be using the
moonshine as a truth serum of sorts. "Can I get a lemon-
lime soda, too?"

"Sure. What should I put in it?"

"Just ice." I wasn't about to indulge in even a drop of
alcohol. I needed to maintain total mental clarity and stay
sharp so I could discern whether Garth inadvertently let
something slip, revealed a clue.

Miranda prepared the drinks with a practiced efficiency
and promptly delivered them to my table. I settled the tab
then and there to relieve my guilt at leading Garth on and
so we could quickly leave the tavern. While waiting for
Garth, I nursed my virgin drink. My gut was tight and my
bones felt as if they carried an electrical current. It was no

wonder. I was about to go on a pretend first date with a possible killer.

The door to the tavern swung open and in came both a bright ray of sunlight and Garth. I raised a hand to get his attention. Miranda glanced over from behind the bar, took one look at the attractive man heading my way, and wagged her brows behind him.

He slid into the seat across from me and looked down at the drink sitting there. "Is this for me?"

"Yep. All yours. I know the owner of the bar. She makes several specialty moonshine drinks using my 'shine. I thought you'd like to try one."

He picked up his glass and raised it in toast. When I lifted my glass, he eyed the clear liquid. "You're drinking water?"

"Soda," I said. "It's got bubbles. See?" I held the glass up higher. "Of course, it's got a shot of my pure moonshine in it, too." I grinned. *Liar.*

We tapped our glasses—*clink*—and Garth took his first sip. He grimaced. "They sure don't go easy on the alcohol here, do they?"

"Nope," I said. "They go through lots of my 'shine. This pub is one of my best customers."

We chatted as we drank. I asked Garth when he first discovered his love of music and his talent for it, which singers and bands he considered to be his musical influences. As he answered my questions, I downed my drink at warp speed, hoping he would match my pace. He didn't. When I finished my drink, he was still only halfway through his.

I pointed to his glass. "Why don't you finish that and we can walk down to the sculpture garden?"

He raised his glass. "If I finish this, I won't be walking. I'll be stumbling." He left what remained of his drink and stood. *Dang it!*

I told him I'd already paid for the drinks but, being both generous and a gentleman, he left a few singles on the table as an additional tip for the server. We walked out the door and headed up Market Street toward the river, walking side by side. I kept an eye out for Marlon and Charlotte, and an ear out for the telltale *clop-clop-clop* that always preceded their arrival. I know Marlon trusted me, but an encounter right now would be awkward.

Garth and I arrived at the Hunter Museum without crossing paths with Marlon, thank goodness. The museum was a modern marvel, all odd angles and glass, poised on a bluff over the Tennessee River. Its signature zigzagging ramp wound its way up from the street to the main level. It was a beautiful day, warm and sunny, the gentle breeze keeping the temperature in check.

Boats floated by on the river below as Garth and I ambled about the exhibit. As we wound our way around the sculptures, I attempted to weave pointed questions into our conversation in order to learn more about the relationships among the Sheridan brothers and about Brody's relationship with Tate and Camille. I also wanted to know more about William, to determine whether he might have easy access to a Caterpillar equipment key.

"I'm curious," I said. "How did you meet William? Do you work with him?"

"We met in high school," Garth said. "We played in the orchestra together."

"I can understand William playing violin," I said, "but do orchestras include jugs and washboards?"

Garth chuckled. "No, but I did play some of the miscellaneous odds and ends. Tambourine. Triangle. Chimes. Bells. Wood block. Basically, if nobody else wanted to play it, the director assigned it to me. He knew I'd be a good sport."

I recalled the conversation we had last night, and used it to learn more about William. "You mentioned that William is good at the business end of things. Did he study business in college?" I asked. "Or did he learn about it on the job?"

"On the job," Garth said, "so to speak. I suppose you could say he taught himself. He's been freelancing with his music for years, giving lessons and playing weddings, bar mitzvahs, and corporate events. He barely scraped by at first. Still lived at home with his folks. But over time, he's figured things out. He's not getting rich, but he's getting by. That's more than most musicians can say."

"He doesn't have a day job like you and Josh?"

"No and, with any luck, Josh and I won't have day jobs soon, either."

If William only worked in music, it seemed unlikely he'd have access to a Caterpillar key. That didn't mean he hadn't scratched one up somewhere, though. But would he even know that heavy equipment keys were universal? That one key would fit every piece of a particular brand's equipment? That odd tidbit didn't seem like something that would naturally come up in conversation.

We passed a horse statue made of driftwood, as well as a collection of statues including a pitcher and a batter engaged in a game of baseball. We meandered on until we reached a comical sculpture depicting two rounded cartoonlike people dancing cheek to cheek atop a bag of cash. The piece was titled *Free Money*. The image made me think of Tate and Camille, and the proceeds from

Brody's life insurance policy. *Had knowing they had a quarter-million dollars coming made them want to dance?*

As we admired the piece, I said, "I was getting moonshine out of the back of my van in the parking lot at the winery the night Brody disappeared. I couldn't help but overhear all of you arguing."

"You did?" Garth looked sheepish. "We must've sounded like a bunch of chickens, clucking and squawking and bickering."

"Pretty much," I teased, hoping my lighthearted response would keep him off guard. "I heard Tate mention something about life insurance. You think he could have killed your brother for the money? The fact that Brody was buried in the pond that Tate dug seems to point to him."

Garth exhaled sharply. "Maybe? But I'm just not sure I'm feeling it."

"He seems to be crazy about Camille and Imogene."

Garth turned to me. "He is. Every time Brody did either of them wrong, Tate would blow a gasket. Brody might have gone too far when he said Tate wasn't Imogene's daddy. Tate's more of a father to her than Brody ever was."

Now we seem to be getting somewhere. "Tate also had a key to the excavator," I pointed out.

"True," Garth agreed. "But Tate was long gone by the time my brothers and I packed up to go."

"He could have come back, couldn't he?"

"I suppose," Garth said, though he still didn't sound convinced. "Seems Josh or I would've seen his truck if he'd been around, though."

"True," I said, musing aloud, "and he wouldn't have been able to drive back through the gate."

Garth cocked his head. "What do you mean?"

"The winery gate. It was closed when you left, right?"

"No. It was open. We drove right through it."

I mulled over what he'd just told me. The gate had been open when I departed the winery, but it was closed when I returned less than an hour later. If the gate had still been open when Garth and Josh left, that meant anyone could have driven back onto the winery property before I returned. Tate. William. The boyfriend of one of the flirty fans. The killer might have even been at the winery before Garth and Josh left. They could have parked out of sight behind a stand of trees or the line of forsythia bushes, planning to follow Brody when he left. When Garth and Josh left before their brother, the killer might have decided to seize on the opportunity to do away with Brody right then and there.

Is Garth lying to me? It seemed possible, maybe even likely. After all, if he claimed the gate was still open when he and Josh left the winery, the implication was that someone else could have driven in and done away with Brody. Maybe he and Josh had acted in cahoots to kill their brother. Two Cains and an Abel. Maybe those two Cains even had help from a friend—William Hill. Maybe he was trying to throw suspicion off himself and any cohorts he might have had.

To test my theory that Garth was lying about the gate, I pressed him for details. "What was Brody doing when you and Josh left?"

"Packing up his instruments. He uses quite a few in our performances."

At least this statement was true. I'd seen him perform on multiple string instruments, and the divers had brought up instrument case after instrument case from Brody's Jeep after finding it in the river. "He was alone?"

"At that point? Yes. The fans had gone. Course, I basically had to shoo the lingerers away. They might've stayed all night otherwise."

Hmm. "Did you and Josh go straight home?"

"I did," Garth said. "Josh says he did, too. But, like I told the detective, we split once we hit Cummings Highway. Josh lives one way. I live the other." He stared at me for a long moment, his eyes narrowing. "It kind of feels like you're putting me through the third degree here, Hattie."

Oops. I'd been too obvious. "I'm sorry, Garth," I said. "I know you had nothing to do with what happened to your brother." *Or do I?* "I just wish we could get to the bottom of things. For the sake of your family primarily, but for my sake, too. I know that sounds selfish. People keep coming into my shop and asking me questions, like I'm supposed to know what happened just because a jug of my moonshine was used in Brody's murder. It would be nice to see justice done, to get answers and closure."

Garth's head bobbed slowly as he eyed me. "I feel the same," he said softly. He turned and stared up at the sky. "But a part of me is afraid of what those answers might be."

Aha! He must suspect someone close to him. But whom does he suspect? Josh? William? Tate?

He was still staring up at the clouds when I gently prodded him. "You think it might have been Josh?"

He hesitated for a moment. "Brody put me and Josh through all sorts of hell over the years. It's hard when your worst bully is your big brother. But, no. I don't think Josh did it. Josh decided long ago that the best way to deal with Brody was to just go along with him. I didn't agree with that strategy, but it probably saved Josh a lot of frustration. Josh got along with Brody a lot better than I did."

"William, then?"

Garth let out a long, shuddering breath. He lowered his head to look at the ground. "I don't know." His shoulders quirked in an uncertain shrug. "I hate to think it, but there's some logic to it. William really wants to make a go at his music. Like I said, he's been busting his hump, trying to build a name for himself. But there's only so far a fiddle player can go on their own. He needed to join up with a band, and the Bootlegging Brothers was on the rise. Brody was the only thing standing in his way. But we've been friends for a long time, and I've never seen William get physical. Not even once. He's a levelheaded guy. It would be out of character for him."

"Brody really messed things up for him, though, didn't he? William had told his fans he'd be playing at the winery that night, and Brody put a stop to that. It had to be aggravating."

"I suppose so. But it wasn't the end of the world. He'd get over it."

We'd exhausted the subject and, because I was pretending this was a real date, I turned to lighter topics. "Max finished painting my great-grandfather's old Ford, and the mechanic is ready to get started on the engine. All that's left for me to do is make a new cushion for the seat." The rusty old springs were exposed. If someone sat on it as is, they could contract tetanus and suffer a case of lockjaw. I'd have to place a thick piece of plywood under the cushion, too, to be safe. I'd enlist Kiki's help. She'd built props for theater productions and would know what to do. "Once the car's all ready, we can get the new photo shoot scheduled."

Garth slid me a soft smile. "You should be in the photos with us. Some of 'em anyway."

"I'm not sure we'd all fit," I said. "Those old car seats are narrow."

"I supposed you'd have to sit on my lap, then." He slid me a sexy smile that made my stomach churn with guilt.

A soft *clop-clop-clop* sounded from somewhere nearby, growing louder. *Uh-oh!*

I pretended to check the time on my phone. "It's later than I realized. I've got to get back to my shop. Thanks for a fun afternoon!" With that, I scampered away as fast my sneakers could take me.

Chapter Seventeen

Having talked to Tate, Camille, and Garth, the only suspects left for me to question were Josh and William. With William working his fiddle freelance, it seemed he'd be the easiest to approach.

On Sunday evening, I searched for William online to see what I might discover about him. I found a Facebook business page with posts detailing his solo appearances at weddings, anniversary parties, and corporate events. He'd posted images of himself in various attire to show his versatility. The bluegrass attire he wore when playing with the Bootlegging Brothers. An embroidered western shirt and cowboy hat. A tuxedo complete with tails, top hat, and a black tie. He'd even trimmed his beard for that last look.

One of his most recent posts was headlined *Big News* and noted that he'd joined the Bootlegging Brothers. The post made no mention of the fact that the position of

strings player had become available only after Brody
Sheridan's death. Not mentioning Brody seemed disrespectful and ill-mannered. On the other hand, perhaps he
wanted to keep things positive on his page. Or perhaps he
didn't want people making the connection that he could
have killed Brody to take his place in the band. The post
noted that, although William would be playing with the
Bootlegging Brothers, he would still be available for lessons and solo performances, his schedule permitting.

Garth had given me William's cell number at the
winery, so I texted him and asked whether he might be
interested in performing in front of my Moonshine Shack.
I also asked William about his rates. I invited him to
come by the Shack at his convenience to discuss the particulars and take a look at the shop.

A reply text pinged a couple of hours later. He charged
$200 per hour with a two-hour minimum. Not exactly in
my budget, but not enough to break it, either. I got lucky.
He'd be playing the River Pearl Winery with the Bootlegging Brothers again on Saturday, the last night of their
four-week run, but he was available Friday night. He said
he'd swing by my shop the following afternoon to take a
look at the store and nail things down. I'd seize the chance
to try to nail him down, too, and determine if he could be
Brody Sheridan's killer.

With the start of the school year just around the corner,
Nora had taken the day off Monday to take her kids
shopping for clothing and school supplies. Granddaddy
had decided to stay home today for the Singing River Retirement Home's weekly bingo tournament. Granddaddy
had always scoffed at the idea before, calling bingo a silly

children's game. I had a feeling Louetta might have convinced him to give the game a try. Smoky was with me, as usual, and Kate was working the store with me, too. Dalton rode around in the carrier on her chest, facing outward today lest he once again coat his mother in baby barf. The look reminded me of the classic scene from the movie *Alien* where the creepy, gooey creature bursts from the person's chest, except in this case the creature was cute rather than creepy. Still gooey, though. In fact, Dalton had a shiny glob of drool on his chin right now. He'd probably get a new tooth soon.

William came through the door at half past four, his fiddle case in his hand and a backpack slung over one shoulder. "Hello, Hattie!" he called.

I circled around from behind the counter and introduced him to Kate, who was dusting shelves and wiping fingerprints from the jars. William was every bit as charming as Garth. He set his fiddle down, put his thumbs in his ears, and wiggled his fingers at Dalton. The baby giggled, cooed, and oohed in delight. *Coo. Ooo. Ooo.*

William turned to Kate. "Got yourself a yodeler, I see."

She beamed down at her son. "Is there any money in yodeling?"

"Not a penny. Send him to technical school for a computer degree."

Laughing, she said, "I'll keep that in mind."

Turning to business now, William glanced around the shop. "This looks like a fun place." He stepped over to read the newspaper clipping on the wall. He pointed to the photo. "Eustatius Hayes? He your kin?"

"Great-grandfather," I said. "I use his moonshine recipe. My granddaddy taught me how to make it."

"My grandfather taught me how to fiddle," William

said. "I was the only one who was interested. All my brothers and sisters and cousins thought it was hokey. Now they're all begging me to play their weddings."

"Same here," I said. "I was the only one who wanted to learn moonshining. Now my family has to buy it from me. I'm tempted to charge them extra."

We shared a conspiratorial chuckle. He walked over to the counter and set his fiddle case and backpack down. He unzipped the backpack and pulled out a folder with numbered song lists inside. He handed me a printout. "I put together a customized song list for you. Classics, mostly. Some country covers. All the songs that mention moonshine. But I'm happy to play any particular songs you might like."

I ran my gaze down the list. He'd nailed the most popular songs the crowd would know. "Mountain Dew," "Daddy's Moonshine Still," "Bootlegger's Boy," "White Lightning," "Mississippi Mud," "Tear My Stillhouse Down," and "Copperhead Road," among others. The choices were perfect. *The guy has done his homework.*

I looked up at him. "Garth told me you were good with the business side of things." I waved the list. "This custom song list is proof."

William gave me a humble smile. "I learned long ago that talent alone won't get you far in the music business. There's lots of people playing around at playing music. To be a success, you've got to treat music making like a real job and you've got to hustle. Opportunities rarely come knocking. Sometimes a person's got to make their own opportunities."

His words had me thinking back to my discussion with Garth the day before in the sculpture garden. *Had William seen Brody as a roadblock to his success? Had he decided to do away with that roadblock and create an opportunity for himself?*

I decided to broach the subject. To that end, I motioned for him to follow me out front. "I thought you could play out here on the porch. Your music would catch people's attention and lure them to the store. They'd enjoy the entertainment."

"They sure would." William's lips spread in a sly grin. "But, truthfully, I'm just bait. What you really want is for them to go inside and buy some of your moonshine, right?"

"Absolutely." *Why deny the obvious?*

"I can wander in and out, get the crowd to follow me."

"Like the pied piper?"

"Exactly. Except with a fiddle, not a flute. I'll be sure to add your jingle to my lineup every ten minutes or so, tell folks to go inside and 'get a jug, get a jar.'"

He'd just provided me the ideal segue. "Seems like just yesterday the Bootlegging Brothers were standing right here on this porch for the photo shoot after they recorded my jingle. I still find it hard to believe that Brody is gone."

"It was a shock, that's for sure. Can't honestly say I miss him, though. Brody was a hothead who thought the world revovled around him. He claimed he was looking out for Garth and Josh, but he duped them into signing that partnership contract. He was holding his brothers back."

I faked a wince. "You think one of them decided to get him out of the picture?"

"Wouldn't blame them if they did," he said plainly. "Garth doesn't have it in him, though. He didn't much appreciate the BS Brody was always throwing their way, but he let his feelings be known, got it out of his system."

The implication being . . . "But Josh did not?"

"Nope. I don't think I've once heard Josh speak out

against Brody in all these years. But like they say, still waters run deep. Things could've built up over time. Besides, Josh had a personal score to settle with Brody."

"Personal score?" William certainly had my attention now. "What do you mean?"

He gave me a knowing look. "Camille."

"Brody's ex-wife? What about her?"

William arched accusing brows. "Brody stole her from Josh."

The news set my senses tingling. "He did?"

William nodded. "Camille and Josh dated for a while seven or eight years ago. Josh was in deep, though he'd never admit it. He made the mistake of introducing Camille to Brody. Brody had no regard for Josh's feelings. He swooped right in with his false charm and swept Camille off her feet. She dumped Josh in a heartbeat and left him looking like a fool."

"That must have been hurtful and humiliating." But was it hurtful and humiliating enough that Josh would kill his brother over it? And, if so, why wait all this time?

Maybe Josh had intentionally postponed seeking his revenge until enough time had passed that he'd no longer be immediately suspected. Maybe he'd been waiting all these years for an opportunity to present itself. Like William had said, opportunities rarely knock. Maybe Josh had realized the freshly dug pond, the available excavator, and the remote location of the winery created the perfect chance for him to even the score with his brother—and then some. Josh could have easily rounded up one of the decorative jugs from the stage and set it aside somewhere out of sight to be used in his assault on Brody. Like Marlon mentioned earlier, he could've used a napkin or shirtsleeve when he picked them up so that he wouldn't leave a fingerprint.

William went on. "Once things soured in her marriage to Brody, Camille realized she'd made a mistake choosing Brody over Josh, but by then it was too late to fix things. Too much water had passed under the bridge."

Now that I knew this history, Josh's mean-spirited grin on hearing that Brody was shorting Camille on child support made sense. He'd likely felt that she was getting her due for dumping him for his unreliable, egomaniacal brother. But I also remembered the look he'd given Brody only a moment later. He might have found the situation funny on one hand, but he also didn't seem to appreciate Brody cheating the woman he had once loved. *Josh still has feelings for Camille, doesn't he?*

As I mulled over the situation, I was struck with the fact that no one else had mentioned that Camille and Josh had once dated. Not Camille. Not Josh. Not Garth. Not Tate. Why would all of them have kept this fact a secret? Did they believe Camille and Josh's long-ago relationship was no longer relevant? Or were they attempting to hide the information in order to protect Josh? Did they think he'd killed Brody in a long-suppressed jealous rage?

I considered the ramifications of William's revelation from every angle. Could Camille still have feelings for Josh? Did Tate know it, and could he have been trying to frame Josh for killing Brody? But, if so, why kill Brody with a jug, which would point to Garth, instead? Did Tate think it would make it appear as if Josh were trying to frame Garth? It was enough to make my head spin as if I'd downed too much moonshine.

"What about Tate?" I asked William. "You think he could have killed Brody?"

"Seems he'd have reason to," William said "From what I hear, Brody was constantly jerking Camille's chain. But

I don't know Tate well enough to form an opinion. We've hung out a few times over the years with Garth, Josh, and Brody, but that's it." He squirmed at little. "I've probably said too much. You'll keep this conversation between us, won't you?"

"Of course," I lied. No way would I keep this revelation from Ace. I'd get in touch with her soon, let her know what I'd learned. I wondered whether William was truly uncomfortable, or whether he'd intentionally tried to plant a seed, to implicate Josh in Brody's death. Did he actually think Josh could be guilty? Or was he trying to deflect suspicion from himself? I had no way of knowing. But I did know that I'd gleaned an intriguing bit of information.

As we walked back inside, Kate looked up from behind the counter, where she was stocking the heavy-duty paper bags we gave to our customers. "Got things all sorted out?"

"We're getting there." William pulled out his fiddle and played a few bars to test out the acoustics in my shop. On hearing the unfamiliar sound, Smoky shot up from his sleeping spot in the front window and darted into the storeroom, earning a laugh from us humans and another coo from Dalton.

William frowned slightly and glanced around. "There's a lot of hard surfaces in your shop. It's got a fun look, but unfortunately, it doesn't make for great acoustics."

"Can I do something about that?" I asked.

"Add a rug or two," he suggested. "You'd be surprised what a difference they can make. Maybe drape some fabric over your counter and sampling table. Anything soft you can add will help, even some plants."

"Smoky treats houseplants like a snack."

Kate chimed in. "What about some hanging baskets? He wouldn't be able to reach them."

"Thanks, Kate," I said. "That's a great idea."

She tossed her head, nonchalant. "I've been babyproofing our house. Pet-proofing isn't much different."

Kate, Dalton, and I followed William as he wandered out onto the porch and played a few bars there, too. "Same here," he said. "Lots of hard surfaces. Maybe throw some pillows on the porch swing and toss a blanket over the rocker."

Kate looked my way. "I see a trip to HomeGoods in our future."

As William packed up his fiddle to go, he said, "See you Friday evening. This is going to be fun!"

"It sure will!" Just in case he was the killer, I'd ask Marlon to come by at closing time Friday. No sense taking a chance, especially with all those jugs of murder moonshine sitting around.

Chapter Eighteen

Kate left at five o'clock. Kiki showed up shortly thereafter to work the evening shift with me, her sketchbook in hand. She'd been hired to paint a mural in a children's dentist office. While she sat at the counter, sketching out some possible themes, Smoky lay next to her sketchbook, reaching out to swat at her pencil. *So helpful.*

Monday evenings were always slow. Only a handful of customers trickled in, which gave me time to design a flyer for Friday night's fiddle performance. My artistic skills weren't nearly as good as Kiki's, but she made some suggestions as I went along. William said I could use the image from his Facebook profile in my promotional materials, so I copied and pasted it onto the page. I added a border of musical notes. When I was finished, I turned my laptop toward Kiki. "What do you think?"

"Not bad," she said. "But let me do a little tweaking."

Once Kiki had resized the images and done some rearranging to make the layout more visually appealing, I printed out fifty copies. I posted one on my door right at eye level, and two more in the windows. The rest I placed in a stack by the register, where I could hand them out to customers. I kept the alarm's panic button in easy reach in the hip pocket of my overalls in the event that Brody's killer came by to do away with me to because they believed I was getting too close. They'd be wrong, of course. Despite my efforts, I still had no idea who killed Brody, whether everyone had told me the truth or fed me lies.

My moonshine business taken care of for the time being, I turned again to the business of solving Brody's murder. I couldn't find Josh's address on the Internet, and I wasn't about to text Garth and ask him for it. I didn't want him to give Josh a heads-up that I might be popping in. I wanted to catch Josh unaware and see if he might slip up. *Hmm.*

It was then I remembered the contracts I'd had the Bootlegging Brothers sign to document the terms of the photo shoot. There'd been a designated line for them to fill in an address, hadn't there?

I scurried back to my storeroom and pulled open the bottom drawer of my desk, which was designed to hold hanging files. I riffled through them until I found the one labeled CONTRACTS. I then fingered through the contracts— my lease, my agreement with the bottling company, my website hosting terms and conditions—until I found the ones for the photo shoot. Per the contract Josh had signed, he lived in an apartment in the eastern part of the city. I snapped a pic of the address line with my phone.

Going to Josh's home alone might be a bad idea. I asked Kiki if she'd be willing to tag along with me.

She pointed her charcoal pencil at me. "You're asking

if I will willingly go to the home of a possible murderer while you confront him? Do you realize how crazy that sounds?"

"Yes. I'm fully aware it sounds insane."

"Okay. Just checking. I'm in. I could use a little excitement. That said, we should arm ourselves."

I pointed to the display of jugs. "Apparently, my jugs make a good weapon."

"They make good *offensive* weapons," she said. "They're too heavy for a quick defense." She glanced around. Noting my grandfather's whittling set on the shelf below the counter, she opened the case. "Maybe we could use these."

Granddaddy's whittling tools were sharp, but they were tiny. "The only thing those tools would be good for is giving Josh Sheridan a manicure."

"Come on. A few thousand jabs with one of the knives would get the job done." She removed an itty-bitty tool with a hooked blade. "We could rip out his intestines with this one. His small intestine, anyway."

"Ew!"

"You got a better idea?"

"Don't people put coins in a sock? So they can swing it? Seems I've heard of that somewhere."

"Great idea." She reached down and grabbed my foot.

"No!" I cried. "If I take off my sock, my sneakers will give me blisters."

"Well, it was *your* idea," she said. "We're not using my sock." She glanced around before raising a finger. "Eureka!" She trotted into the storeroom and returned with one of the bright-yellow latex gloves I used for cleaning. She handed it to me and said, "Hold it open."

While I held the open end of the glove wide, she jabbed a button on the cash register to open the till. *Cha-ching!*

She proceeded to scoop quarters, dimes, nickels, and pennies out of the till and into the glove. When the coin slots were empty, she snatched one of the rubber bands I kept in the till for securing stacks of bills. She fastened the band tightly around the wrist of the coin-filled glove so the change wouldn't fall out. The improvised weapon complete, she demonstrated with a light slap to my cheek.

I put my hand to my face. "Ow! You could've broken my molar."

"Buck up, buttercup. At least we know it's effective."

"We've got another problem," I said. "We can't just show up at his house unannounced for no reason. What's our story going to be?"

"Easy." She grabbed one of my bags and shoved a mason jar of apple pie moonshine in it, along with one of my promotional T-shirts and a pour spout. She held it out to me. "It's a care package. You've been concerned about the guys who sang your jingle and just wanted to check in on him."

It was a good ruse. I just hoped I could pull it off.

After we closed the store, I loaded Smoky's carrier into my van and set off for Josh's apartment. Kiki followed in her Mini Cooper with the coin-filled glove.

When we arrived at Josh's apartment complex, I circled the lot until I spotted his number on a door. Fortunately, we found parking spots within a quick sprint should Josh become enraged and we had to make a quick getaway. We'd use the glove only as a last resort.

Kiki and I walked up to Josh's door, which was on the first floor of the building. There was no welcome mat, no potted plant, not even a pair of muddy boots. Just the number, 8G. *Could G stand for guilty?* Kiki stood by my side, one arm crooked up behind her to hide the coin-filled glove she held at the ready, just in case it would be needed. Taking a deep breath, I raised my hand and knocked. *Rap-rap-rap*.

A few seconds later, the door opened. Josh stood there in a pair of dingy socks and lounge pants, no shirt. He held a can of beer in his hand. A big dog stood next to him, the ubiquitous mix of pit bull and some other breed that resulted when irresponsible owners failed to neuter or spay their dogs, then dumped the puppies at a shelter. I was glad this dog had found a home. Josh was surprisingly fit. Six-pack abs led up to rock-hard pecs and well-formed biceps.

"Wowww," Kiki said on a breath. "You do not miss a workout, do you?"

A grin tugged at Josh's lips but, as usual, he said nothing.

I thrust the bag at him. "I brought you a care package. I was at the store, wondering how you were doing, and I thought this might cheer you up."

Josh took the bag from me and uttered an almost inaudible, "Thanks."

He looked from me to Kiki and leaned over to try to see what she was hiding behind her. She shifted, lost her grip on the heavy glove, and dropped it to the cement stoop behind her. The force caused the glove to split open, sending a bombardment of coins clinking to the pavement. *Clink-clink. Clink. Clink-clink.*

Josh snorted. "A latex glove makes an odd piggy bank."

Think quick, Hattie! "We ran out of paper coin rolls at the store. We had to improvise."

"Yep." Kiki nodded, backing me up.

Josh's face was tight with skepticism. "Why didn't you leave the coins in your car?"

I'd come here to ask him questions, not the other way around! "We were afraid someone might steal them."

He issued a soft snort, but at least he stopped the interrogation.

Kiki bent down and cupped the dog's face in her hands. "Hello, boy." The dog returned her greeting by wagging his tail and swiping her from chin to ear with his speckled tongue. Kiki didn't mind. She looked up with a smile. "I think he likes me!" She released him and started gathering the coins, shoving them into her pockets.

Josh said, "Thanks again," and went to close his door. When I threw out a hand to stop him, he stared at me expectantly.

"Um . . ." I didn't know how to raise the subject of him and Camille naturally. "Um . . ."

Kiki realized I was struggling, stood, and having filled her pockets, shoved the last handful of coins she'd retrieved into her bra. "Hattie was worried about your family and was looking over everyone's Facebook pages. We saw a post on a page from a few years back. It said something about you and Camille dating?"

He gave a half shrug with one shoulder.

He wasn't going to meet us halfway, was he? I said, "I'm sorry if that made Brody's death harder for you. You must've had some very mixed feelings about everything."

He said nothing, just did the half shrug again.

My patience was running out, though I tried to keep it in check. "Why didn't you mention to the detective that you and Camille had once been involved?"

He gave another half shrug.

I fought the urge to reach out and throttle him. "Are you just going to shrug after every question I ask you?"

Finally, he gave me a real answer. "No. After that

question I'm going to shut my door." He slammed the door in our faces.

I turned to Kiki and rolled my eyes. "Well, that went well."

We left the remaining coins scattered all over his stoop. My financial records wouldn't reconcile, but so be it.

Kiki and I parted ways in the parking lot. As soon as I was back in my van, I pulled out my cell phone and called Ace. "I learned something from William Hill, but he told me in confidence and asked me not to repeat it."

Ace barked a laugh. "Whenever a suspect says to keep something secret, it usually means they hope you'll spread the information far and wide. They're hoping to deflect suspicion."

"I'd wondered that, too." *Could the theory be true in this case? Is William trying to implicate Josh when William himself was the one who'd killed Brody?* I couldn't know. At any rate, best that Ace be brought into the loop. "William told me that Josh and Camille used to be a thing."

"A thing?"

"They dated for a few weeks years back, but then Josh introduced Camille to Brody, and Brody made a move on her. That's how Camille and Brody first got together. You told me that people kill for love or money. Maybe Josh killed for love. Lost love."

"I could see how it would be particularly painful for a guy to lose a girlfriend to his brother. He'd be forced to relive it every time he saw them together." The line went silent for a moment as she seemed to be pondering the situation. "Then again, it's been years. Camille and Brody have been divorced since Imogene was a baby. Maybe Josh got over it long ago, especially since it didn't last."

She was thinking out loud, and having the same thoughts that had run through my mind. I felt proud that I'd been thinking like a true detective.

The fact that Josh and Camille had once been a couple until Brody stepped in not only gave Josh a motive to kill Brody, but the fact that nobody had mentioned this history was also suspicious. Were Garth, Camille, and Tate covering for Josh? Garth might have felt that Brody did their brother wrong, and that Josh was warranted in seeking retribution. Camille might feel guilty for coming between the two brothers. Tate might have kept quiet about his wife's former boyfriend for her sake. Maybe they thought that Josh didn't intend to kill his brother, that things had simply gotten out of hand somehow, and they didn't want to see him rot in prison for decades over a mistake.

Ace said, "I'll talk to Josh again. See how he reacts."

I winced. "About that . . ."

She sighed loudly. "Let me guess. You've already confronted him."

"I took him a care basket," I said. "It happened to come up."

"Because you brought it up?"

"Well, yeah," I admitted.

"Your curiosity could get you killed one day," she said. "You're like a cat. Unable to leave things alone."

It was true. And like a cat, I couldn't change my nature.

Chapter Nineteen

Ace called me Tuesday morning while I was still at home, sipping coffee at my kitchen table and Smoky was noisily chomping on his kitty kibble. I tapped the screen to accept her call. "Hi, Ace."

As usual, she got right down to business. "I spoke to Josh earlier this morning. He said he got over Camille a long time ago. He said things were never that serious between the two of them, that she was just another pretty face."

"You think he was telling the truth?"

"Not for a second. His grip tightened so hard on his doorknob it's a wonder it didn't break."

Whoa. "Did you arrest him?"

"Couldn't. There's not enough evidence against him. And it was hard to say what he was getting upset about. That long-ago love affair with Camille or the fact that you went to his apartment last night to badger him about it and I showed up this morning to go through it all over again."

It was clear this bridge was burned now. Josh had to know it was me who told Ace that he'd had a relationship with Camille years ago. He'd probably never speak to me again—not that he'd ever said much in the first place. *Would this case ever get solved?*

We ended the call, I rounded up Smoky, and the two of us went down the mountain. I picked up my granddaddy at the retirement home, and we headed to the Moonshine Shack.

Later that afternoon, Granddaddy was napping in his recliner when I heard the door of the shop open. I looked up to see Marlon coming in the door. He was off duty today and dressed in civilian clothes—a short-sleeved western shirt, a pair of jeans, and boots, the consummate cowboy. "Hey, you," I said. "What are you doing here?"

"Just came by to say hello." He hiked a thumb at the flyer taped to the door and gave me an incredulous look. "William Hill is playing his fiddle here Friday night?"

"Yep. I think he'll draw a lot of people to my shop."

"Hattie, the guy could be a killer."

"*Could* be. This is America. Innocent until proven guilty."

"That rule only applies to our legal system. It doesn't mean you throw your common sense out the window."

I sent him a squinty-eyed look of warning. "You're coming awfully close to calling me 'stupid.'"

His mouth spread into a mischievous grin. "I like the 'awfully close' part."

He stepped over, pulled me to him, and gave me a warm kiss. Having delivered the smooch, he wandered over to say hello to Smoky, too. The cat had left his usual perch in the front window and decided it would be fun to hop up onto the shelf where I displayed my grandfather's Whittled Critters, which we sold for seven dollars each. They made an inexpensive souvenir for tourists and a simple toy for children. Customers often bought one or two to keep their kids occupied while the adults sampled my 'shine. The critters also brought in some extra pocket money for my grandfather, who was on a fixed income.

Smoky successively knocked each of the wooden animals to the floor. *Clunk. Clunk. Clunk.* Marlon picked them up and put them back into place only to run through the routine again. *Clunk. Clunk. Clunk.*

My grandfather woke up, scrubbed a hand over his face, and sat up in his chair, peering out the door of the stockroom. "Is that cat knocking my critters around again?"

"He is," I said. "He's bored."

"He needs a box," Granddaddy said. "I'll get him one." He lowered the footrest on his chair and stood to grab an empty carton.

As Marlon slid a whittled kitty back onto the shelf, he cast a glance my way. "If I didn't know better, I'd swear I saw you down by the sculpture garden Sunday afternoon with Garth Sheridan."

Uh-oh. I wasn't sure what to say. I didn't want to lie outright to him, but if he only suspected it was me and didn't know for sure, I didn't necessarily want to confirm it, either. I settled for simply saying, "Oh, yeah?"

"Yeah." He picked up the carved squirrel Smoky had

slapped off the shelf and put it back in place. He turned and stared me down. "You saying it wasn't you?"

He knows. No sense continuing to pretend. I sighed. "I was only trying to see if I could get some more information out of him."

He exhaled sharply. "Getting information is Ace's job."

"I know," I said, "but people are careful when they talk to cops. Tight-lipped. I thought maybe he'd have his guard down with me and slip up. I was only trying to help."

Marlon strode back my way and stepped up close, bending over to look me in the eye. "Trying to help could get you killed, Hattie."

"Or it could solve the case!"

He shook his head and backed away. He released another breath, this one louder and longer. "You are as stubborn as a mule."

Granddaddy walked out of the back room with the box in hand. "She sure is." He set the box on the floor. Smoky immediately jumped into it. My grandfather closed two of the flaps to give Smoky some privacy.

"I'm not stubborn," I insisted. "I'm determined."

"Nah," Granddaddy insisted. "You're stubborn. You get it from me."

"No fair ganging up on me." I sent a scowl his way before turning back to debate the matter with Marlon. "I'm . . . tenacious."

Marlon shook his head. "Stub. Born."

I crossed my arms over my chest. "Well, you're not perfect, either, you know."

"Okay, I'll bite," Marlon said. "What's wrong with me?"

Not a darn thing. Marlon was hardworking, compassionate, smart, and handsome. I couldn't think of one thing I'd change about him, except for the fact that he called me out when I was doing things I shouldn't. "Well, you call people names, for one thing. You just called me 'stubborn.'"

Marlon shook his head. We set our disagreement aside and enjoyed a quiet evening together in my shop. Marlon challenged my grandfather to several games of chess and dominoes. He dusted the model train track that ran around the wall up high. I usually had trouble reaching it, but it was easy for a tall guy like him. He stuck around until the end of the evening to make sure I got the shop locked up, and that Smoky, Granddaddy, and I made it out to my van safely.

Before climbing into my van, I stood on tiptoe and gave him a warm goodbye kiss. "Thanks for coming by tonight."

He cupped his hand under my chin and looked me in the eye. "Be careful, Hattie. Chances are that someone you've interacted with killed Brody. If they realize you're digging, they might kill you, too."

"I'll be careful," I said, but even I didn't believe me.

I woke Wednesday morning feeling itchy and restless. Brody's murder investigation was moving too slowly. I knew Ace had done all she could, and that there wasn't enough evidence against any one person for her to make an arrest. Everyone's finger-pointing seemed to go in a circle, much like the new man-made river at the River Pearl Winery. Maybe everyone had all been in on it together, like the suspects in Agatha Christie's *Murder on the Orient Express. Who knows?* I decided to make one last visit to the person I considered the most viable suspect before throwing in the towel. I called Nora to let her know I'd be late coming into the shop, but that Kate was also on the schedule so she'd have some help.

"No worries," Nora said. "We know what to do. In fact, you should take a day off now and then. Working seven days a week must wear you out."

My schedule was indeed exhausting. But she was right. Now that I had a full staff, I could take some time off. Maybe I'd even start scheduling days off so that I worked only a normal five-day, forty-hour workweek. I loved my job, I loved my moonshine, and I loved my Moonshine Shack, but all work and no play make Hattie a dull girl.

After an early lunch of a clementine orange and a peanut butter and jelly sandwich, I bade Smoky goodbye with a kiss on the head and a scratch under the chin. "I love you, fluffy bum." The irritated swish of his tail told me he didn't appreciate my latest nickname for him.

I climbed into my van and aimed for the winery, where Tate would be finishing up the work on the pond. I still considered him the most likely person to have killed Brody. Only Camille could corroborate his alibi, and she had a vested interest in making sure her husband didn't go to prison. He had the best motive for killing Brody. Brody had caused both his wife and stepdaughter a lot of grief and had cheated both them and Tate financially by not paying his fair share of child support. I didn't truly expect anything new to come from speaking with him but at least, if I questioned him one more time, I'd feel that I'd done all I could. As hard as it might be, I'd force myself to move on and stop obsessing about the case.

As I approached Shirley Byrd's old farmhouse, I slowed and raised a hand in hello. She was sitting on her rocker, as always, the shotgun leaning against the wall to her side and her dog at her feet. The jug of moonshine I'd given her sat on the wood railing beside her. Once my van had come to a full stop, I unrolled my window and called, "How's your moonshine supply holding up?"

She reached over, picked up the jug, and turned it upside down to indicate that it was empty.

"We can't have that!" I called with a smile. I eased over to the side of the road, turned off my motor, and retrieved a jug from the stash in the back of my van. I carried it up to her porch and held it out to her. "Here you go, Ms. Byrd. A fresh jug."

She took it from me. "Thank you kindly. I'll put it to good use."

"I'm sure you will."

The two of us shared a conspiratorial chuckle. *Amazing how moonshine can bring people together.*

The gentle breeze carried the scent of smoke to our noses. Shirley frowned and fanned a hand in front of her face. "I'm so glad they're nearly done burning that brush. Every time I smell that smoke and see those flames, I worry an ember is going to blow over here and catch my house on fire."

In light of the fact that her ramshackle farmhouse was little more than dry kindling, her worries were well founded.

I glanced over at the smoldering fire. The tall brush pile I'd seen on my first visit to the winery had since been reduced to little more than a few charred coals. The winds today were relatively calm, but they'd been generally high the last couple of weeks, especially in the mornings. The weather had probably slowed things down. Brush couldn't be burned when the winds were brisk. The risk of starting a wildfire was too great.

As we looked across the road, I spotted Darren coming out of the prefab metal barn. Through the open doors behind him, I could see assorted farming equipment parked inside, all of it John Deere brand painted the company's trademark green. Darren carried two five-gallon buckets with him, one in either hand. From the way he walked, they appeared to be full and heavy. He carried them over to a two-seater green all-terrain vehicle with a flat cargo box on the back. He set the buckets down on the ground, then heaved them one at a time into the cargo space. He climbed into the driver's seat and drove the ATV over to the brushfire.

There, he slid out of the vehicle and proceeded to splash water out of the buckets onto what remained of the fire. The dark smoke mingled with steam as the hot coals turned the water into vapor. Once Darren had emptied the buckets, he retrieved a rake from the vehicle and dragged it over the coals, spreading them about so they'd extinguish faster.

I turned to Shirley. "He's doused the last of it. Looks like you won't be bothered by the fire and smoke much longer."

She harrumphed. "I'll still be bothered. They should've left the trees. I'd much rather look out on woods than that fake fountain. What do they think this is, Las Vegas?" She harrumphed a second time. "I hollered at Darren Kemp when he first started clearing that land. I told him he was crossing Mother Nature and that she'd get her revenge."

"Wait. Darren cleared the land?" I asked. "Not the crew from the pond company?"

"It was Darren," she said. "I'm sure of it. I know because he wore that bright-orange University of Tennessee ball cap while he was working. My grandsons went to school there, too. Studied engineering. Smartest boys you'll ever meet."

"You must be so proud."

Though it surprised me that Darren would take on such a large task as clearing the land, I realized that hiring someone to do the work would be quite costly. Clearing the land himself would be a way to keep expenses down. Besides, it didn't require special skills like building a pond would.

"I'd better get going," I told Shirley. "Enjoy your moonshine."

"Don't you worry." She patted the jug sitting on her lap. "I will."

Chapter Twenty

As I made my way back to my van, I spotted Tate standing near the pond. I felt myself grow hot as my frustration level rose. *He has to be the one, doesn't he?* After all, he had all kinds of motives for killing Brody. The guy had repeatedly upset his wife and stepdaughter, and cheated him out of child support. He made Tate look bad to Darren Kemp after Tate had gotten the band the winery gig. With Imogene being so young still, Tate and Camille would have been forced to endure a dozen more years of Brody's bad behavior had he not died. A quarter-million dollars was waiting for Tate and Camille, if only Brody passed. The front of that SUV or truck I'd seen in the parking lot when I'd returned to the winery for my cell phone looked a lot like Tate's pickup. He could have slid one of my decorative jugs into Amelia's diaper bag or surreptitiously secreted it somewhere, maybe under the stage, to bash Brody's head with later. He had a key to the excavator that was used to bury Brody. All signs pointed to him. Unfortunately, all of the evidence was circumstantial, not conclusive. *What will it take to get him to break?*

I climbed into my van and continued on to the winery. I drove through the gate and parked near the front door. But rather than going inside, I headed out into the vineyard, making my way to the pond. It was a hot day, and trudging across the large vineyard was an unpleasant slog. Before long, my T-shirt was glued to my back with sweat. *Maybe I can cool off in the fountain's mist.*

When I reached the pond, I found Tate putting the final touches on the water feature, tossing in small pebbles coated in pearlescent paint to simulate river pearls. The excavator sat idle on the far side of the pond. I supposed a big piece of machinery like that wasn't needed to complete the finer final touches on the pond project.

As I approached Tate, my aggravations and unanswered questions surfaced. "Why didn't you or Camille mention that she had a relationship with Josh years ago?"

Tate looked up from the pond and scoffed. "Well, hello to you, too, Hattie."

I raised a palm. "Sorry. That came out harsher than intended. I'm just frustrated. I need Brody's murder to be solved so customers will stop coming in and asking me macabre questions. I can't take it anymore. I don't like that people have withheld important information."

"And I don't like what you're implying." He closed his fist around the pearlescent stones that remained in his palm and frowned. "Look. Neither Camille nor I withheld any relevant information. She dated Josh for a few weeks. Like you said, it was years ago. Before things got serious between the two of them, she met Brody and called things off with Josh. She told me things were a little uncomfortable for a while between the three of them, but that Josh got over it and started dating someone else. Heck, he's had a dozen girlfriends since then."

Yet he's never married any of them. Had he been pining for Camille all this time? Only moments before, I'd convinced myself that Tate had to be the killer, but now I wondered once again if it was Josh, instead. "You think Josh could have killed Brody out of jealousy?"

"I don't know." He raised his palms. "I mean, why now? Years have passed since Camille left Josh for Brody. It's been years since her breakup with Brody, too. In all that time, Josh never sought revenge against his brother. Josh might not have liked what happened, but he seemed to have accepted things and moved on."

I wasn't sure I agreed with Tate's assessment. Time doesn't necessarily heal all wounds. If Josh felt wounded when Camille dumped him, that wound could have festered over all these years.

"Besides," Tate added, "Brody apologized to Josh about it. He said he never should have moved in on Camille and that he regretted it, that brothers shouldn't treat each other that way. Josh forgave him."

"Really?"

"Really. Camille apologized, too. It was all part of the same conversation."

I thought aloud. "I wonder why Josh didn't tell me that when I went by his apartment."

Tate snorted. "Maybe because it's none of your business."

I flinched. Tate had a point. Admittedly, I was a bit of a busybody.

As I mulled things over, a dust cloud in the distance caught my eye. Darren Kemp was operating the grape

harvester again. I returned my attention to Tate and gestured around the immediate area. "The woman across the
street told me that Darren cleared the space for the pond.
I would've thought your crew had cleared the land as part
of the pond job."

"We could've," he said. "We included the cost of clearing the land in our initial bid, in fact. But the Kemps decided to do that part themselves. Guess they thought they
could do it cheaper."

I gestured toward the metal barn. "Because they already had the equipment?"

"Some of it, sure," Tate said. "But they'd need a forest
machine to deal with the downed timber."

"A forest machine?" I'd never heard of such a thing.

"It's got a grapple to grab and lift logs so you can move
them." Tate formed a *C* with his hand, as if he were a
Lego person, and moved his arm about in demonstration.

"Where would they have gotten a forest machine?"

"Rental outfit, most likely. Our pool company rents
specialized equipment for jobs on occasion, too."

My gaze went back to the metal equipment barn then
shifted to the Kemps' house, where their dark pickup
truck sat in the driveway. An icy chill filled my veins as
horrible thoughts flooded my mind.

Could the dark pickup truck now sitting in the Kemps'
driveway be the one I'd seen in the winery's parking lot
when I'd returned for my cell phone the night Brody was
killed? Could Darren or Pearl have killed and buried
Brody? But what reason would they have? After all, they
hardly knew Brody. They didn't seem to have a motive.
Then again, as many had said during their interviews,
Brody had a way of getting under the skin of nearly every
person with whom he crossed paths. He'd hassled me

about what I was paying him for the jingle and the photo shoot. Could he have upset the Kemps in some way, too? Enough that one or the other of them would resort to killing him?

Of course, that wasn't the only question that had to be answered. Another was, assuming the Kemps killed Brody, would they have had a key to the excavator that was used to bury Brody's body? *They might if the forest machine they'd rented was a Caterpillar brand.*

My investigative senses tingling, I bade Tate goodbye, but not before suggesting he and Camille bring Imogene to the Moonshine Shack to put on a solo show. "I'd love to have her play and record some videos for social media. I'd even pay her. You could put the money toward her music lessons." The kid had clearly inherited her biological father's musical talent. It was the one good thing he seemed to have done for her. Best not to waste it.

Tate gave me a nod. "We'll do that."

I headed back across the vineyard. Rather than entering the tasting room, I climbed back into my van. How could I determine whether Darren Kemp might have rented Caterpillar-brand equipment? I supposed the best way to find out was to make some phone calls.

Using my cell phone, I pulled up a browser and searched for *heavy equipment rental* in Chattanooga. More than two dozen rental outfits popped up. I worked through them in order, pretending to be a winery employee.

"Hi, there. I'm calling from the River Pearl Winery. I do the bookkeeping." For some reason, I talked with an exaggerated twang, as if playing some kind of character. It was silly and pointless. None of these people knew my voice, so there was no need to disguise it. But, once I got started, I couldn't stop myself. "My boss rented some equipment from y'all a while back, and I can't make out the total on the invoice. I spilled some coffee on the printout. I was wondering if you could tell me the amount?" I figured once any of them bit, I'd have them confirm what type and brand of equipment had been rented.

A half hour later, I was almost at the end of the list and my tongue was all twanged out. I was beginning to think that maybe Darren had borrowed a forest machine from a neighbor or friend rather than renting one. But then a customer service agent said, "I've found the River Pearl Vineyard account." She rattled off the total rental expense figure. "That includes the rental fee, taxes, and a five-dollar charge to replace the key that wasn't returned."

Holy crap! I took a deep breath, steeling myself for what I might hear. "Can you also confirm what equipment that invoice covered?"

"Sure," she said. She noted that the rental had included something called a wheel loader—whatever that was—as well as a mulcher, stump grinder, and the coup de grâce, a forestry machine.

I assumed a mulcher and stump grinder were smaller machines, ones that could be moved by hand or hauled on a trailer, and might not require a key, so I didn't bother to ask about them. "The forestry machine. That was a Caterpillar brand, correct?"

There was a brief pause as the woman seemed to be checking her records. When she came back, she said, "That's right. It was a Caterpillar."

"Thanks." I ended the call and sat back for a moment, trying to process the information. I'd confirmed that Darren Kemp had rented Caterpillar equipment and failed to return the key. Had he lost the key? Or had he simply forgotten to return it and sucked up the small charge? Tate had landed the Bootlegging Brothers the gig at the winery, so the Caterpillar equipment was gone by the time the Kemps even met Brody. *Do these pieces add up?* I wasn't certain.

As I sat there, movement reflected in my rearview mirror caught my eye. I glanced up at the mirror to see a car driving through the winery's automatic gate, which stood open since it was business hours for the tasting room and shop. As I eyed the gate, another thought occurred to me, a thought that got my heart racing. Pearl and Darren claimed that they'd exited the back of their shop and driven home in the golf cart without coming around to the front of their shop. That's why they claimed not to have known who remained at the winery after closing time. But wouldn't they have had to come around to the front of the tasting barn to close the entrance gate?

It sure seemed that they would have. And, when they did, they should have seen any people and cars remaining in the parking lot. Didn't Garth say that, other than Brody, he and Josh were the last to leave? And that the gate was still open? If Garth had been honest, that would mean that only Brody and the Kemps remained at the winery. Darren or Pearl Kemp, or perhaps both of them, must have gone out front to close the gate.

I sat back and pondered this new revelation. The last thing I wanted to do was wrongfully accuse the Kemps of anything. But someone had closed that gate between the time Garth and Josh left the winery and the time I went back for my cell phone and had to squeeze through the bars. If not the Kemps, then who? As far as I could tell, all the staff had gone home by the time Pearl and I had finished our sales reconciliation. She and Darren were taking care of the final closing tasks themselves.

But surely there had to be an explanation. The woman who dressed like an angel couldn't be a killer, could she? Or her friendly grape-farmer husband? I didn't want to believe it. I *couldn't* believe it. Surely, they'd have a simple explanation for me.

I decided the best thing to do was to run the news by Ace, let her decide where to take things. I pulled out my cell phone and called her. The phone rang once, twice, three times, before going to voicemail. *Darn.*

I left her a message. "Hi, Ace. It's Hattie. I'm at the winery. I just learned some interesting information that pertains to the murder case. Please call me back right away."

Having no luck reaching the detective, I tried Marlon. My call to him also went to voicemail. Seemed that everyone was tied up at the moment. *Ugh!* I left him a similar message, telling him I'd come across new details and asking him to call me immediately.

I sat in my van and waited. Three minutes went by with no return call. Then four minutes. Then five. I'd never been a patient person, and waiting here, doing nothing, felt like pure torture. Against my better judgment, and against the warnings both Ace and Marlon had repeatedly given me, I decided to go on into the tasting room and get some answers myself. I didn't truly think I was at risk here. I just wanted to hear Pearl's explanation. Even so, I grabbed a jug of my granddaddy's moonshine from my van. After all, it was proven to be a deadly weapon. It would be heavy to wield, but it was all I had. If Pearl asked why I had it in my hands, I could tell her it was a gift.

I walked into the tasting room with the jug tucked in

the crook of my arm. A glance around the space told me that Pearl was working alone this afternoon.

Pearl looked up from behind the counter, where she was assisting a customer. To my surprise, she went stiff and her face clouded when she spotted the jug in my hands and the determined look on my face. She turned back to the customer and stammered when handing them the bagged bottle of wine they'd just purchased. "Thank . . . thank you. Come back s-soon."

Had Pearl reacted oddly on seeing the jug because she'd witnessed Brody's head being clobbered with one just like it? I'd felt only an inkling of concern on my way inside, but now I suspected the woman had lied, both to me and to law enforcement.

Pearl looked my way again and smiled at me, but it appeared forced. "I'll be right with you, Hattie." She turned and stepped into the walk-in wine cooler.

I felt fairly certain she'd gone into the cooler to collect herself. I figured I'd have better luck getting real answers if I cornered her before she had time to gather her wits. I circled around the counter, followed her into the refrigerated space, and confronted her. "Is there something you're hiding?"

She made a face. "What do you mean? What would I have to hide?"

"Maybe the fact that Darren has a key to Caterpillar equipment."

She froze for a long moment, then swallowed hard, staring at me, her eyes wild with panic.

"Pearl," I said softly, "did Darren kill Brody Sheridan?"

Pearl gasped and put a hand to her chest. "Of course not! How could you say such a thing?"

Before I realized what was happening, Pearl shoved me aside with all her might and darted past me. As I stumbled into the chilled bottles of wine, she ran out of the cooler, slammed the door, and dropped the locking security arm into place. *Clang!*

Chapter Twenty-One

Pearl had lowered the metal lever, but she didn't take the time to lock it with her key. While the security arm would hold me inside the cooler, it wouldn't prevent someone from lifting it from the outside.

I rushed forward and put my face to the glass, only to see her take off running. As she bolted toward the deck doors, she slammed her shoulder against that of a bewildered female customer who'd been coming into the tasting room.

"Help!" I cried to the customer. I set down the jug of 'shine and banged my fists on the glass. "Help! Raise the lever and let me out!"

The customer's eyes went wide and wild. She bit her lip, uncertain whether to release me. She probably assumed there was a good reason Pearl had decided to lock me in the cooler and run away. *Argh!* She whipped her phone from her purse and dialed 911. I could hear her through the glass door, but just barely. "A clerk locked a woman in the cooler at the River Pearl Winery. I have no idea what's going on. Can you send help?"

Clearly, this woman was going to be of no use to me. I'd have to help myself. I picked up my jug, held it tight with both hands, and used it as a battering ram against the glass. *BAM!* The jug broke into a half-dozen large pieces, spilling moonshine all over the floor, but it had done the job. The inner glass door of the wine cooler bore a web of lines. I tossed the broken jug aside and yanked a bottle of wine from a shelf in the cooler. I jabbed the bottom of it as hard as I could against the glass and the web of cracks gave way even more. Another jab and the wine bottle broke, too, adding a shower of chenin blanc to the moonshine already pooled around my feet. Holding on to a shelf lest I slip in the wet mess, I raised my foot and kicked at the glass. It shattered, large shards falling to the floor. *Tinkle-tinkle-tinkle!*

The woman ran out of the tasting room, probably afraid the crazed, cold woman from the refrigerator would attack her. *She has it all wrong.* I still had to get through the metal mesh security panel to the outer pane of glass. Luckily for me, the handle and mouth of the jug had broken off in one piece. I picked it up from the floor. Clutching the handle, I jabbed the mouthpiece through one of the diamond-shaped holes on the metal security screen between the two panels of glass, aiming for a spot just below the crossbar. *BAM!* When the first jab was insufficient to break the outer glass, I did two more in quick succession. *Jab-jab!* The glass splintered. A few more jabs and I was able to create a hole big enough to slide the neck of a wine bottle through. I used the narrow neck to shove the bar upward, but with the small hole in the glass limiting my range of movement, it lifted only an inch or two. I tried again, this time shoving the door open at the same time. I got the door open just before the arm came down again. *I'm free!*

I'm not sure what possessed me. I should've joined the customer and driven off, leaving law enforcement to sort things out here. But my adrenaline had other plans for me. I tossed the bottle of wine aside—*Smash! Tinkle!*—and ran outside after Pearl. I looked around and spotted her rushing through the grapevines, heading for her husband's harvester. I ran after her, making much better time in my sneakers than she could in her wedge heels. The tractor rolled down a row away from her, Darren's back to us as he sat at the controls.

Pearl had nearly caught up to Darren and I'd almost caught up to Pearl as he turned at the end of the row and started up the next row in my direction. By then, Pearl had emerged at the far end of the row and was now behind him again. Darren didn't seem to realize his wife was on his tail. He made eye contact with me through the windshield of his machine. I raised my hand in a halt gesture and hollered. "Stop!"

But Darren didn't stop. The frantic look on his face told me he realized that I now knew what happened to Brody—or at least who was involved. Him and his wife. I was onto their lies. He shoved the throttle forward and roared past me down the row, hooking a sharp turn at the end and aiming for the white barn Pearl and I had come from.

By then, Pearl had run partway down the row her husband had just emerged from. I turned around in my lane so that I could intercept her at the end of it. She was a few feet ahead of me in the adjacent row, but I was gaining on her. Her loose white blouse flowed out behind her. But while I'd once thought she'd looked like an angel in her white garments, I now realized she was no heavenly angel, but rather an angel of death.

She came around the grapevine just as I reached the end. She'd intended to run after Darren but, seeing me blocking her path, she turned and ran in the other direction down the edge of the vines. She ducked down a row. I sprinted after her, my sneakers pounding the ground.

She looked over her shoulder and realized I was gaining on her once again. She slowed down. I expected her to give up and reached out to grab her. But she wasn't ready to give in yet. She ducked down and went under the vines into the next row over, where she took off running again.

I repeated her movements, ducking under the vines and support wires to pursue her. It was like chasing someone through a fruit-bearing hedge maze. As I closed in, Pearl executed another dodge. Rather than following directly in her footsteps, I attempted to duck under the vines where I was. A wire scraped across my forehead and scalp, taking three layers of skin and some of my hair with it. "OUCH!"

Darren had since reached the winery's shop, realized his wife was not there, and climbed back into his tractor. He must have spotted me chasing Pearl, his partner in crime, through their vineyard. He aimed for us, careening across the vineyard in the harvester, grapevines be damned. While Darren left a path of smashed grapes and destruction in his wake, I gave up my pursuit of Pearl and simply ran for my life lest I be plucked to pieces between the tractor's mechanisms.

I zigged. I zagged. I ran straight. I circled around. But, try as I might, I couldn't outrun the harvester. *Darren is gaining on me!* The tractor bore down on me, its engine a deafening growl. If not for some miracle, I would be squashed to death. *So, this is how I go.* I might not be able to have an open casket, but at least my death would be memorable.

All seemed lost until I heard another engine bearing down. I looked up to see Tate barreling across the field on the excavator, the arm raised as if it were a boxer ready to throw a punch. He motioned with his hand, directing me to get behind him. I ran for all I was worth and had just made it past the excavator when the machines collided and engaged in battle. *CLANG! SCREECH! BANG! BAM! EEEEERKKKKK!*

When I reached the pond, I stopped and turned around. The tractor and the excavator fought in a metal-wrenching battle as if competing in some sort of warped monster truck rally.

Barely audible over the sounds of the heavy equipment engines and clashing metal was the *woo-woo-woo* of law enforcement approaching. *Thank goodness!* I turned to see Marlon's Chattanooga PD SUV racing up the road. He was followed by a Hamilton County deputy sheriff's cruiser.

Tate pulled the arm on the excavator as far as he could to the side and swung it in what would be a right cross in boxing. The force knocked the narrow vineyard tractor onto its side, with Darren still in the cockpit. The throttle must have been stuck because the wheels continued to turn, causing the tractor to spin on its side as if it were attempting to break-dance. The machine churned up dust, dirt, and rocks. The vision would have been comical if it wasn't so terrifying.

Darren managed to throw open the side door and climb

out vertically. He took off running toward Pearl, but Tate wasn't about to let the man get away. He went after Darren in the excavator, lowered the bucket, and scooped the winemaker up from behind. Darren folded inside the bucket before grabbing the edges and hanging on for dear life lest he plummet to the ground. Tate raised the bucket as high as he could in the air and turned the excavator around, heading for the pond. Once he arrived at the edge, he maneuvered the bucket upward and tipped it. Darren fell out, performed an inadvertent backflip in the air, and belly flopped into the pond with a loud *SPLASH!*

The vintner came up sputtering. Marlon barreled up in his SUV and hopped out, his gun at the ready. "Put your hands up!" he hollered. "Come out slowly!"

Tate climbed down from the excavator to stand next to me. We watched as Darren Kemp slogged through the shallow pond, both the pond water and his own tears running down his face. Marlon had the man in cuffs by the time Ace rolled up in a police cruiser. She slid out just as the deputy sheriff hauled Pearl Kemp over, also in handcuffs.

Ace tossed up her hands. "What in the world went on out here?"

Pearl was bawling like a baby, and Darren sobbed, too. I still didn't know the story, exactly, but I could at least tell Ace what had happened since I arrived.

"I stopped to speak to Shirley Byrd on my way to the winery and she told me that Darren cleared the property before Tate and his crew started the pond project. When I arrived here, I talked to Tate and he confirmed what Shirley had told me. He said Darren had probably rented specialized equipment for the job. I made some calls and tracked down the rental company by phone. They confirmed that

Darren had rented Caterpillar equipment and told me he'd been charged an extra fee for failing to return the key."

Ace ducked her chin and shook her head, incredulous.

I went on. "I was sitting in my van, wondering if the Kemps could have killed Brody, when I had an epiphany about the gate. Garth told me earlier that the gate had still been open when he and Josh left the night of the murder. At the time, my only thought was that either he was lying to hide his guilt or, if he was telling the truth, that the open gate would have allowed someone else to sneak back onto the property to kill Brody. But I later realized that the Kemps' explanation of the sequence of events didn't make sense. The gate was closed when I came back to get my phone. The Kemps must have closed the gate at some point and, when they did, they would have noticed whether Brody was still around. Their claim that they hadn't come around the front of the barn had to be a lie. I went inside to confront Pearl. I asked if there was something she was hiding. She played dumb. I said I knew Darren had a Caterpillar key, then I just came right out and asked her if Darren had killed Brody. She panicked and locked me in the wine cooler."

Marlon's jaw dropped. "How did you get out?"

"I had one of my moonshine jugs with me. I used it to smash the glass. When I escaped, I went after Pearl."

Marlon shook his head. "That wasn't smart, Hattie."

"I know!" I cried. "But I was so angry I couldn't stop myself. Anyway, Darren saw me running through the vineyard, realized the jig was up, and raced his tractor over to the tasting room to find Pearl. He didn't notice that she'd run into the vineyard ahead of me. When he returned, he came after me on his tractor." I gestured to Tate, who was still standing by my side. "Tate climbed into his excavator and got between Darren and me. He saved my life."

When Marlon heard how close I'd come to being crushed by the tractor, he scrubbed a hand over his face and took a shuddering breath. He then stepped forward and extended a hand to Tate. "Thanks, bro." Tate took Marlon's hand, and they did that handshake–back pat combo that men do in place of a hug to show affection.

When they released each other, I grabbed Tate shamelessly in a tight hug. "I can never thank you enough! You could've gotten hurt. You took a big risk for me."

He brushed things off, humble. "When I saw Darren coming after you, I knew then and there that he must've killed Brody. I never cared for my wife's ex, but he was Imogene's biological father. That meant something. Or at least it should have."

With Pearl and Darren still out of sorts, Ace decided to forgo questioning them on-site and instead took them straight to the station. Once Marlon had put Darren in the back of his vehicle and the deputy had secured Pearl in his cruiser, Ace turned to me. "I'll be in touch, Hattie."

Tate and I were left to watch the cars drive off together. Ace stopped briefly at the tasting room to string cordon tape around the barn. Once she'd finished and returned to her car, I turned to Tate. "I hope you got paid in full for the pond."

He patted the breast pocket on his work shirt. "Got the final payment today."

"If I were you," I said, "I'd leave right now and take that check to the bank. This winery is likely to get tangled up in a legal battle."

He chuckled. "That's darn good advice. Thanks."

Chapter Twenty-Two

As I drove away from the winery, Shirley Byrd stood from her porch and waved me down. When I pulled to a stop in front of her house and unrolled the window on my van, she said, "Did my eyes deceive me, or did I see you nearly get run down by a tractor over there?"

"Your eyes did not deceive you."

"Goodness, girl! Come have some moonshine and tell me all about it."

While I turned around and pulled my van into her driveway, Shirley rounded up a spare chair for me from her kitchen. The two of us sat on her porch sipping iced tea spiked with 'shine as I gave her the rundown.

"I still don't know exactly why the Kemps killed Brody Sheridan," I said. "I only know that they did it. I'm sure Ace will get the story out of them at the station."

Shirley tsked. "What a shame. I am glad this murder

case is wrapping up, though. Every time I looked out at the river I got a creepy feeling, wondering if the killer might return to the scene of the crime. I had no idea the killers were at the scene of the crime this whole time."

I glanced over at the winery. "I wonder what will happen to the vineyard." Even if someone bought the property now, the grapevines would have to be replanted. Darren had destroyed most of the vineyard chasing after me on the harvester.

Shirley said, "I don't know what will happen on that side of the road, but there's soon to be some changes over here."

"Oh, yeah?"

"Remember those grandsons I told you about?"

"I sure do."

"One of them is going to bring his family here and move in with me. He's got plans to fix up the house so it'll look nice again. I'll enjoy having family close."

"That sounds wonderful."

"My grandson said the first thing he's going to do is take my shotgun and lock it away. I told him he didn't need to bother. It's not loaded. I don't even have any shotgun shells. But I suppose if it makes him more comfortable, I'll go along."

"Sounds like a good plan." I raised my glass of tea. "To family."

"To family."

We clinked our glasses together in toast.

When we finished our tea, I stood to go. "It's been nice talking with you."

"You, too," she said. "Come back again soon. And bring more moonshine with you."

I gave her a smile. "I'll do that."

* * *

Facing attempted murder charges for their attack on me, Pearl and Darren realized the best thing they could do was come clean and hope for mercy. They admitted to killing Brody Sheridan and burying his body in the pond. Ace took me and Marlon out to dinner that night at my favorite Italian restaurant to celebrate the resolution of the case. She filled us in over salad, linguine, and glasses of red wine.

On the night in question, Brody waved the Kemps down as they drove their golf cart around the front of the tasting barn to lock the gate. "Pearl still had her cleaning gloves on, and she had a rag and spray bottle with her so she could wipe the dust from the gate."

"That gate was always shiny," I interjected, remembering how I'd thought it resembled heaven's pearly gates the first time I saw it. "She must've cleaned it every night."

Ace went on to tell us that Brody had argued with the Kemps. "Brody told the Kemps that the Bootlegging Brothers brought in a big crowd and deserved more than a measly one hundred dollars apiece for a full night's work. Darren told Brody that it was anyone's guess whether the customers had come for the Wine and 'Shine event, to see the Bootlegging Brothers, or to see William Hill. William has racked up quite a following on his own and had told his fans he'd be playing at River Pearl Winery that night. Darren told Brody that if he'd wanted more money, he should have asked for it up front when they were negotiating the contract."

"That's similar to what Brody did to me," I said. "He pulled a bait and switch, of sorts. Tried to, anyway." He'd changed his tune when I'd flashed the cash at him.

Ace said, "Darren told me Brody had scoffed and called them 'cheap.' When Darren told Brody that he did not appreciate being insulted at his own place of business and that the Bootlegging Brothers were no longer welcome at the winery, Brody had laughed and demanded the remaining nine hundred dollars the Kemps had agreed to pay the band, three hundred dollars for each of the next three weeks. Brody threatened to sue for breach of contract if they didn't pay up. Darren was fed up by that point and demanded that Brody leave immediately. When Brody stood his ground, Darren took him by the arm to escort him to his Jeep. Brody wrenched out of Darren's grip and pushed him. Darren fell back and hit his head hard against the barn. He got a big knot, which he later hid under a sun hat with flaps."

I gasped. "I saw Darren in that hat!" If only I'd realized he'd been wearing it to hide an injury. I thought he'd been trying to prevent a sunburn on his neck.

Ace continued to fill us in. "Pearl feared things would escalate, so she ran back inside to look for a weapon. Your jugs were the first thing she spotted in the storage closet. Darren had rounded up the two jugs from the stage along with the amps and microphones. Pearl grabbed one of the jugs and ran back outside with it. By then, Brody had turned to go. Darren had stayed on the ground rather than get up and risk the fight escalating. Pearl didn't realize the altercation was over. When she saw her husband on the ground with a hand to the back of his head, she feared he'd been hit again. She lifted the jug of moonshine and swung it with all her might at the back of Brody's head. Turned out all her might was more might than she or Darren would have ever dreamed she could muster. When the Kemps realized the blow had killed Brody, they panicked.

They feared they wouldn't be able to claim self-defense given that Darren had been the first to lay a hand on Brody, and that Pearl had hit Brody on the back of his head as he was leaving. They decided to get rid of the body and evidence, and devised a scheme. They thought if they dumped Brody's Jeep in the river and buried his body deep in the pond, neither would ever be found. The area where they dumped the Jeep wasn't suitable for swimming, and boat traffic doesn't come close to shore there. They drove to their house in the golf cart and returned to the tasting room in their pickup truck. After loading Brody's body into the bed of their truck, they went to ditch his Jeep in the Tennessee River."

I gasped again. "You mean Brody's body was lying in the bed of their pickup truck when I returned to the winery to get my cell phone?"

Ace nodded. When my head went light and teetered on my neck, Marlon put a supportive hand on my shoulder.

Ace said, "The Kemps saw that you had returned to the winery. They hunkered down in the tall grass on Ms. Byrd's property, out of sight. They said they could hear you calling at the doors." Ace gave me a pointed look. "You're lucky they didn't decide to do away with you, too."

Yikes! The thought had me reaching for my glass of wine. I tossed back a big slug.

"Once you left," Ace said, "they drove Brody's body to the pond. Darren still had the Caterpillar key from when he'd rented the equipment to clear the land. He'd added it to his key chain and forgotten to return it when the rental company came out to pick up the machinery at the end of the lease. He said he called the rental company once he realized he still had the key, but they told him not to worry about returning it. Because the keys were universal, they could easily replace it and they had plenty of keys on hand, anyway. He used the Caterpillar key to start up the excavator, dug a deep hole, and rolled Brody's body into the improvised grave."

Marlon frowned. "Seems to me they could've claimed self-defense. Even if Darren was the first to lay a hand on Brody, all he'd done was try to get the guy to leave. He didn't strike him."

"They eventually came to that conclusion, too. A few hours later, when they'd had time to settle down and think more clearly, they realized they'd made a big mistake not calling law enforcement right away. But how could they explain burying Brody and rolling his Jeep into the river? They feared that they wouldn't be believed. They decided the best thing they could do was continue their charade, to pretend they had no idea what happened to the guy."

I shook my head. Brody might have been an obnoxious jerk, but it wasn't right to just let him disappear without a trace.

Ace scooped up a forkful of pasta. "When Pearl realized that Garth, Josh, William, Tate, and Camille were coming under suspicion, she attempted to spread doubt around so that no single one of the others would seem clearly guilty. She didn't want anyone else going to jail for her and her husband's actions. The Kemps decided that they'd come clean if someone else was arrested and charged with the crime, but they realized that with so many potential suspects, the chances were slim to none."

In other words . . . "They expected to get away with it. To take it to their grave."

She nodded. "It's ironic, really. Despite everything, if Darren hadn't come after you on the tractor today, they might still only be facing minor charges. Abuse of a corpse is just a Class E felony, punishable by one to six years in jail and a three-thousand-dollar fine. The D.A.'s office might have even negotiated that down since the Kemps have no priors. A person can get as little as two years for reckless homicide, just one year for criminally negligent homicide. But Darren going after you today? You weren't armed. You were just playing tag with his wife. He's going to have a hard time claiming he was defending her. He'll be facing attempted murder charges."

Chapter Twenty-Three

With the mystery solved, I could focus again on marketing my moonshine and my developing relationship with Marlon.

William Hill and his fiddle were a big hit that Friday night at the Moonshine Shack. We had our best night ever, and not a single customer referred to my wares as *murder moonshine*. Looked like we could all finally move on and put Brody's death behind us.

The mechanic finished restoring the engine on the flathead, and the motor purred like Smoky when I scratched his ears. Using a plywood base, a foam pad, and vinyl fabric, Kiki and I fashioned a new seat for the car so people could sit in it comfortably. It was good to have a friend with creative skills.

So as not to violate the terms of my antique automobile registration, I waited for the first Saturday to come around once it was completed, and I drove it down to the Singing

River Retirement Home to pick up my grandfather. He was sitting on a bench out front, chatting with Louetta and friends, when I rolled up in his father's car. I activated the horn. *Aaooogah!* The group turned in unison and their mouths fell open.

Granddaddy stood, his eyes wide and bright with joy. He raised his cane to point. "That's my daddy's car!"

I hopped out of the driver's seat and walked over to him. "What do you think?" I asked, though I already knew the answer. He was over the moon to see his father's car running again.

He walked over to it and I helped him into the passenger seat. "I feel like a kid again!" he cried. "I remember sitting between Mother and Daddy and going for rides on Sunday afternoons. Daddy would make lots of stops to see friends."

"Let me guess," I said. "He was delivering moonshine?" And using his wife and son as props to make it look to law enforcement like they were just out for a leisurely Sunday drive.

Granddaddy laughed. "Sometimes he'd send me to a door with a jug."

"He was training you to work in the family business."

Granddaddy nodded. "I'll never forget the time we outran some guys from a rival bootleg gang. Mother and I had to hang on for dear life!"

His friends gathered round, running a hand over the hood or bending over to take a look at the shiny grille. My grandfather beamed with pride.

Once the men were done admiring the classic car, I gave the horn another go—*Aaooogah!*—and off we went to the Moonshine Shack. I repositioned the game table and rockers out front to make room for the car and then carefully backed the old Ford up and over the curb. I parked it at an angle so it wouldn't block the sidewalk and earn me a citation.

Granddaddy sat in that car all day, a glass of moonshine-spiked lemonade in his hand, chatting up passersby. He regaled them with stories from his youth. Before I knew what was happening, the raven-haired reporter had pulled up in her van. I went out front to find out what was going on. Apparently, someone had called the station and suggested they send a crew to interview my grandfather for one of their feel-good filler segments. She and her cameraman asked if he'd be willing to do an interview.

"Why, sure!" He patted the seat beside him. "Take a seat right here and I'll tell you all about this car and my daddy and his moonshine business."

The woman climbed into the cab. "Mind if I honk the horn?"

Granddaddy said, "Be my guest."

Aaooogah! The reporter giggled like a schoolgirl. I bit my lip to keep from grinning like a fool. The segment was sure to bring more customers to my store.

The next few days were especially busy. Not that I was complaining. It was nice to do something other than think about Brody Sheridan's murder for a change.

We scheduled a photo shoot with the new Bootlegging Brothers. They posed around the car with their instruments and jugs and jars of my 'shine. The images were a great way to promote both my brand and their band. It was a good partnership, a smart business decision for all of us. We took some videos and photos of Imogene and her jug, too. My favorite pic showed her sitting on the hood, blowing into her jug, her eyes big with effort. She made an adorable hood ornament.

Under William's management, the Bootlegging Brothers were skyrocketing to fame. People came by my shop asking to buy empty jugs to play in their bluegrass bands. Apparently, my jugs had developed a reputation for having the best sound around. I was happy to sell empty jugs for half the price of ones filled with moonshine.

As I locked up the store one night, I stopped and stared at the display of Granddaddy's Ole-Timey Corn Liquor, once again thinking about Brody's obsession with blood, how it was thicker than water. My family, my blood, had been making moonshine for generations—out of yeast, corn mash, and water. Our jugs were filled with spirits, both literal and metaphorical. I had no idea where the currents of life might carry me in the future, but wherever they did, I knew it would be an exciting ride.

ACKNOWLEDGMENTS

Cheers to everyone who had a hand in getting this story out of my head, onto the page, and into the hands of readers. I appreciate you all!

Thanks to my agent, Helen Breitwieser, for finding a home for this book series at Berkley.

Thanks to Michelle Vega for bringing me into the Berkley fold. Thanks to my editors, Miranda Hill and Candice Coote, for your insightful suggestions and guidance through the editorial process. Thanks, also, to the rest of the Berkley team, including Dache Rogers, Kim I, and Megha Jain for all of your hard work in getting the book to readers, and to Sarah Oberrender and Auden George for the adorable cover.

Last but not least, a big thanks, as always, to you wonderful readers who chose this book. Have a great time with Hattie and the gang!

Recipes

Each recipe makes one serving.
Use 12-ounce or larger glasses. A shot
glass equals 3 tablespoons, or 1.5 ounces.

Blueberry Bluegrass Tea

- 8 ounces of plain tea
- Ice
- 1 shot of blueberry moonshine
- 7 fresh or frozen blueberries
- Orange wedge

Pour the tea over ice in a tall, clear glass. Add the shot of blueberry moonshine and blueberries, and stir to completely mix the 'shine into the tea. Garnish with the orange wedge.

Rosemary Lemonade

- 8 ounces of lemonade
- Ice
- 1 shot of unflavored moonshine
- Sprig of fresh rosemary
- 1 lemon for peeling

Pour the lemonade over ice in a tall, clear glass. Add the shot of unflavored moonshine and stir to completely mix the 'shine into the lemonade. Add the sprig of rosemary. Make a lemon peel curlicue by slicing a lemon. Cut through the slice on one side, making sure to cut through the peel and pulp. Using a paring knife, gently separate the peel from the pulp until you have a long semi-circle of peel. Using your hand, twist the peel to form a curlicue. Or, if you prefer, wind the peel around a chopstick to form a curlicue. Note that the peel will be easier to twist if you warm it first with your hands or by running it under warm water. Garnish the glass with the lemon peel curlicue.

Sucker Punch

- 6 ounces of fruit punch
- 3 ounces of ruby red grapefruit juice
- ½ shot of cherry moonshine
- ½ shot of peach moonshine
- ½ shot of apple pie moonshine
- Ice
- One strawberry

Pour the fruit punch, grapefruit juice, and moonshine over ice in a tall, clear glass. Stir until well mixed. Garnish with the strawberry.